TOR BOOKS BY DAN WELLS

I Am Not a Serial Killer
Mr. Monster
I Don't Want to Kill You
The Hollow City

THE
HOLLOW
CITY

DAN WELLS

TOR®

A TOM DOHERTY ASSOCIATES BOOK / NEW YORK

This is a work of fiction. All of the characters, organizations, and events portrayed in this novel are either products of the author's imagination or are used fictitiously.

THE HOLLOW CITY

Copyright © 2012 by Dan Wells

All rights reserved.

A Tor Book
Published by Tom Doherty Associates, LLC
175 Fifth Avenue
New York, NY 10010

www.tor-forge.com

Tor® is a registered trademark of Tom Doherty Associates, LLC.

ISBN 978-0-7653-6871-3

Tor books may be purchased for educational, business, or promotional use. For information on bulk purchases, please contact Macmillan Corporate and Premium Sales Department at 1-800-221-7945, extension 5442, or write specialmarkets@macmillan.com.

First Edition: July 2012
First Mass Market Edition: November 2013

Printed in the United States of America

0 9 8 7 6 5 4 3 2 1

To Janci Patterson.

When I was ready to throw this book away, she convinced me it was worth saving, and then she showed me how to save it.

ACKNOWLEDGMENTS

As with all novels, this one owes a great deal to a great many people. First are my professional accomplices: my agent, Sara Crowe; my editor, Moshe Feder; my in-house advocate, Paul Stevens; and my publicist, Alexis Saarela. Without their work on this and all of my previous novels, *The Hollow City* would still be a poorly written file on my hard drive.

Great thanks also go to my writing group and various other readers, who helped shepherd the early versions of this book from "Dan's weird imagination" to "something people actually want to read." In no particular order: Brandon and Emily Sanderson, Peter and Karen Ahlstrom, Ben and Danielle Olsen, Alan Layton, Ethan Skarstedt, Kaylynn Zobell, Janci Patterson, Steve Diamond, Nick Dianatkhah, Will Groberg, and Rob Wells.

Special thanks go to Dawn Wells, my wonderful wife and the best support I could ever ask for, and to Philip K. Dick, who I gave up trying to emulate but who continues to inspire me. When the world makes sense it's because of her, and when it doesn't I think of him.

Oh dreadful is the check—intense the agony—
When the ear begins to hear, and the eye begins to see;
When the pulse begins to throb, the brain to think again;
The soul to feel the flesh, and the flesh to feel the chain.

EMILY BRONTË, "The Prisoner"

THE
HOLLOW
CITY

PROLOGUE

AGENT LEONARD KNELT down by the body, carefully lifting his coat up out of the blood.

"Do we know his name yet?"

Agent Chu shook his head. "Nametag says Woods, but ChemCom has a lot of janitors and the guy who found him didn't recognize the name. Visual ID is, obviously, impossible." He gestured at the police officer standing beside him. "Chicago PD is interviewing the night watchman, we're hoping he knows."

Leonard surveyed the body carefully: two bullet holes in the chest, trauma to the back of the head, and nothing but a shattered, bloody mess where the face should be. *Just like all the others.* He pulled on a rubber glove and touched the head carefully, rolling it upright for a better view of the wound. "This definitely looks like our guy," said Leonard, releasing the head back into place. He probed the corpse's bloodstained coveralls with a gloved finger, and cocked his head in surprise when he found a hole in the sleeve. "What's this?"

Agent Chu crouched down to look over his shoulder, and Leonard opened the tear. There was more blood inside.

"He's got a wound on his arm," said Leonard. "Probably the same slash that opened the sleeve."

Chu raised an eyebrow. "Cool."

The officer behind them cleared his throat. "Excuse me?"

"Sorry," said Chu, "I'm not trying to be insensitive, it's just that . . . well, the Red Line Killer's been virtually untrackable so far. He's too careful. None of his victims have ever had the chance to fight back before, but these kinds of wounds—knife cuts on the forearms—are probably defensive, which means he saw the attacker coming." He shrugged. "Probably."

"That's an awful lot of probablies," said the officer.

Agent Leonard stepped over the body to examine the other arm. "Yeah, similar thing over here. Victim almost lost a finger." He looked up at Chu. "This guy definitely fought back."

Chu looked down the hallway, taking stock of the angles. "This corner was probably the ambush point—victim comes around the edge, Red Line's waiting with a gun, boom. Two in the chest, then go to work on the face, or at least we assume that was the plan. That's how he's done all the others. Why didn't it work this time?"

Leonard peeled off his gloves. "The defensive wounds would come first, which means the knife hit before the gun. Maybe he couldn't pull it out in time?"

"But if he was lying in wait he would have had it out already," said Chu. He walked the few steps to the end of the hall, his shoes tapping lightly on the concrete floor. "See? My footsteps were audible, and it's not even quiet in here. In the middle of the night, without a whole forensics team in the background, they would have been pretty loud."

"So the victim comes this way," said Leonard, walking toward Chu, "approaches the corner, and the Red Line Killer lashes out with a knife; the victim fights him off, runs back the way he came. . . ." He paused, looking at the floor. "Except there's no blood here, only back by the body."

"And the shots are in the chest," said Chu, "not the back. We're going to need the whole team in here to figure out how this fight went down—kinetics, blood splatter, everybody."

"Or you could just ask the rent-a-cop," said the policeman, pointing down the hall. "Looks like ChemCom has security cameras."

Chu and Leonard looked where he was pointing, following his eye-line to a small glass bubble on the far wall.

"You've got to be kidding me," said Leonard. "He's never been on camera before."

"You think the camera works?" asked Chu. "The body was found by another janitor, not a security team watching on a monitor."

"This hallway looks like it's just storage," said the policeman, glancing at the wide, evenly spaced doorways. "The cameras probably don't even go to a live feed, just a hard drive somewhere to keep a record of who's been in and out."

"This is huge," said Leonard. "We've never even caught a glimpse of this guy before—he's too careful. If we've got him on film . . . This is huge."

Chu nodded and started off down the hallway. "Then let's stop talking about it and find the tapes."

The night watchman was in the main ChemCom lobby with the remaining janitors, giving statements to the local police. Chu and Leonard listened in—the man knew nothing, or claimed to—and then walked him into the security office to look at the tapes.

"When do you think it happened?" the watchman asked, pulling up the security footage.

"Around one o'clock, one-fifteen," said Leonard.

"Just play the whole thing on fast-forward," said Chu, "and stop when you see people."

The man nodded, loaded the file, and the long, empty hallway appeared on the screen in black and white. He clicked fast-forward and the time code in the corner started racing, but nothing else changed. The man accelerated the fast-forward, then again, until suddenly a dark shape shot across the screen in a blur and exploded in a flash of light. The three men swore in unison. The image collapsed into fuzzy snow, as if the signal had been completely lost.

"Back it up," said Leonard, peering closely at the screen. The watchman reversed the video, found the janitor's first entrance, and hit play. He pointed at the time code.

"One-thirteen. You guys are good."

"Quiet," said Chu.

There was a burst of static on the screen, as if the signal died and came back just for an instant, and then the janitor came into view beneath it, walking toward the far corner. He stopped at a door, fiddled with the lock, then continued on.

"That's Brandon all right," said the watchman.

"You know him?" asked Leonard.

"Not very well," said the watchman. "He's not exactly a talkative guy, but I'm the one that has to check him in every night. Name's Brandon Woods, lives . . . outside the city somewhere."

Leonard and Chu glanced at each other, then looked back at the screen.

Brandon Woods continued down the hall to the far corner, but just before he reached it, he stopped abruptly and clutched his head, as if he'd come down with a sudden, unbearable migraine. His lips moved, but the recording had no sound, and the image was too small to make anything out. He retreated several steps toward the camera, still clutching his head and screaming.

"Has your company done any recent drug testing?" asked Agent Leonard.

"Once a year," said the watchman, "but it's different for every employee, on a randomized schedule. You think Brandon's on drugs?"

"I don't think anything yet," said Leonard. "I'm just collecting information."

Brandon Wood's pain seemed to ease as he moved backward, and just then another figure stepped around the corner—a man all in black, a ski mask pulled over his face, and a gun in his hand. Agent Leonard's breath caught in his throat: *this is the man we've been hunting.* He raised the gun to fire, the janitor saw him, and suddenly the image flickered—once, twice—and the space between Woods and the attacker seemed to ripple. The attacker staggered back, dropping the gun, as if the ripple had shoved him against the far wall.

"What on Earth?" whispered Chu.

The attacker staggered to his feet, reaching for his gun, but Woods was running toward him and he didn't have time. The man planted his feet, bracing for impact, and right before Woods reached him a jagged bolt of light leapt out between them, bridging the gap between the two bodies like an electrical arc. The man in black shook as it struck him, but shoved the janitor away and pulled a long hunting knife from a sheath on his belt. The janitor regained his footing, squaring off against his attacker, and once again the screen flickered and a ripple of distortion flew across the hall—not directionally, like the first time, but everywhere, emanating out from the janitor like a wave. It struck the attacker almost instantly, and his body shook with the contact; a second later the wave reached the camera, the image exploded in light, and the feed collapsed once more into static and snow.

The three men stared at the screen in silence. After a long moment Agent Chu spoke.

"What was that?"

"Well," said the watchman, hesitating, "obviously, it was a janitor shooting a serial killer with his mind. That . . . that seemed pretty clear to everyone else, right?"

Agent Leonard flipped open his badge and held it in front of the watchman's face. "I'm showing you this to remind you how serious I am when I tell you that everything you've seen in this room tonight is a state secret. We're confiscating the file, the camera, and any and all backups that may exist. You do not say anything to anybody at any time. Am I clear?"

The watchman swallowed nervously and nodded his head. Agent Chu leaned forward, grabbed the mouse, and rewound the video. He froze it on an image of the man in black, knife in hand, crouched at the end of the hall. He stared at the man intently.

On the screen, the man stared back.

ONE

"WHO ARE YOU?"

I'm in a hospital bed; I can tell by the rails on the sides, and by the white coats on the people gathered around me. Their heads are haloed by bright fluorescent lights, still indistinct as I struggle to wake up. There's a needle in my elbow, an IV tube reaching out behind me. I feel nauseous and slow, and the light burns my eyes. How did I get here? Where's Lucy?

"You're awake," says one of the men, "good, good. You gave us quite a scare, Mr. Shipman."

He knows my name. I stare at the man, forcing my eyes to focus. He's older, sixties maybe, in a long, white hospital coat. Two other men and one woman stand by him, probably also doctors, pressed around my bed. There's a guard by the door—a guard? Or just an orderly? I don't know what's going on.

My throat is dry and I struggle to talk. "Why don't I remember coming here?"

"My name is Dr. Murray," he says. "You had a fall—do you remember falling?"

Do I remember anything? I remember hiding out, and then ... a chase? Someone found me. Yes, I'm sure of it; I remember running. And there was an empty city, full of empty houses, and a deep, dark hole, like a well or a mine shaft.

The people I was running from were bad—that much I know. Did they catch me? Are these doctors part of it? I slow down and try to think.

"Where's Lucy?"

"Who?"

"Lucy, my girlfriend, she was with me in the ... where was I?"

"What do you remember?"

"I remember a pit," I say slowly, watching their faces. "I fell down a pit."

Dr. Murray frowns; he thinks I'm wrong. Am I? But I remember a pit, and he said I had fallen, and ... My head aches—not just my head, my mind aches. Dr. Murray leafs through a slim folder, holding up a page to read the one below it. "You fell, or jumped, out of a window. Do you remember that?"

I say nothing, trying to remember. Think, Michael, think!

"We were worried you'd hurt yourself," says one of the other doctors, "but nothing's broken."

"If he's lost his memory," says the woman, "he might have hit his head harder than we thought."

I scan my eyes around the room, trying to get a better sense of where I am—a regular hospital room, with cabinets and curtains and hand sanitizers lining the walls. No computers that I can see. Good.

"We would have seen more damage to his head," says another doctor. "The abrasions were grouped on his legs and arms—he landed about as well as you could hope to."

"Mr. Shipman," says Dr. Murray, catching my eye and smiling. "Michael. Can you tell us where you've been for the past two weeks?"

I frown, my suspicions rising. I'd been trying to disappear, and I think I thought I had, but now I'm in here, surrounded by prying eyes and equipment. I shift my legs imperceptibly, testing for restraints under the covers. It doesn't feel like they've tied me down. They might just be normal doctors—they might not be part of the Plan. Just helpful doctors who don't know who I am or who's after me. Maybe I can still get away.

Maybe I can, but not with five people between me and the door. I need to take my time.

"We're only trying to help you, Michael." The doctor smiles again. They always smile too much. "Once we knew who you were and we looked up your file, well, you can imagine that we started to wonder."

I stare at him, my eyes cold. So they do know who I am, or at least part of it. I start to tense up, but I force myself to calm down. Just because they know who I am, that still doesn't mean they know about the Plan. "No," I say firmly, "I can't imagine." The men I was running from had been watching me for years—if they gave the doctors their file, they'll know everything about me. I shift my legs again, bracing myself to bolt for the door if I have to make a move. "What does the file say?"

He raises the folder in his hands, an old manila folder with a curling green sticker on the tab. "Standard things," he says. "Medical history, hospital stays, psychological evaluations—"

"Wait," I say. "Is that it? It's just a medical history?"

Dr. Murray nods. "What else would it be?"

"Nothing." So they don't have the real file, just the fake one from the state. That's good, but it could cause problems of its own. "None of that stuff matters."

The doctor glances at the man beside him. "We're doctors, Michael, it matters a great deal to us."

"Except that it's all false," I say. I know I can trust them now, but how can I explain what's going on? "The state file was created . . ." It was created by Them, by the people who've been following me. Except I'm too smart to tell the doctors a truth they'll never believe. I shake my head. "It was created as a joke," I say. "It doesn't mean anything."

Dr. Murray nods again. "I see." He flips to a page in the file. "Ongoing treatment for depression and generalized anxiety disorder." He turns the page. "Two weeks in Powell Psychiatric Hospital, fourteen months ago." He turns the page. "Multiple prescriptions for Klonopin, paid for by state welfare." He looks up. "You say this is all part of a joke?"

How am I supposed to explain this to him without looking crazy? I close my eyes, feeling the early flutters of a nervous panic. I roll my hands into fists and take a deep breath: it's okay. They're not part of the Plan. They don't even have me tied down. I can probably walk right out of here if I can just find a way to defuse their suspicions. I glance around again; no computers, and the TV's off. I might be okay.

"It's just the . . . state doctors," I say. "You need to talk to my personal doctor, my family practitioner. Dr. Ambrose Vanek. He can straighten this out."

"We'll contact him right away," says Murray. He nods to one of the other doctors, who makes a note on his pad and steps out of the room. "I'm afraid his information wasn't included in your report or we would have called him already. We've called the only number on here, someone named L. Briggs, but we haven't been able to reach her. Is that your friend Lucy?"

"She's my girlfriend," I say again, trying to look helpful. Have They gotten to her yet? Do I even dare drag her into this? "I'm afraid I don't know her number."

Dr. Murray raises an eyebrow. "You don't know your girlfriend's phone number?"

"I don't use phones."

"Ah." He nods and makes a note. "Is there anyone else we can contact?"

"No."

He waves the folder slightly. "This says you live with your father."

"Yeah, but don't call him."

"His son is in the hospital; I'm sure he'd appreciate a call."

I clench my fist tighter, trying to breathe evenly. "Just . . . please."

Dr. Murray pauses, then nods. "If that's what you want." He looks at another sheet in his folder. "It says here that your Klonopin was prescribed by Dr. Little, after your stay at Powell last year. Have you been taking your pills, Michael?"

I nod. "Of course, Doctor." It's a lie—I fill my prescription every few weeks, just so no one asks questions, but I haven't taken it in months. I'm not convinced the pills are part of the Plan, but I'm not taking any chances.

"Excellent," says Murray again, but I can see his smile falter. He doesn't believe me. I scramble to find something else to soothe him—what's in that file? It probably mentions my job at Mueller's; the state got me that job. Maybe I can convince him I'm nothing to worry about.

"You said I wasn't injured in the fall, right?" I smile, trying to look normal. "Because I really need to get back to work soon—Mr. Mueller really relies on me." There's no response, so I keep going. "You know Mueller's Bakery, on Lawrence? Best doughnuts in the city, you know. I'd be happy to send you a box once I get back there." I liked working at Mueller's: no punch-card machine, and no computers.

"Yes," says Dr. Murray, flipping to another page of the file, "it was Mr. Mueller who reported you missing." He looks up. "It seems you didn't show up for work for nearly two weeks and he got worried. Tell me, Michael, can you tell us where you've been during the last two weeks?"

They got to Mueller. I'm nervous now, and I glance around again. No machines; the room might be clean.

"I need to go, please."

"Do you remember where you've been?"

I don't. I rack my brain, trying to remember anything I can. Empty houses. A dark hole. I can't remember. I still feel nauseous, like I'm thinking through syrup. Did they drug me? I look around again, trying to see what's behind the bed.

"Is everything okay, Michael?"

I raise up on my arms, craning my neck around the edge of the bed, and recoil almost instantly, like I've been struck. An IV stand looms over my shoulder, with a small black box just inches behind my head. Red digital lines turn in circles as clear liquid drips slowly into my arm.

I try to jump off the other side of the bed, but the doctors move in, holding me in place.

"Easy, Michael. What's wrong?"

"I have to get out of here," I say, grunting through clenched teeth. My chest feels painfully tight. I scrabble at my elbow, rip up the tape, and pull out the IV needle before they can stop me; pain lances through my arm.

"Frank!" says Dr. Murray, and the big man by the door rushes over and grabs me by the shoulders.

"No!" I shout, "No, it's not like that, I just need to get out of here!"

"Hold him down!"

"What's wrong, Michael?" asks Murray, leaning in over my face. "What happened?"

"You don't understand!" I plead. "Get it out, please, get it out of the room."

"Get what out?"

"The IV stand, the monitor, whatever it is—get it out!"

"Calm down, Michael, you've got to tell us what's wrong!"

"I told you what's wrong, get it out of here!"

"Dr. Pine," says Dr. Murray, nodding at the IV stand, and the female doctor lets go of my leg and wheels the IV stand to the door, gathering up the trailing plastic tube as she moves it into the hall. It helps, but I can still feel it watching me. Do the doctors know? They can't know—they can't know or they wouldn't be in here. That means they're friends, but only if I act fast. My freakout over the IV monitor was too much, and I've tipped Them my hand. The woman comes back. We don't have long.

"What else is in here?" I ask, falling back against the pillow and allowing the orderly to hold me still. Don't fight; they have to trust you. "Any other monitors? Computers? Cell phones?"

"Michael, we all have cell phones, we're doctors—"

"Get them out."

"Please, Michael, calm down—"

"This is important!" I close my eyes, struggling to estimate the time: how long have I been here? Three minutes since I woke up, give or take a few seconds, and who knows how long I was unconscious before that. How long do we have before They get here?

I don't have time for games, and there are too many of them to fight. I need to lay out the truth and hope for the best. I take a deep breath. "I'll tell you everything, but not until the room is clean. No electronic devices of any kind."

Dr. Murray nods, but smugly, as if he's heard it all before: I'm just another crazy guy. "Why do electronics frighten you, Michael?"

It's the same as last year—the same arrogant assumptions that landed me in a psych ward. Once the system decides you're crazy, there's not much you can do to fight it. I shake my head. "Cell phones outside."

Murray looks at me for a moment, glances at the others, then shrugs. "Okay, Michael, whatever makes you comfortable, but you have to talk to us."

"Hurry." I try not to sound desperate. Murray gathers their cell phones, takes them to the hall, and a moment later he comes back. He opens his mouth to speak, but I cut him off. "Listen very carefully, all of you, because I don't know how much time we have. I'm very sorry you got dragged into this, but

I'm being followed by some very dangerous men, and I need to get out of here as fast as I possibly can. They can track me—They can track all of us—through electronics: computers, cell phones, TVs, radios, everything. I know this is hard to believe, but you've got to trust me. Now, does that window open?"

Murray is nodding again. "Easy, Michael, just take it easy—"

"You don't understand," I say. "They will be here any minute. Look, if the window doesn't open we can get out through the halls, but only if we stay far away from anything dangerous. Back stairs usually have cameras, so we can't risk—"

"Please, Michael, no one is chasing you."

"Yes they are," I say, "They're men, Faceless Men, and they can track us through your cell phones, through computers, through anything that sends or receives a signal. They're not looking for you, so you don't have to come with me, just let me slip out the door—"

"The Red Line," says the woman, and I glance up to see that all four doctors and the orderly have backed away.

I try to look behind me. "What red line?"

"When you say 'faceless,'" asks the woman, "do you mean, like, the face has been . . . destroyed?"

"No." I turn back to them, watching their faces. What are they thinking? "No, it's nothing like that at all. They're faceless, literally faceless, no eyes, no nose, no mouth, nothing, just . . . blank." I pass my hand over my face, willing them to understand. They stare at me a moment, and I dare to hope.

"This is more than just anxiety disorder," says one of the men, and the others nod.

"I'm not crazy," I say.

"Brain damage?" asks another doctor. They're not even acknowledging me anymore.

"Could be," says another, "or it could be all mental. Schizophrenia?"

The woman eyes me warily. "There was another one just last week, you know. We can't take the chance."

I feel myself start to tremble, the nervous vibration on my chest making it hard to breathe. "Please— what are you talking about?"

Dr. Murray stops, looks at me carefully, then whispers in another doctor's ear. The other doctor goes into the hall, and Murray steps forward. "Michael, I need to ask you a question, and I need you to answer me as carefully and as honestly as you can." He pauses. I look at the door—where did the other doctor go? What, or who, was he sent for?

Dr. Murray stares at me, eyes intense. "Have you seen any bodies, anywhere, with the faces destroyed?"

"Why do you keep asking that? Where would I have seen something like that?"

"Can you remember where you've been for the last two weeks?"

"No," I say, "I can't remember anything! Tell me what's going on!"

Dr. Murray glances at the other doctors, then

back at me. "Have you ever heard of the Red Line Killer?"

I freeze. "Some." I've heard the name, but I don't know much. Some kind of serial killer. I get a deep, sinking feeling in my gut—not just from the name, but from the faces of the doctors as they watch me. They're nervous and scared.

They're scared of me.

"Over the past eight months," says Dr. Murray, "the Red Line has killed nearly ten people in and around Chicago. Nobody has any idea who he is, but his story has been all over the news. Are you sure you've never heard of him?"

"I don't watch TV," I say, glancing at the darkened set on the wall. Can it see me while it's turned off? "Why are you asking me about this? What does it have to do with me?" And why are you so scared?

"If you'd seen the news, Michael, you'd know: when the Red Line Killer kills someone, he . . . mutilates the bodies." He frowns and continues. "He kills them and then he destroys their faces—skin, muscle, bones, everything."

And there it is. A killer on the loose, a tenuous link, and the floodgates of suspicion break open in a torrent. I'm still the same person, but in their eyes I've changed—no longer just a man brought in for a fall, but an unbalanced psycho who might be a murderer.

"I haven't done anything wrong," I say carefully.

"We're not saying you have."

"You wouldn't have brought this up if you didn't

think it was me." I have to get out now. I have to run before this goes any further.

"We don't think anything, Michael, no one's accusing you of any—"

I leap up suddenly, catching them by surprise, but I only get halfway out of the bed before the orderly grabs me; the doctors are only a few steps behind. I fight like a caged animal, kicking wildly with my legs, and feel a horrifying crunch in my foot as one of the doctors grunts and falls backward. They're screaming now, calling desperately for nurses and sedatives, and all I can think to do is bite the arm wrapped tightly across my chest.

"Where's the Geodon!"

"Frank, dammit, hold him down!"

Someone lets go and I struggle to my feet, almost clear of the doctors, and then suddenly my arm's getting twisted around and my shoulder's nearly popping and I howl at the pain. My legs go limp and I whimper, all of my attention focused desperately on my arm.

The room has more people in it now, and I feel hands picking me up and positioning me back on the bed; there's a sharp prick in my arm, and I know they've given me a shot. A sedative. I don't have long.

"Please," I say, "you've got to get me out of here. I'm not who you think I am, and They'll be here any . . . any minute." Images swirl in and out of each other, and I squint to catch them before they fade.

"Find Dr. Vanek," says one of them; Murray, I think. There's something on my arms, and I try to lift them up to see, but they won't move. My head weighs a ton, ten tons, but I steel myself for the effort and raise it up, just enough to look down at my body.

"The drugs are hitting quickly—how much did you give him?"

"It's just the standard dose—it shouldn't work this fast."

"He can barely move."

I squint again, my head as empty as a balloon, my body slipping away down a tunnel. I can feel it drawing out, stretching like putty, but there's something I have to see, someone standing in the back of the room. I fight my way out of the tunnel, struggling for just one glimpse, and—there it is.

A man with no face.

They've found me.

TWO

I WAKE UP with a scream, suddenly, as if I were never asleep and the Faceless Man was still right there, coming for me. He is gone, and the room is empty.

"Whoa," says a voice, and I shout again. "Are you okay?"

"Who's there?" I'm still disoriented. I lunge forward, looking for the speaker—a woman—but there's something on my arms and I stop short, jerked back by heavy leather restraints.

"Calm down," she says. Is it Lucy? "Just take it easy; looks like you had a nightmare or something." She steps into my view and she's not Lucy; she's young, about the same age, but wearing a sort of suit jacket that Lucy would never wear. "My name is

Kelly Fischer, I'm a reporter with the *Sun*. I didn't mean to startle you."

"What do you want?" I slowly grow more centered, as if my higher functions are only just now waking up. I test my restraints subtly; my legs are tied down as firmly as my arms, with just a few inches of give in any direction. The TV is still off, but it looms over the room like a darkened eye.

"I'm writing a piece on the Red Line Killer," says the woman. "I heard you might know something, and I thought maybe I could ask you some questions."

I freeze. How does she know who I am? How does she know anything about me? I study her carefully, looking for clues: she has a face, for one thing, and a large handbag slung carefully over her shoulder. Is she one of Them? Does she work for Them?

I narrow my eyes. "How did you find me?"

"One of the nurses is a friend of mine; she tips me off when big stories come through."

"I'm not a big story."

"You're under investigation in connection with the Red Line killings," she says.

"Great." I throw my hands up, or try to, but the restraints stop them with a jerk. I close my eyes and growl under my breath. "I need to get out of here."

"You're not a suspect," she says, shaking her head, "or at least you're not a suspect yet. If you were I'd be breaking the law just being here. As it is . . ." She glances at the door quickly, nervously. I look at it too, then back to her, realization dawning.

"You're not supposed to be here," I say.

"I can help you," she says, holding out her hand to quiet me. "Listen, just give me two minutes, and I can try to keep you out of Powell. I don't have a lot of pull, but—"

"Powell?" My eyes go wide. "They're sending me back to Powell?"

"You didn't know?" She glances at the door again, then bolts for the back corner. "Someone's coming— don't say anything, I'm *begging* you." She jogs through the bathroom door, without even time to close it before the hall door opens and a nurse comes in—the big orderly from before, the one named Frank.

"Thought I heard you scream," he says. He glances at the wall behind me. "You have a nice nap?" There's a bandage on his forearm that wasn't there before. He sees me looking at it and raises his eyebrow, all humor gone from his face and voice. "Looking for a repeat? You bite me again and I will make you re- gret it."

"I bit you?" The details of the fight are hazy, but I remember kicking someone. "In the . . . earlier, when everyone tackled me?"

"When you tried to escape," says Frank. "You bit me and you broke Dr. Sardinha's nose."

"I didn't mean to."

"You guys never do."

"What do you mean, 'you guys'?"

"I mean 'mentally divergent,'" says Frank. "Well, technically I mean 'crazy,' but I'm required to say 'mentally divergent' in front of the crazy people. Makes you feel better."

"It's not working."

"I get that a lot." He leans forward, resting his forearms on the bed railing. "So listen, you're gone in a few hours, and I don't want any trouble between now and then, so let's make a truce, okay?"

"I'm not crazy."

"You stop screaming," he says, ignoring me, "and whatever else you were doing in here, and I'll leave you alone."

"You can't let them take me."

"I'm not letting them, I'm helping them. I'm doing everything I can to expedite the process."

"But I'm not crazy!" I say again, my voice rising. "I have depression and some kind of anxiety disorder—you can't lock me up for either one of those."

"You've been upgraded to schizophrenia," says Frank, "mostly thanks to the evil face monsters or whatever you said was chasing you. I don't remember—in two more hours it won't be my problem anymore."

I fall back into the pillow, shocked. I've heard of schizophrenia before, in passing, and none of it was good; the diagnosis falls like a sentence of execution.

I glance at the bathroom door; if Frank won't help me escape, maybe the reporter will. "No trouble," I say, looking back at him. "I don't bother you, you don't bother me."

He stops. "You guys usually put up more of a fight. You planning something?"

"Yes," I say, nodding firmly. "The evil face monsters are going to cut these restraints off and carry me away in their magical flying car."

Frank stares at me a moment, then shakes his head and turns to the door. "I don't know why I even talk to you people." He stops by the door and shoots me a final look. "No noise, no funny stuff, and in two hours we'll be out of each other's way forever."

I nod. He closes the door and walks away.

The woman peeks out of the bathroom. "He's kind of an asshat, isn't he?"

"You said you could help," I say, and tug on my arm restraints. "Can you get me out of these things?"

"Whoa," she says, stepping into the room. "That would really be crossing a line."

"You don't understand," I say. "This hospital, and apparently Powell, are run by . . ." And now we're back to the same old problem—if I tell anyone the truth, I sound completely crazy. It's the trickiest part of the Faceless Men's Plan, to hide themselves so well from the world that no one will ever believe they exist. "I have to get out of here."

"Let me ask you a few questions first," she says, "and then I'll see what I can do about the restraints, okay?"

"Do you promise?"

"I can't promise I'll get you out, but I promise to look into it. You're asking me to break the law, Michael; you're going to have to trust me first."

I look at the door to the hallway, then up at the TV. "Fine," I say, "but make it quick."

"Great." She smiles and opens her handbag, pulling out a small black device. I draw back as far as I can and shake my head.

"Get rid of that."

"It's my digital recorder," she says. "I'm just recording the interview."

"No," I say more firmly, pressing myself as far back into the pillows as I can. "Put it in the hall, or back in the other room, but it can't be in here."

She looks at it, then at me, then shrugs and walks into the bathroom. "I'm leaving it on the sink," she says, "is that okay?"

"Yes." I take a deep breath, forcing myself to calm back down. It's just a recorder—it might not send a signal at all. "If you've got a cell phone, leave that in there too."

"All right," she says, walking back in with a notebook and a pen. "Let's get started. The doctors here suspect that you may have witnessed a crime scene related to the Red Line killings. Can you describe that scene for me, please?"

"I don't remember anything like that."

She frowns. "But they said you were talking about it."

"I was talking about . . . something else," I say. I don't dare mention the Faceless Men; I need her to believe me, not think I'm crazy. "I may have seen something, but I don't remember a crime scene. Certainly not any bodies or anything like that."

"Okay," she says slowly, tapping her pen on the notebook. "If you don't remember a crime scene, maybe you remember something else? They obviously think you saw something or they wouldn't have called the police."

"They called the police?"

"Nothing fancy, just a tip. My source placed the call, that's how I knew to come here. Let's try to figure this out. I take it you lost some memory?"

"About two weeks," I say, nodding. "I was in some kind of a fall."

"Were you pushed?"

"I don't remember."

"Where were you?"

"I don't remember."

"You're not being very helpful."

"I remember some kind of a . . . hollow city," I say. "Streets full of houses with nobody in them, like an empty skeleton after all the flesh has gone away."

She jots it down. "That's creepy, but it's a start. Can you remember who you were with?"

"I don't think I was with anybody. Maybe Lucy— definitely Lucy, because I can't imagine going away without her." I look up, intense and sincere. "We're going to get away—get to a small town somewhere, maybe a farm. I think I'd like to live on a farm. The hospital couldn't find her, though, so I don't know where she is." For the first time it occurs to me that something might have happened to her, and my stomach clenches into a knot. "You've got to find her: Lucy Briggs."

"Girlfriend?"

I nod. "I don't know her phone number, but she works in a Greek place on Grand Avenue. I think something may have happened to her."

"I'll find her. Anyone else?"

"No one I can think of."

"Have you recently associated with any members of the Children of the Earth?"

My heart stops beating—the entire world seems to freeze—and then everything snaps back into place. I stare at her carefully, cautiously, suddenly wary. "What do you know?"

She looks up, eyes wide. "What's wrong?"

"Why are you asking about the Children of the Earth?"

She makes a note on her pad. "Is that a problem?"

"How much do you know about me?" I demand. "What's really going on here?"

"I . . . ," she stumbles over her words, brow furrowed in confusion. "I don't know anything, why? Are you a member of the Children?"

"The Children of the Earth are a murder cult," I say. "They kidnapped my mother while she was pregnant, and when I was born they killed her. I wouldn't associate with them for anything. I'd kill them first."

Her face goes white. "You did not just say that."

"What do the Children of the Earth have to do with the Red Line Killer?"

She sucks in a breath. "Almost all of the victims have been members."

I curse.

"Someone is hunting down the Children of the Earth and cutting off their faces," she says. "Someone who hates them as much as you do."

"So they do suspect me," I say, watching her carefully. "You said they didn't, but they do."

"Well, yeah, *now* I know that." She clicks her pen and drops it in her purse, folding up her notebook and shoving it in after. "I could get in so much trouble for being here."

"You can't leave," I say quickly. "You can't leave me with them."

"Listen, Michael." She stands, glances at the door, then steps toward me and lowers her voice. "I promised I'd look at getting you out of here, and I will—if you're as innocent as you say I'll do everything I can to get you out of here. But until then you've got to be careful, okay? And please, don't tell anyone I was here. I'll try to visit you at Powell, as soon as I'm allowed to, but please—just keep me a secret, okay?"

"You promise you'll come?"

"I'll do everything I can, but if you tell anyone I was here I could get cut off completely."

"I won't tell."

"Thanks." She steps to the door, listens carefully, then cracks it open and slips into the hall.

I sit in silence, staring at the blank TV. It stares back. I hear a voice in the hall, loud and familiar, and look anxiously at the door.

My last hope has arrived: Dr. Vanek is here.

THREE

DR. VANEK THROWS open the door, nearly filling it with his bulk. I allow myself to hope that I might be released, but he seems to sense my optimism, and frowns and shakes his head.

"You made quite a splash here, they tell me." He grunts slightly as he drops into the nearby chair. He has dark hair, ringing his face with a dark beard, and the frames of his glasses look thin and fragile. "I wish you'd have come to see me sometime in the past six months—it's one thing to get a call from the hospital announcing your long-lost patient has finally surfaced, and it's quite another to learn that said patient has managed to injure two members of the hospital staff—one of them, I might add, the head of the psych ward. You did not make any friends with your outburst yesterday, I assure you of that."

"You're in a mood," I tell him. Dr. Vanek has always been gruff, much more so than any of the other psychiatrists I've dealt with. Some of them were great; I even had a crush on my old school counselor, a young, pretty woman named Beth. She's the one who first diagnosed me with depression. She loved her job; loved helping people. On the opposite end of the spectrum, sometimes I think the only reason Vanek got into medicine was to show off how smart he is.

"Didn't I warn you about this, Michael?" Vanek rubs his forehead with thick, sausagelike fingers. "Didn't I tell you, when you started missing a session here and there, that a lapse in treatment or medication could result in a heightening of your symptoms?"

"Do you have a cell phone?"

He sighs. "No, Michael, I never bring my cell phone to our sessions, you know that. Though now I understand that your distaste for technology has grown some new and interesting dimensions. Tell me about these Faceless Men."

"They think I killed them. They think I'm this . . . Red Line Killer."

Vanek raises his eyebrow. "Where did you get that idea?"

I open my mouth, but say nothing. I promised the reporter I wouldn't say anything. I shrug. "It just . . . seems obvious."

"Well," says Vanek, nodding, "that saves me the trouble of breaking it to you gently. If we're going to do anything about it, though, I think you ought to tell me where you've been for the last two weeks. The Red Line Killer killed a janitor in an industrial park last week, and it would be nice to be able to prove you were somewhere else."

"Hiding," I say. Vanek has a poor bedside manner, perhaps, but he's not dumb. He might be able to see the truth. "You need to get me out of here. We can talk about all of this back in your office, or wherever you want, but not here."

"I'm not here to get you out," he says, staring at me intently. "I'm here to oversee your transfer and readmittance to Powell Psychiatric. Dr. Sardinha is recommending high security, intensive therapy, and neuroleptics."

"Neuro . . . what?"

"Antipsychotic medication," Vanek explains. "You're not just a violent patient anymore, Michael, you're a violent, schizophrenic patient. That is not a good combination in the eyes of our medical or legal systems."

"I'm not crazy."

"Please, Michael, we prefer the term 'mentally divergent.'"

"I don't have multiple personalities."

Vanek laughs, a rough sound, like a bark. "Double damnation on whoever started that misconception. Schizophrenia has nothing to do with multiple personalities; it means that your brain responds to stimuli that don't exist. You see and hear things, like these Faceless Men of yours, and you believe things, like this paranoid plan of persecution and surveillance, that are not real."

I sit up desperately, but the arm restraints stop me from leaning very far forward. "I'm not crazy," I say quickly, "and I'm not paranoid."

"Please, Michael," he says, peering at me over the tops of his glasses. "You've been paranoid your entire life. That's a reasonable enough reaction for someone who was kidnapped before he was even born, but 'reasonable' and 'healthy' are very different things."

"This has nothing to do with my mother," I say, angry at him for bringing it up. "Now listen, you've got to believe me. The Faceless Men are real—there was one in here last night. I saw him!"

"Well of course you saw him," says Vanek, "that's what I just explained—you see imaginary things that your brain perceives as real. It's called a hallucination."

"It was real," I insist. How can I make him believe me? "He was as real as . . . as that wall, as the chair; he was as real as you and me."

"Reality," says Vanek, frowning. He leans forward and gestures with his hand. "Think of it this way: the human brain does not have a direct connection to reality—not yours, not mine, not anyone's. We can only perceive something after it's been filtered through our senses—our eyes, our ears, etc.—and then communicated to our brain. Our brain takes that information and reconstructs it to create the most accurate picture of reality that it can. That's good enough for most of us, but schizophrenia breaks the system—the signal from your senses to your brain gets corrupted somewhere along the line, so when your brain puts together its picture of reality, that picture is full of extra, artificial information. Some people hear voices, others see faces or colors or other things. Put simply, the reality you perceive is separate from the reality that actually exists."

"That's ridiculous," I say. "My brain doesn't do that."

"Everyone's brain does it to some extent—what do you think a dream is? It's a false reality that your brain creates out of remembered stimuli, extrapolating where necessary to fill in the gaps. The difference, of course, is that a dream is usually healthy, while a hallucination is not."

I shake my head. On top of being trapped, now I'm being disbelieved and studied and who knows what else. My chances of escape are slipping away with every word that comes out of his mouth. "This is . . ." I don't know what to say. "This is stupid and unfair and . . . illegal." I tug on the arm restraints. "You can't say I'm crazy just because I saw something you haven't seen. What about . . . what about God? Can you lock someone up for believing in God? You've never seen him, so he's probably just a hallucination, right?"

"It's times like these I wish I had an assistant to explain things sensitively," says Vanek. "I don't have the patience for it."

"Obviously not," I say, "or you wouldn't have jumped straight from 'Michael's saying strange things' to 'Michael's a delusional psychotic.'"

"It wasn't my diagnosis, Michael." He sighs and rubs his forehead again, his eyes closed. "It was Dr. Sardinha's."

"The one I kicked? They said I broke his nose—no wonder he wants to lock me up."

"Thank you for arriving at the point I started this conversation with ten minutes ago."

"And his diagnosis doesn't seem suspicious to you?"

"Listen, Michael, it's more than just you saying strange things. Hallucinations and delusions are the most visible symptoms of schizophrenia, but they're not the most important. The big ones, the ones at the core of the disease, are depression—which you've had for years—and 'disorganized behavior,' which is a fancy way of saying . . . well, of describing the way you've been living for the past six months: you stopped taking care of yourself, you wander around and get lost, you do bizarre things like carry faucet handles in your pockets—"

"I didn't do any of that."

He holds up a small metal lever—the knob from a bathroom sink. I recognize it instantly as mine, though I have no idea where it came from.

"This was in your pocket when you were admitted, though I suppose it's not damning in itself. Shall we enumerate the other points on the list?" He ticks off his fingers one by one. "You stopped coming to our sessions, you stopped going to work, you eventually stopped doing everything—the cops found you living under an overpass. You haven't shaved in months, you haven't bathed in weeks, and the police report suggests that you'd been pissing in your pants for days."

"I was being chased," I say, gritting my teeth. "We were trying to get out of town, and sometimes . . . sometimes hiding from the bad guys requires sacrifices. What else was I supposed to do?"

"How can you be sure you were hiding?" he asks. "Do you even remember where you were? Or why you went there?"

I look at him silently, trying desperately to remember anything about the last two weeks, but all I get are quick snatches—meaningless bits of sight and sound and smell that I can't piece together into anything coherent. It's like trying to look at the world through a dirty glass, smeared and warped and blurry.

He sighs. "You had no money and no ID; the only thing you did have, in fact, was the water faucet."

"I remember the faucet!" I say suddenly, shocked at my own outburst. Excitement wells up inside of me—the first memory to return from the two missing weeks. "I can't remember much—I think something happened to my head—but I remember the faucet handle. I was defending myself."

"You're lucky you didn't hit a cop with it, or you'd be in even more trouble than you are now."

"Not like that," I say. "It was to keep the hot water turned off. The Faceless Men had tracked me down, but they couldn't get to me through the wires like they usually did, so they filled the water heater with cyanide instead. I took the faucets off to make sure it couldn't get out."

Vanek is watching me, stubby fingers folded across his round chest. "You removed your father's faucet handles? No wonder they found you living on the street."

"I . . ." I stop. He's right—my father would never have allowed it. He was not a patient man. "I wasn't living there. Did I get kicked out?"

"When did you leave your father's house?"

"Two weeks ago, I think. I . . . I remember I tried to take the TV outside, to make the house safe. I think he threw a fit."

"That sounds like him. And you." Vanek pulls off his glasses and rubs his eyes. "If your father cared half as much about his son as he does about his television, some of this behavior might have been reported early enough to make a difference."

"I got away from home," I say, not really paying attention. "They had no reason to poison me unless I'd escaped from the web of electronic surveillance—and they were trying to poison me, which means I'd done it. I'd found a place without any wires." I laugh. "I think it scared them." So little of the past few days made sense to me, but this did. The Faceless Men were on my trail, and I'd almost gotten away. It was just a chance encounter with the police that got me back on their radar—which means that if I can get away again, and avoid the police this time, I can escape completely.

Except I can't leave without Lucy. Are they holding her hostage to keep me from running? Where is she?

"Listen to yourself, Michael," says Vanek, leaning forward. "Inconsistency is one of the best ways to spot a delusion, so let's consider: first the Faceless Men are tracking you, and then when they lose track of you they decide to kill you in the most obtuse, convoluted way possible. How did they know which water heater to spike with cyanide if they didn't know where you were? And if they did know where you were, why not just plant more listening devices and continue observing you? And the biggest question of all: if they wanted you dead, why not just kill you outright? Why bother with such a roundabout plan?"

"I don't know," I say. "If I knew all the pieces of the Plan, do you think I'd be strapped to this hospital bed?" I tug again on the restraints for emphasis. "I have been running from these people for months. What do I have to do to convince you?"

"Why are they observing you: a jobless, homeless nobody?"

"I have a job," I shoot back. "And a home, and a girlfriend, and everything. I have an entire life, and they are trying to take it away."

"You haven't done anything important," says Vanek. "You don't know anything important. You're nothing."

"I have something they want."

"You have nothing."

"But I do," I say, "I know it. I think I'd found something, right when I disappeared—a thing or a place or maybe a person. Something they didn't want anyone to ever find, and I found it. But now . . ."

Vanek leans forward. "Where is it?"

"Look, I don't know why I can't remember anything, and I don't know what I have, but I know that they want it, which means that they want me. They want me more than anything in the world."

Vanek smiles. "Narcissism is the other best way to spot a delusion." I try to talk, but he stops me with his hand. "Paranoid schizophrenia involves, inherently, a heightened belief in your own importance—that all of these vast, hyperintelligent superorganizations have nothing better to do than watch your TV and poison your water heater."

"Dr. Vanek, you've got to believe me. They want me because they're scared of me. I'm the key to their whole Plan, or I found the key to their Plan, and they don't dare let me loose because they think I'm going to stop them, but I don't care anymore. I don't need to stop them, I just want to get away." I pause. "Lucy and I were going to go to a farm."

"It's a reflection of the fact that your reality exists solely in your mind," says Vanek, brushing past my comments as if they weren't even there. "The Faceless Men don't have anyone better to spy on because, to them, no one else exists. You're both the center and the circumference of their entire, imaginary world."

"Stop saying that!" My face is hot, and I feel rage boiling inside me. I take a deep breath, and realize my fists are clenched. "If you're not going to help me, just get out of here." If Vanek doesn't believe me, and something horrible's happened to Lucy, who's left?

Vanek stares at me for a long time, watching silently. Finally he nods. "You're right," he says. "I can't convince you your reality is false any more than I could convince anyone else in the world. That's what's going to make this so difficult to treat."

"So let me go."

"I already told you, Michael, that's not my call. Once you're at Powell they're going to do some more tests—not physical tests, don't worry—and if they agree with Sardinha's diagnosis, they'll start you on antipsychotic medication."

"I don't want drugs."

"Then don't be schizophrenic," he says. "Those are really your only two options right now."

"We could do therapy."

"Oh, you'll get therapy," he says, "but not until after the drugs make some headway. Psychotherapy is designed to cure unhealthy thought processes, and unfortunately for you your thought processes are completely healthy—they're just reacting to false thoughts."

"So I'm sane and insane at the same time?"

"Welcome to schizophrenia," says Vanek. "Your brain's ability to talk to itself—which is how it does its job—is dependent on the substances dopamine and serotonin. No amount of psychotherapy can change the way those substances interact with your brain, but drugs can. Once they find the right drug, at the right dose, the corruption in your thought patterns will disappear, and the hallucinations and delusions will disappear with them. Then they can start some social therapy and life skills and that sort of thing; teach you how to live in the real world again."

"So they're just going to drug me until I stop telling them I see things."

"You can look at it that way if you want," says Vanek, holding up his hands. "What you think about it doesn't really matter, does it? Your brain's broken."

"Are you the worst therapist ever?"

Vanek frowns. "I'm not your mother," he says.

"No one is."

"Tragic but irrelevant. You're twenty years old, Michael, and I'm not here to coddle you. I'm here to smile at the staff and sign some papers and check you into Powell."

"You're coming with me?"

"Not to stay. They have their own doctors."

"But I'm your patient, right? You're my personal therapist."

"I'm a therapist you haven't visited in six months; I've had my shot and failed. If you want to get better, you need to pay better attention to Dr. Little than you did to me." He stands up. "I'll go tell them you're ready." He steps toward the door, and it feels like part of me—my life, my freedom—is being ripped away. I can't let them lock me up in a psych hospital; I have to think of something.

"Wait!" I shout. He stops and turns to look at me. "Tell them . . . tell them I can't leave yet! That there's something wrong." I rack my brain. "The memory loss! Go with that; my memory's been screwed up and you think I should stay in a regular medical hospital until they figure out why."

"Two minutes ago you were begging to get out of here, and now you want to stay?"

"It's better than a psych hospital."

"There's nothing I can do."

"Does schizophrenia explain the memory loss?"

"No . . ."

"Then tell them I can't leave until we find something that does. Maybe I got brain damage in the fall."

"They've gone over the MRI scans a hundred times, Michael, there's no sign of trauma—"

My pulse thunders into overdrive, and I feel my head going light. "I had an MRI?" My voice is louder than I expect; almost a screech.

Vanek's eyes widen at my outburst. "You fell," he says, keeping his voice calm. "An MRI is the best way to test for cranial and spinal injuries—"

"An MRI is like a—" I don't even know how to talk; my heart's pounding in terror, my head's going cold and light. "They're trying to control me through electronic devices, and you shove me inside the biggest device you can find? An MRI is designed to

bombard your body with an electric field; that's
what it's for. Who knows what they did to me while
I was in there!"

"An MRI is completely harmless, Michael."

"Why can you not understand this! They could
have read my mind, or put something in it, or—or
just cut chunks of it right out! That's why I can't
remember anything! That's why I'm going crazy!"
Dr. Vanek opens the door and walks into the hall,
calling for Dr. Sardinha, and I shout after him desperately. "You've got to get me into surgery, right
now! Find whatever they put in my head and cut it
out! That's why I have a false reality—I can only
think what they want me to think!"

Dr. Vanek doesn't come back. About thirty minutes later Frank and another orderly prop open my
door and start wheeling me out.

"Listen, Frank," I say, "I'm sorry, I didn't mean to
do it, so no hard feelings, right?" He ignores me.
"Frank, you've gotta help me, you've gotta get me
out of here—don't let me go to Powell, don't . . .
just take me somewhere else, just wheel me into a
closet and untie me and you'll never see me again, I
promise."

Nothing.

"Come on Frank, no hard feelings, right? You can
bite me back if you want, if it makes you feel better,
or you can punch me in the face or whatever you
want to do—I'm serious, man, just help me out here.
Help me—" We push through the outer door, and
they wheel me toward an ambulance.

I'm crying now. "Come on Frank, we're friends; you know I didn't mean to bite you, I was just scared is all, and you know I'd let you go if it was me, right?" They bump me up into the back of the ambulance, medical equipment whirring and blinking around me. "Please, please, please don't let them take me. Please. You don't know what they're going to do to me in there."

Frank clamps the gurney into place. "They're going to make you better." He steps out. "Good luck."

He shuts the door, and we drive away.

FOUR

"HELLO, MICHAEL," SAYS Dr. Little. I'm in the commons room at Powell, untied and standing up, flanked by a nurse named Devon and a burly security guard who didn't bother to introduce himself.

"I'm Dr. Little," says the doctor. "We met before, do you remember?"

"Yes," I say. He was my doctor the last time the state threw me in here. In many ways Dr. Little is the exact opposite of Dr. Vanek—he's a small man, with a kind smile and a pair of thick glasses that make his eyes look huge. He's also nicer, or at least better at pretending to be nice.

"Good, good!" He talks a little too slowly, his facial expressions a little too broad, like he's talking to a child. I remember disliking him, and now I remember why. "You were here a year or so ago, as I recall; we determined that you had generalized anxiety disorder, and I prescribed Klonopin. Have you been taking your Klonopin?"

"I stopped six months ago," I say quickly, hoping to persuade him to try it again. Klonopin annoyed me, but at least it didn't mess with my head; if he tries something stronger, who knows what it will do to me? "I kept picking it up, but I wasn't taking it. I'm sorry, I really am. I'll do better this time."

"Very good," he says, grinning like a doll. "That's excellent news, Michael, excellent news. You're really going to like this new medication. I'm really looking forward to it—"

"Wait," I say, "new medication? Seriously? I thought we were going to have some more tests and therapy and talk about this some more." I inch away from him—not even an inch, maybe a half inch. The restraints are gone, but I don't want to give him any reason to bring them back. "We don't have to go straight to the drugs."

"I assure you, Michael, you have nothing to be afraid of. In some ways Loxitane is just a different kind of Klonopin. Did the hospital explain to you about dopamine and serotonin?"

"Yeah," I say, swallowing hard. I can see the pill now, a green blob in a small plastic cup. He holds it casually, but I shy back like it's a snake.

"Excellent," says Dr. Little. "The Klonopin you used to take stops your brain from overusing serotonin, and that worked more or less okay while you were taking it—though not, apparently, well enough to keep up with the progress of your condition. Loxitane," he holds up the plastic cup and shakes it, rattling the pill inside, "reduces your brain's use of dopamine, and we anticipate that it will work much better. Your medical history shows a very strong susceptibility to drug effects, so we'll start you small with ten milligrams and see where we go from there. Are you ready?"

"Wait," I say, pulling back farther. "Can't we start with something else first? Can't we talk about this and decide if I even need drugs at all?"

"Your diagnosis already recommends drugs," he says, smiling, "and the fact that the Klonopin had a positive effect, however minor, suggests that drugs will continue to be beneficial. On top of that, your repeated outbursts at the hospital suggest rather strongly that your condition, whether schizophrenia or something else, has become urgent. We will talk, just like you suggest, but there's no reason to delay the medication."

"But are you sure it's safe?" I think about the MRI and shudder involuntarily. "You're sure there's nothing in it, or that it won't, I don't know, like . . ." I close my eyes. What am I trying to say?

"Every drug has side effects," says Dr. Little, stepping toward me. He has a glass of water in his other hand. "But we will be monitoring you constantly, and we'll make sure nothing happens. Say 'ah.'"

I start to protest but he dumps the pill in my mouth, pouring a quick shot of water in after it. I splutter, soaking my front, but the pill's already gone down. It's inside me; I feel it like a hole in my gut.

"Excellent," says Dr. Little, smiling broadly. "Now, you get some rest, and I'll see about scheduling you for some of our group sessions."

I nod, and the doctor walks away. The security guard goes with him.

"Well," says the nurse, clapping a hand on my shoulder, "welcome to Powell. What do you want to do first?"

I almost say "escape," but I stop myself, think for a minute, and smile. If this hospital is part of the Plan, and the Faceless Men really are watching me here, this might be my best chance to learn what the Plan actually is. It won't do me any good to escape until I know how they're tracking me, but if I stick around and keep my eyes open, I might learn something important.

"Show me around," I say. "Show me everything."

THE THING ABOUT Powell, or any psych hospital, is that nobody believes anything you say. This is maddening, but it is also predictable, and if you can predict it you can use it for your own advantage. They've done nothing to protect themselves from the Faceless Men, because they think I'm crazy, and that lack of precaution means there are holes in their security. If I can find those holes I can use them, and the best way to find them is to think backward: how are the Faceless Men getting in? If I can retrace their steps in reverse, I can get out the same hole and disappear forever.

Devon walks me through the large commons room, dominating the center of Powell's secured wing. The longest wall is marked with windows, just slightly taller than I am, framed with old, painted metal and covered with a grate of woven steel. The only view is another building, another wing of the hospital I think. From the way the shadows track left to right across the floor I assume that the sun is moving right to left, which means the windows face north. This information is not useful, but I feel better for knowing it.

Most of the commons room is full of tables, long cafeteria-style tables with simple metal chairs. This is where the patients eat their meals and put together puzzles and shuffle mindlessly through the aisles, tiny, scrubbing steps in worn-out slippers. I stay away from these patients. The west end of the room is carpeted, with sofas and cushioned chairs and a large TV bolted onto the wall. I stay away from those patients too.

The south wall of the commons room has doors for patient rooms, and hallways running east and west. The east hallway leads past more patient rooms, then branches again to even more rooms, including the restroom and a large, communal shower. The west hallway is much shorter: a few feet down there's a nurse's station, with an open door and a window cut into the south wall at chest height, and then a wide metal gate to block us off from the rest of the world. I peer at the gate from a distance, eyeing the electronic keypad that opens the lock, but I don't dare get too close. The window to the nurse's station has a computer monitor, and I need to keep my distance.

Devon leads me toward my room, but one of the patients walks over quickly to intercept us.

"Hello, Steve," says Devon.

"This the new guy?" asks Steve. He's tallish, and very skinny, with a black scraggly beard and a bright red ball cap turned backward on his head. "What's your name?"

"Michael," I say.

"Just got in? Just got out?" He knocks his wrists together a couple of times, signing handcuffs. I nod. "Where you gonna put him, Devon? You can't put him in Jerry's room."

"Jerry doesn't have a room anymore," says Devon, still walking calmly. "Remember? Jerry went home."

"But he still has a room," says Steve. "He won't like it if you give it away. Right? He won't like it."

Devon smiles. "We already gave his room to Gordon," he says, and Steve frowns.

"Gordon? Which one's Gordon?"

"You know Gordon, Steve," says Devon. "We have this conversation every week."

"You gave him Jerry's room?"

"A couple of months ago."

"Gordon!" shouts Steve, spinning around. He pauses a moment, scanning the room, then storms off. "Gordon, come here!"

Devon chuckles. "Jerry left in February; guy can't get it through his head."

"He's been here that long?"

"Five months," says Devon. "Don't worry, though, most people are in and out of here a lot quicker than that."

I nod. "Anything else I should know?"

Devon looks around the room. "It's pretty mellow in here, all things considered. That bald guy is Dwight; if he starts talking about ammonia, he's about to get violent, so keep your ears open."

"I will."

"Here's your room." He opens a door and shows me in; it's a pretty standard hospital room, with a raised bed and a wheeled table and a small dresser in the corner. There's no TV, but there is a small clock radio bolted to the dresser. I don't say anything about it.

"Everything look good?" asks Devon.

"Great," I say, nodding. I need to get rid of that radio, but other than that it looks great.

"You're a little late for dinner, but I could probably rustle up a snack if you want one."

"No thanks," I say, shaking my head. "I'm fine. I'll see you later."

"I'm taking off soon," says Devon, "but if you change your mind the night nurse can take care of you. Sorry you don't get a window, but there's only—"

Suddenly I'm on the floor, gritting my teeth and clutching my head in agony. Devon buzzes, a low electronic hum, and he drops to his knee next to me.

"Mike, are you okay, man?" He buzzes again.

"Get away!" The pain is blinding—I feel like my head is swelling and compressing all at once, kneading my brain like bruised dough. Devon buzzes again and I shove him away, pushing myself back into the corner. "Don't touch me!"

My skull feels like it's breaking apart, cracking open like an egg, and I grab it desperately, trying to hold the pieces together. The buzz comes again, stronger this time, and I scream to drown it out.

"Come on, Mike," says Devon, and then he leaves at a run. I stay in the corner, clutching my head until it feels normal again. Nothing's broken. I hear a voice at the door.

"New guy."

I look up. My door is closed.

"Hey new guy, you awake?"

"Who's there?"

"Not the best way to start your freedom, shoving a nurse."

"I didn't mean to, he was . . ." He was buzzing. "He was attacking me."

"You're acting like an idiot, and they don't let idiots leave."

I raise my head. What was that guy's name—the one from the hall? "Are you Steve?"

"They are always watching us," he says. "Always watching."

"The doctors?"

His voice is a thin whisper. "The Faceless Men."

I scramble to the door, half crawling, slipping on

the slick linoleum. Footsteps run away, pelting down the hall, and when I yank open the door the hallway's empty.

I whisper as loud as I can. "Steve!" There's no answer. I poke my head out into the hallway and look down through the commons room to the TV on the far side; there's a swarm of activity by the nurse's station. I slide back into my room and push the door closed.

Someone's trying to warn me, which means I'm not the only one who knows. I don't think it's Steve. Is the hospital part of the Plan? Are they in on it, or just pawns? Whoever it was was right; the Faceless Men are here. Somehow, maybe in the MRI, they put something into my head that lets them control me, and whenever they want they can flip a switch and make me see things and hear things and do things—whatever they want me to do. Even if I leave I'm a prisoner.

Unless I can find out how it works, and how they find me.

I pull the blanket off my bed and cover the radio. With the sensors neutralized, I reach behind the dresser and pull out the plug, killing it completely. But a lot of these clock radios have batteries, in case of a power outage. Can it still broadcast without being plugged in? I grab the blanket, take a deep breath, and yank it off. The screen is blank; it doesn't have batteries.

Unless the batteries only power the transmitter, with no juice left for the screen.

I need water; with a glass of water I could short it out. What would the doctors say—do they know I'm being watched? Are they part of the Plan, or just pawns in it? I throw the blanket back over the clock, just in case, and probe the rest of the room, looking for cameras—for anything else they might be using to watch me. I can't find anything.

"Michael?"

I turn around; Devon's back, with Dr. Little and another nurse. I stand up, tense and embarrassed from being caught. Do they know what I was looking for?

Dr. Little steps forward. "Are you okay, Michael? Devon said you were having a seizure."

I glance at Devon; he caused it, didn't he? Is this an act, to make me trust them, or do they really not know? Maybe Devon has an implant as well, and they use him to get to me.

"Michael?" asks Dr. Little.

"I'm fine," I say quickly. Whatever they did to me was real—it hurt, it was a real pain—but I don't tell them. "It was just . . . it was nothing."

"You pushed Devon," says Dr. Little sternly. "Do you think that's an acceptable behavior?"

My heart sinks. "No, sir."

"We let you out of your restraints, despite your violence at the hospital, because you promised to act peacefully. Do you need to be restrained again?"

"No sir, no I don't." I swallow hard, trying not to look at Devon. "It's just that . . . it's not going to happen again."

"See that it doesn't," says Dr. Little, and then the smile comes back to his face. "I'm glad we have an understanding. While I'm here, you'll be pleased to know that you already have a visitor, or at any rate a visitor request. I told her that our visiting hours were over for the evening, but she'll be back first thing in the morning."

"Who?"

"A friend of yours."

FIVE

LUCY ARRIVES JUST after breakfast—oatmeal and apple juice and Loxitane, served on a tray and delivered from a thick plastic cart, like a rolling cupboard. I think I could fit inside that cart; if I was able to crawl in when nobody's looking, I could hold very still and they'd pull me right through the gate to freedom.

"Michael!" Lucy runs across the commons room, grabbing my hand for a moment before throwing her arms around me in a massive hug. I close my eyes, feeling her heart beat against me. She kisses my ear, and I feel her tears wet against my skin. "Oh, Michael, Michael," she says. "I'm so sorry. I came as soon as I heard."

"It's okay."

She pulls back and takes my hand in hers, looking down with concern. "It's not okay." She's beautiful. She's dyed her hair again—back to black this time, covering the bright purple streaks she had a few weeks ago. She sees me looking at it and shrugs, reaching up to twist a strand in her fingers. "I didn't know if they'd let me in here any other way. I don't mind; I like black." She pulls up a chair and sits next to me, comforting and familiar: her worn black jeans, her old black T-shirt, the smile in the corners of her mouth.

I hold her hand. "Where have you been? The hospital couldn't reach you, and I thought something had happened."

"They probably have an old number," she says. "I had to move kind of suddenly. But where have you been, that's the question. I've been looking for you for weeks. I thought you'd had another depressive attack or something, but your dad said you hadn't come home."

"He actually talked to you?"

She rolls her eyes. "Sort of. He still hates me. But this time he wasn't ignoring me, he was accusing me of running off with you. I put two and two together and figured he couldn't find you either."

I look around quickly; we're getting some looks from the other patients, but none of them are close enough to hear, and the only doctor in the room is on the far side, holding some kind of therapy session by the TV. I lean in close to Lucy, whispering softly.

"I was running from someone."

Her face goes solemn. "Who?"

I gesture discreetly at the room around us. "Who do you think? I'm not sure of the details, but . . ." I lean closer. "Do you remember when I used to tell you there were people watching me?"

"Yeah, but you never told me who. Is it these guys—the hospital?"

I've never told her the truth before. Will she believe me? Will she think I'm crazy? I don't know if I dare tell her everything. "I'm not sure of all the details, because I've lost some memory, but about two weeks ago They made some kind of move—or at least I think They must have, because something prompted me into action, and I went on the run. I left home, I stopped going to work, I was hiding out . . . somewhere. Dr. Vanek said the police found me under an overpass, but I must have run because I fell out of a window. That's when they finally caught me."

"You fell?" She puts a hand on my head, feeling for lumps. "Are you okay? Is that why you lost memory?"

"I think so, or it might be the . . ." It might be the MRI, reacting with the implant, but I don't say that out loud. I can't bear the thought of her looking at me the way the doctors do, like I'm some kind of helpless head case. "Listen, it's not important how they caught me, what matters is that I need to get out of here. This is not like last year when I spent two weeks in recovery for anxiety—this is serious. They've trumped up a big fake diagnosis so they can hold me indefinitely; something called schizo-phrenia."

She shakes her head. "Multiple personalities?"

"No, that's something else. Schizophrenia is like I'm hallucinating or something—like an official stamp that invalidates everything I say. As long as they tell people I'm crazy, they can hold me in here and observe me and do anything they want with me. I think they might even be experimenting on me."

Lucy snarls. "Bastards. Why do they want you?"

I say nothing, staring into her face. She stares back, angry and worried and trusting. I take a deep breath—I won't tell her everything, but I can tell her some.

"They think I have something to do with the Red Line Killer."

"What?" She practically shouts it, and I quiet her quickly, hissing through my teeth.

"Keep it down!"

"They think you're the Red Line?"

"Dr. Vanek said they did, but no one's asked me any questions yet. How much do you know about the case?"

"Not much," she says, "just stuff I've overheard in the restaurant. Why do they think it has anything to do with you?"

"Because the victims were all . . ." I can't mention the Faceless Men—she doesn't know about them. "They were all from the Children of the Earth."

"Milos Cerny's cult?"

I nod. Milos Cerny was the man who killed my

mother. "I need you to find out more," I say. "Find out everything you can—who the Red Line's killed, and when, and how, and what the Children have to do with it. I'm going to do what I can to get out of here, but I don't want you tied up in that—I don't want to give Them any excuse to come after you too."

"I'll do my best," she says, "but . . . who are They?"

"I can't tell you right now," I say, "just please, trust me, and I'll tell you as soon as I can. You should go now."

And suddenly there's the look—not as bad as I'd feared, not as blatant, but it's there. She's doubting me. I feel tears growing hot behind my eyes. "Please, Lucy—please. I'm not crazy."

She purses her lips, thinking, then finally nods. "I believe you."

"Thank you. Now go, and be careful."

She leans in and kisses me, then squeezes my hand and turns to go. There are tears in her eyes. The other patients in the room are watching me, some quick and sharp, eyes darting to and fro, others staring slack-jawed, like they're not even seeing me at all. Which ones should I be afraid of?

I take another bite of oatmeal, but it's gone cold. I scan the room subtly, looking for Faceless Men, looking for cameras, looking for anything they might use to trigger my implant or read my mind. There's a clock on the wall, black hands like scissors snapping closed on the number 10. Can a clock send a signal? What's hiding behind it? They call it a clock face—what if it means—

"Michael?"

I turn with a start. The woman from before is standing behind me: the reporter.

"I'm sorry," she says, "I seem to be making a habit of startling you. I don't mean to."

"You . . ." I feel wordlessly uncomfortable.

"Kelly Fischer," she says, holding out her hand, "from the *Sun*."

I don't take her hand. "You're here."

"Thanks for keeping quiet about me." She pulls up a chair and sits. "You kind of freaked me out before, about you being a suspect, but my editor said to talk to you anyway—you're not officially a suspect yet, so if I interview you now, before they announce it, we can scoop everybody else."

Something about her feels wrong, somehow. I watch her carefully. She watches me, waiting for something, and when I don't speak she leans forward, putting a hand on my knee. "Obviously we're going to do everything we can to get you out of here, just like I promised."

"How can I trust you?"

"We're on your side, Michael, you've got to know that." She pulls her notebook and pen from her purse and holds them up. "No recorder, like you said; just the pen. Now my friend at the hospital tells me you've lost some memory, is that correct?"

I watch her carefully, trying to analyze her words. What is she really after? It doesn't give her anything to confirm what she already knows, so I shrug. "Yeah."

"About two weeks' worth?"

I nod.

"Listen, Michael, you're going to have to be a little more talkative than this. Do you have any idea where you might have been during the two weeks you can't remember?"

I study her face, warring with myself—do I say nothing? Do I say everything? How do I know where to stop in the middle? "Most of it's a haze," I say. "I can remember some things, silly things I guess, like a water faucet handle, but I don't know where I was or why. I was under an overpass when the police found me, but I must have run because I fell out of a window. That's when they finally . . . caught me."

I get the most horrible feeling of déjà vu, and feel myself grow nauseous.

"Let's go back further, then," she says. "Have you had any contact with the Children of the Earth since you were an infant?"

"No, none."

"You haven't gone looking for them, or found any members of the cult?"

"Why would I go looking for them?"

"I'm grasping at straws here, Michael; if you'd say something substantive I wouldn't have to drag it all out of you like this."

"What do you expect me to say?"

"You told me before that you hated the Children of the Earth," says Kelly, "and you said you'd sooner kill one than associate with him. What I'm asking is, did you ever act on that?"

The nervous flutters swirl sickly through my chest. "What?"

"You obviously hated them, you've obviously thought about it, and you proved at the hospital that you're more than capable of violence when something sets you off. I don't think it's out of the question to ask if you ever thought about acting on your hatred."

"I don't want to talk to you anymore."

"This is very important."

"I'm not a killer!"

People are looking at us now. Even the doctor in the corner looks up from her therapy session.

"I'm not a killer," I hiss. "They're the ones who are following me—I'm the victim here!"

"Whoa," says Kelly, her eyes going wide, "you say they're following you? The Children of the Earth?"

I grumble and shake my head, feeling the nervous flurry rising in my chest. "Not them, it's . . . I'm not crazy, okay? All I wanted was to get away. I didn't hurt anyone, I just left, and I need to leave again before they get what they want—"

"What do they want?"

"I don't know!"

"Excuse me," says a woman—the doctor from the therapy session—"is there a problem?"

"I'm fine," I say, struggling to calm down. I can't let them see me like this—I'm not crazy. "I'm fine."

"Why don't we go to your room, alright?" asks the doctor. She helps me to my feet. "You're doing great, Michael, you're not in any trouble, we're just going to have a little rest."

"I don't need a rest."

"I know you don't, but some of the other patients do, and we don't want to disturb them with shouting."

"Wait," I say, "I have one more—"

I turn to ask Kelly a question, but she's gone.

SIX

THE DRUGS, AS far as I can tell, do nothing. It's been a week now—seven days—and I've had no more visits from Lucy or the reporter. I've tried to contact my secret ally, whoever he is, but he doesn't answer. I'm alone.

They give me oatmeal, they give me pills, they come and they go. The doctor who took me back to my room, Linda Jones, invites me to her therapy sessions, but I'm too smart for that. She's just trying to get me into the corner where the TV can mess with my head.

I've cataloged every electronic device in the secured wing: a computer and a TV in the nurses' station, an electric lock on the gate, a TV and an analog clock on the commons room wall, a digital clock in every bedroom, two security cameras in the main hall, two smoke alarms in the main hall, and another smoke alarm in the restroom. Every angle is covered; every corner is filled. There's nowhere They can't see me.

When I pour water on my digital clock they replace it; that's how I know that it worked. If I ever need to disappear again, I can kill the clock with just a little cup of water.

On the seventh day I'm standing in the hall, watching Devon on the far side of the room. Is he watching me? Is he real—is his face real? He smiles, and the muscles move believably under the skin. Another nurse walks past me toward the gate, and I turn to watch as she types in the code on the keypad: 6, 8. She shifts to the side and I lose my view; the gate clicks open and she walks out, closing it firmly behind her. 6 and 8. How many more numbers are there? The nurse turns a corner out of sight and another form steps into view—a Faceless Man, tall and straight in a slim gray suit, standing just beyond the gate. He looks at me—even with no eyes I can tell he's looking straight at me, his face a distorted blur. I don't move, and neither does he.

Something touches my shoulder and I spin around, frightened, but it's only Devon.

"Someone's here to . . . whoa, Mikey, are you okay? I didn't mean to scare you."

"There's someone there." I spin back, pointing at the Faceless Man, but he's gone, and in his place are two men standing just beyond the gate, their faces calm and normal, their suits black instead of gray.

"He was right there," I say, stepping forward anxiously. I try to see behind the men, but I feel the buzz of the computer monitor and shy back. I look at Devon. "Did you see him?" I look back at the men in the hall. "He was right there—did you see him? You must have walked right past him!" I'm shouting now. "He was a man without a face—did you see him?"

The men look at each other, and one of them, an Asian man, raises an eyebrow. They think I'm crazy.

"Easy, Mikey, there's nobody there. Okay? Just take it easy."

"Don't tell me to take it easy." I'm supposed to be convincing them I'm sane, not freaking out like this. "It was just . . . a joke, Devon, it was just a joke." That's a stupid line, of course he won't believe it. I crane my neck to see over the men to the hall beyond. The Faceless Man might be just out of sight behind a corner.

"These are the men I told you about," says Devon, walking to the gate. I hear the beeps as he punches in the code, but they all sound the same; I can't guess the numbers from the sounds. The men come through and Devon closes the gate behind them. "They're here to see you, Michael, they're from the FBI."

My blood grows cold.

"I'm Agent Leonard," says the tall one, and points to the Asian. "This is my partner, Agent Chu. We'd like to have a word with you if we could."

"I didn't kill anyone."

"We never said you did."

"You think I'm the Red Line Killer, that's why you're here, but I'm innocent—I've never killed anybody. I've never even hurt anybody."

"We just want to talk to you," says Agent Chu. "We're hoping you might be able to help us."

Devon stands next to me. "He's not exactly . . . healthy . . . right now. I don't know what you expect to learn from him."

"Dr. Little explained his condition when we spoke with him," says Agent Leonard. "We understand that he's crazy—"

"We don't use that word," says Devon quickly.

"I apologize," says Leonard. "Is there a room we could go to?"

Devon leads them to one of the private therapy rooms, a small room with a round table and a ring of plastic chairs. I don't follow, but Devon comes back and pulls me toward it, coaxing me with a promise of candy.

"Does that work on the other patients?" I ask.

"Just come on," says Devon, "they're not going to hurt you, they just want to ask you some questions."

I stand in the doorway, bracing myself against the wall so he can't push me in. "Cell phones out first."

"What?"

"No cell phones, no recorders, no electronic devices of any kind," I say. "You want to talk to me, I want to make sure they're not listening." Unless the whole room is already wired—who knows what that man in the hall was doing here.

"Is it alright if we just turn them off?" asks Agent

Chu. I stare at him, wondering if he's part of it—if you take off his face, would he look like the other man in the hall? But no—even faceless, I feel like I can recognize them, and this man is different. They both are. I nod, and they turn off their phones.

I slip in carefully and sit down, pulling my chair to the door so I can run if I need to. Devon comes in as well, closing the door behind him.

"Let's start by saying that this is not an interrogation," says Agent Leonard. "We know about your condition, we know about the hallucinations and delusions, we know that everything you say here might be completely imaginary. Nothing you say today will be used as evidence against you, okay? We just want to ask you some questions."

I sit still, waiting. After a moment he speaks again.

"You say you see Faceless Men," he says. "Can you please describe them?"

"Why, do you know about them? That's what this is, isn't it—you're FBI, you know all about the conspiracy." I look at Devon, grinning. "I told you they were real."

"Please just describe them, Michael, so that we know we're on the same page."

"They're . . . men without faces."

"I need you to be more specific than that. If the face is gone, what's there instead?"

"Nothing."

"There has to be something—even a hole is 'something.'"

"It's not a hole," I say, "it's like their face is just . . .

blank. There're no features, no eyes and nose and mouth."

Agent Chu passes his hand over his face. "You mean just smooth skin?"

"It's more like a . . . like a blur," I say. "Like a smear."

"Red?"

"It's skin-colored," I say, "not blood or anything like that. Their faces aren't destroyed, they're just . . . not there. That's why I'm not the killer."

"When was the last time you saw one of these men," asks Agent Leonard, then shakes his head slightly, "not counting the one in the hall?"

"There was one in the hospital."

"Standing up, like the one you saw today?"

"Of course."

"And before that?"

"There was one that came into the bakery," I say. "I have a job at Mueller's Bakery, and there was one that came in there every week."

Agent Chu writes that down. My pulse quickens, and I try to control my breathing. "Is that important?"

"We just want to get all the information we can," says Agent Leonard. "Can you tell us the last time you saw the man in the bakery?"

"It was a woman."

"A faceless woman?" He looks confused.

"She bought bread."

"That doesn't sound very ominous," says Agent Chu. "I thought this was a secret cabal watching

your every move, not just people in the neighborhood."

"She was checking up on me," I say. I don't like
his tone—he's not joking with me, he's serious. He
sounds . . . suspicious. "That was part of how they
kept tabs on me."

"And the last time you saw her?"

"About a month ago, I guess. Right before the
two weeks I can't remember. I'm not exactly sure—
it's hard to keep track of time in here."

"Can you describe what they were wearing?"
asks Agent Leonard.

"The one at the bakery had just regular clothes,
I guess. A dress, with like . . . flowers, I think." It's
hard to remember. I never got a good look, because
I always hid in the back when she came.

"Not a lot of housewives wear dresses these days,"
says Agent Chu, writing it down. "If she's real, she
should be easy to find."

"She's real," I insist.

"Did anyone else see her?"

"Of course they did, they sold her bread every
week."

"Did they think it was weird that she didn't have
a face?"

I hadn't thought of that. Was Mr. Mueller in on it
too? Were they paying him to keep quiet, or maybe
threatening him? Or could he really not see it?

What if I'm the only one who can?

"Michael?"

I snap back. "What?"

"Did you hear my question?"

"I don't want to answer that question."

"Fair enough," says Agent Leonard. "How about the one in the hall—what was he wearing?"

"A gray suit," I say. "A hat, like the . . ." I gesture at my head, struggling to describe the hat. "Kind of shaped like a cowboy hat, I guess, but with a small brim, and really nice. Like a classy gray hat that you'd wear with a suit."

"A fedora."

"I guess."

The two agents looked at each other. Agent Chu stands up. "I'll see if I can catch him before he leaves the building."

"You did see him! I knew it!"

"Yes, Michael, he passed us in the hall. He had a face, though."

Agent Chu left, and Devon went with him to help with the gate. I looked back at Agent Leonard.

"You've got to get me out of here. When you find that guy and question him you'll know—this whole place is part of the Plan, They're keeping me here against my will, and you've got to get me out."

"Can you describe any other Faceless Men?"

"You're not listening to me," I say. "You've got to believe me. That man's probably an administrator or an owner or something—he runs this place, I guarantee it, and as soon as he finds out I blew the whistle on him I am going to disappear—he might already know. Is your cell phone turned off like I asked?"

"We're going to talk to him," says Agent Leonard,

"but not because we suspect him of anything. We just want to figure out why you see certain people as faceless."

"Because they're trying to kill me!"

"Tell me, Michael, have you ever seen one of these faceless people in a custodial uniform? Like a brown jumpsuit?"

"No, why?"

"Does the name Brandon Woods mean anything to you?"

"Should it?"

"How about a chemical company called Chem-Com?"

"No—where is this all going?"

Devon comes back. "Is everything okay, Michael?"

"We're actually done here," says Agent Leonard, standing up. "We'll see if we can find either of these people he's talking about—see if they're real, see if they have any connection at all to the murders. No sense going any further if all we're getting from him is made-up junk."

"I'm not making it up."

"At least not on purpose." He walks to the door. "Dr. Little says your treatment's working, so when your mind's cleared up a bit we'll be back with more questions."

Devon holds the door open. "You mean if these leads check out?"

"No, we're coming back either way. This is a psych hospital, right?" He looks at me. "Sounds like the perfect place to ask about your mother."

Devon walks him to the gate. I can't see the numbers when he types them in.

"Come on, man," says Devon, walking back to me, "it's time to get cleaned up." I let him turn me and lead me to the shower.

If the FBI are here then the reporter was right, and they really do suspect me. And if the Faceless Men are here, traveling openly, then the hospital really is working with Them. Or for Them. That would explain Devon's buzzing. Is Linda in on it as well, or Dr. Little?

What about the other patients?

I need to be more careful. When we get to the shower I leave the hot water turned off, just to be sure, and brace myself for the frigid blast.

SEVEN

SOMETHING TOUCHES MY arm and I jerk awake, shouting wordlessly. A light blinds me, and I throw up my hands to shield my face.

"Easy," says a woman's voice, "it's just me." I feel a hand on my arm, soft and feminine, and when my eyes adjust I see a pretty woman holding a small penlight. At first I think it's Lucy, but she shines the light on her face and I see that it's not. "I'm sorry to wake you, Michael. I didn't mean to scare you."

"Who are you?"

"I'm Shauna, the night nurse. Are you feeling okay?"

"Yeah, just . . . scared is all. Just startled. I'm fine."

"Sorry about that. I didn't want to wake you up, but I guess I did anyway, huh?" She holds my wrist and shines the light on her watch, taking my pulse. I wait, watching her count. When she finishes she keeps her hand on my wrist, holding it lightly.

"How are you feeling?"

"You can turn the light on if you want," I say. "It's better than the . . ." I look at the flashlight in her hand, wondering if the Faceless Men can tap into it the way they do with the other devices—it creates an electric field, at least a small one, but it can't really send or receive a signal. Or maybe this one can, if the Faceless Men have infiltrated the hospital. I want to tell her to keep it outside, but I also want to look normal. I can't escape if they keep suspecting me. "I'm great," I say, nodding. "I'm fine."

"Okay," she says. Her fingers on my arm are cool and calming. "Is there anything you need?"

I pause. It's been too long since the reporter was here—she said she'd be back in a few days, but it's been over a week. What went wrong? Was it too hard to find evidence in my favor?

"Do you know . . . Is there some kind of list of people who come to visit? Like a sign-in sheet or something?"

"There is," she says, nodding. "Would you like me to check on something?"

"I'm just . . ." I don't know what I'm just. "I was expecting a friend, and she hasn't come, and I just wonder if . . . I don't know."

"You think she might have come when you were asleep?"

I look at the window in the door, showing faint

light from the hallway. "I guess I'm just worried that she might have come and looked in and decided not to come inside. You know? Like I'm all . . ." I realize my eyes are wet, and I wipe them with the back of my hand. "It's like I'm a monster. I can't do anything, I can't see anyone, I can't go anywhere. . . . It's like I'm in a zoo."

"Easy, Michael," she says, and squeezes my wrist. I feel stupid and weak. "I know it's hard in here," she says, "but you've got us. We're your friends." She smiles, and I try not to flinch away from the penlight. "You like peaches?"

"Peaches?"

She laughs, warm and cheerful in the darkness. "I love peaches—my parents used to have an orchard, and my mom would can them every year. They always cheer me up. I know it's not much, but if you want some peaches for breakfast I can put a note on your chart and see if the kitchen can send any up in the morning. Make you feel a little more . . . like a person. You know?"

I feel stupid and embarrassed, but it does sound nice. I nod. "That'd be good. I like peaches."

"Great." I can't see her in the dark, but I imagine she's smiling. I smile back.

IN THE MORNING my oatmeal comes with peaches, but they taste wrong—sweet but superficial. I can't place it exactly. I also have an extra pill; they've doubled my dose. I feel depressed, like I've somehow ruined everything. The commons room buzzes with conversation, but from what I can tell most of the patients are talking to themselves, not to each other. Which one is my secret ally? I scan the tables silently, trying not to look suspicious, but it's impossible to tell.

"Michael."

I jerk my head up, surprised, and see Dr. Vanek settle into a chair beside me. "You're rather deep in thought; I could barely get your attention."

"Sorry," I say, "just . . . thinking."

"Which is why I said you were deep in thought."

Another patient sits at our table, a small man with wide eyes and frizzy hair, but Vanek shoos him away. "I hate these hospitals."

"Seriously," I ask. "How did you ever become a psychiatrist?"

"You might call it a survival mechanism."

"You hate everyone here."

"I hate everyone out there as well, so psychiatry is no worse than anything else."

"Great." I take a bite. "What brings you here, anyway?"

"Your psychoses. I find myself increasingly fascinated the more I learn about them."

I nod and click my tongue. "I'm glad I'm entertaining."

"Tell me, Michael, is there some specific memory of a phone that you find particularly horrifying?"

"What?"

"Phones," he repeats. "You're scared of them, and

I want to know why. Many schizophrenic delusions are based on specific events from the patient's past—it may be that you see Faceless Men, for example, because of some childhood abuse by a man with an obscured face."

"I was never abused," I say quickly.

"Yes you were," he says, "at least emotionally, by that disaster you call a father. It may be that your delusions of Faceless Men somehow come from him."

"My father has a face."

"I can see that you're missing every point I try to make," he says. "We will retreat from the general and return to the specific: why are you afraid of phones? Is it all cell phones? Is it the mere idea of them, or is it their usage? Is it a specific ring that holds some kind of buried meaning for you?"

"You already know why."

"Yes, yes," he says, "but that explanation applies to all devices generically. Your outburst a few weeks ago, when you attacked Devon, was focused on a specific device. You didn't react to the clock radio in your room, but the cell phone scared you terribly."

"Wait," I say, setting down my fork with a frown. "There was a cell phone in the room?"

"Of course there was; what did you think was buzzing?"

"That buzzing was a cell phone?"

Dr. Vanek raises an eyebrow, drumming the table with his pudgy fingers. "He keeps it set to 'vibrate' to avoid disturbing the patients, though that obviously didn't work in your case. Tell me, Michael, what did you think it was?"

"I thought it was . . . I don't know."

"Surely you thought about it long enough to concoct some kind of explanation. Pants don't just buzz for no reason, and your intense reaction to the sound makes it obvious you were aware of it."

"I thought it was—" I stop. I can't tell him what I thought it was. For all I know Vanek is part of the Plan as well. "I didn't know it was a cell phone."

"But it was," he says, "which returns us to my question: why are you afraid of phones?"

"It's not all phones," I say, "just cell phones—it's not even cell phones, it's the signals they send and receive. Normal phones keep their signals trapped in cords, but cell phones just shoot them through the air." I glance around nervously. Is there another doctor listening? I don't want them to hear anything they think is crazy. "Why are you asking me this?"

"Because I'm a psychiatrist."

"But not my psychiatrist; not anymore."

"I have arranged a research agreement with the hospital," he says. "I have limited access to all patients, pending doctor approval."

"And Dr. Little approved your visit to me? He doesn't seem to like you."

"And I don't like him," says Vanek, shrugging. "Thank goodness we manage to act like professionals regardless."

Devon had a cell phone. Everything happened because of a cell phone signal. Is that the switch that lets them control me—an external signal from a nearby phone? I smile. That might be a good thing— if they have to use an outside source, that means I don't have a transmitter actually on me. That means I can escape and be free, as long as I stay clear of their signals. This could be the break I've been waiting for.

"So?" asked Vanek. "Why do you think you're afraid of cell phones?"

I click my tongue and take another bite of oatmeal. "I'm not crazy."

Vanek nods. "Saner words were never spoken. Tell me, Michael, have you seen any more of the Faceless Men?"

I shake my head. "Of course not. You told me yourself they aren't real." I click my teeth. "I'm not crazy."

He smiles thinly. "Two weeks ago you used their reality as evidence of your sanity; now you use their unreality as evidence of the same. You can either be crazy then or crazy now, but given that you've mentioned the Faceless Men at all you have to be one or the other." He stands up. "Think about your story more carefully the next time you talk to Dr. Little."

He walks away, and I stare at my tray. He's right: I can't claim to be cured without acknowledging that I was sick, at least for a while. I nod, twice, searching for an answer.

"Medicine time," says Devon, and I shy back reflexively. Will his cell phone go off again? He sets a small plastic cup on the table next to me; there's two

Loxitane in it, half green and half tan, like camou-
flage. "Everything going okay?"

"Great," I say, picking up the cup. It doesn't matter what they think; I can escape now. I click my
teeth. "I'm great, thank you for asking." I swallow
the pills and wash them down with apple juice. It's
time to get out of here.

EIGHT

SOMEONE WALKS THE halls at night. It's not Shauna, the pretty nurse, though I know she's there as well; her footsteps are soft and gentle, like she's wearing slippers. I can hear her go up and down the halls, checking our vitals and meting out drugs. But when she stops, and the halls fall silent, that's when the other footsteps come. They're heavy, and loud, and the space between them is wider; whoever they belong to has longer legs, and a longer stride. His shoes click on the floor like the ticks of a clock.

I use more soap than the other patients, scrubbing my hair and body extra hard to make up for the cold water. I don't dare use the hot, and I never go in the showers when someone else is already there. They can control which spigot is connected to the cyanide, just like they can control which devices are watching me.

I sit in the commons room, waiting for Lucy, watching the patients and the nurses and the doctors and wondering who they are. I watch them walk around, all stiff limbs and floppy joints and bodies so solid they block the world right out. I'm surrounded by water and meat, by dead hair and slow, shuffling circuits. I listen to them talk and the words make no sense: tile. Tile tile tile tile tile. Words lose all meaning. I wonder how these creatures can communicate at all.

And then I'm back, and I wonder what it was that bothered me so much.

It's been almost three weeks since Lucy came in, and I haven't seen her since; I have to assume They got to her. I have to find her. If I can figure out the key code for the gate, I can escape.

I start by setting up a chair in the lunch area, with a clear view of the gate, but it's too far away—I have pretty good eyesight, but at that distance everything melts together and I can't tell one number from another. I need to get closer. I try walking right up to the nurse in the side office, hoping to make small talk until someone walks up and uses the keypad, but I can't do it—the nurse's computer is right there, just a few feet away. I can feel it like a buzz in my head, burrowing in, trying to get control. I wave at the nurse and go back to the commons room.

It's the TV that eventually gives me my chance;

irony's like that sometimes. Every morning at ten-thirty Dr. Linda holds a group therapy session in the TV area, where all the nice couches are; not only do they turn off the TV, but the group is big enough that it spills just slightly into the hallway. I watch them from the cafeteria tables, calculating the distance. If I pull over a chair and sit right *there,* I'd have a perfect view of the keypad from only a dozen feet away. I stand up and drag my chair across the room.

"Hello, Michael," says Linda. "Thank you for joining us this morning."

I sit down. "Hi."

"This is a social therapy group, Michael. Today we're talking about jobs and responsibility."

"I had a job," says Steve. "I worked in a bookstore. I could sell anything."

"That's wonderful," says Linda. "Tell us about it."

I zone out while Steve talks about how important he used to be, and subtly turn an eye to the hallway. I can see the keypad clearly. All I need is for someone to use it.

"I could sell anyone a mystery," says Steve. "It didn't matter what they came in for, I could send them out with a mystery."

"Why do you think that was?"

"They always want to know how it ends."

Devon walks past me toward the nurses' office. He stops and chats with the lady by the computer. Just use the gate! He says something too low for me to hear. She laughs. I flex my arm: open, close, open, close.

"What were some of your responsibilities in the bookstore, Steve?" asks Linda.

"I did everything," he says. "I had to do everything because nobody else ever did anything."

"Did you help open the store?"

"No, the manager did that before I got there."

The nurse by the computer says something else, and it's Devon's turn to laugh. He waves good-bye and reaches for the keypad. 6. 8. 5. Another nurse joins him, blocking my view.

"Michael?"

I spin my head around, my heart beating rapidly. Linda and the patients are looking at me. Do they know what I was looking at? Do they know what I'm doing?

"Did you have a job before you came here, Michael?"

"Um, yeah," I say. I try to soothe my nerves and pull myself together. I nod. "I worked in a bakery. Mueller's Bakery, the place with the coal oven."

"I've never eaten there," says Linda, "but it sounds delicious. What did you do there?"

I hear the gate click; Devon's already through, and I missed the numbers. I click my teeth a few times. "I helped load and unload stuff, like bags of flour and trays of bread and stuff like that. Mr. Mueller did everything by hand—all the mixing and the kneading and everything, like in the old days. No machines at all."

"It sounds like you had a lot of work to do, then," says the doctor. "What was your favorite part?"

"Don't answer that," says a voice. "You don't have to tell them anything without a warrant." I look around, but it doesn't look like any of the other patients said anything. I flex my arm.

Why am I flexing my arm?

"I wish I'd worked in a bread store," says Steve. "I hated that bookstore."

"Please be respectful, Steve," says Linda. "It's Michael's turn to talk."

I look back at the gate. There's nobody there. I glance the other way and see another orderly walking toward us from the back rooms. Is he coming to us, or to the gate?

I turn back to Linda. "My favorite part was the heat." I try to drag it out—to tell her everything I can about the bakery so that she can't ask any more questions until I'm done, and nothing can distract me from the keypad. "I know that sounds weird, but I liked it." I nod. "It was hot and dry, like a cave in the desert, and you could just sit there and enjoy it, the heat and the smell of yeast, and pretend you were a lizard hiding under a rock. Maybe a dinosaur." The orderly walks past us to the gate; I turn my head just far enough to see the keypad, and try to make it look like I'm staring into nothing. "I used to stand in the back, in the red dark by the ovens, and listen to the sound of the walls popping as the heat pressed out against them." 6. 8. "I'd pretend I was in a balloon, filling up with hot air, and eventually I'd just float away." 5. His arm moves and I miss the last number—a 1? Maybe a 2? It had to be one of those. 6851. Or 2. If I enter the wrong code, will it set off an alarm?

"Wow," says Linda. "That's very nice. I'm glad you had something about your job you liked."

"Buildings can't float away," says Steve.

"Please, Steve, it's Michael's turn."

"I'm done," I say, nodding. I flex my arm again.

"Thank you for sharing with us," says Linda. "Edward, how about you?" The frizzy-haired guy looks up, terrified, and Linda coaxes him gently. "Did you have a job, Edward?"

I keep my eye on the gate, waiting. No one comes. After several minutes someone steps into view on the far side of the gate—the same gray suit, the same blurred distorted nothing where his face should be.

He has no eyes, but I can feel his gaze boring into me. I look back and we watch each other for a moment, waiting. I can feel my breathing, calm and controlled. We say nothing. He's the same one as before; somehow I can tell, I can *recognize* him, as if I've seen him a hundred times.

He walks away.

I have to get out tonight. I can't wait. They know I'm here, and they know I've seen them. If they're going to make a move, they'll make it soon.

I have to make mine first.

I LIE AWAKE, listening to the footsteps. I have to time this very carefully. First I hear Shauna go by, soft shoes padding lightly on the hard, slick floor. Her footsteps grow louder as she nears, then softer as she disappears down the hall. I wait. One of the other patients is singing, tuneless and distant. I hear a train in the background, a bass rumbling that grows and fades. Silence.

Then the other footsteps come, echoing loudly in the hallway. I see a light bobbing up and down the walls, and a dark figure pauses to peek in the small window in my door. I close my eyes and try to breathe steadily, faking sleep. The footsteps move on, and when I open my eyes I see the light receding down the hallway. I slip out of bed silently, repeating the number code in my mind: 6851. 6852. I don't know which one to try first. The footsteps in the corridor pause occasionally, as the dark figure peeks through the doors. When they stop completely, I grip the doorknob tightly, turning it slowly and carefully so it makes no sound. I hear no reaction. I open the door quietly and release the knob just as slowly, so it doesn't snap back with a click.

The hall is empty. I nod and slip out, closing the door behind me. I crouch as I walk, ducking below the windows in each door I pass. Ahead of me is the gate, and next to it the nurses' office. Bright light floods into the hall. How can I get past them without being seen?

The hall fills with a faint clicking noise and I freeze, looking behind me. Nothing. Where's it coming from? I flex my arm, thinking, and I realize I'm clicking my teeth. Click click click click click click. I clamp my hand over my mouth and find that I'm nodding, up and down, up and down. I take a deep breath and force myself to hold still. Why am I doing this? It's like my body is moving on its own, completely out of my control.

It's Them—they know I'm escaping, and they're trying to take over.

I start walking again, and my arm is flexing at the elbow: back and forth, back and forth. It hits the wall with a soft thud and I grab it with my other hand, trying to hold it still, but now I've let go of my teeth.

Click click click click.

I stagger forward, keeping my eyes on the gate; it bobs up and down as my head nods furiously. Five steps closer. Ten steps closer. I hear footsteps behind me, far away; I spin around, but there's nothing behind me. He's still around the corner—hurry up!

Five more steps. Five more after that. My arm flexes against my chest, held tightly by my other arm. Click click click click click. My body is turning against me, part by part, as Their buried control system batters itself against my mind. Five more steps. I'm almost to the nurses' office.

I release my arm and grab my mouth, shoving my fingers between my teeth to muffle the noise; if I keep away from the walls my arm won't hit anything and give me away. My teeth keep biting, too soft to draw blood. The footsteps behind me grow louder. I creep forward, nodding wildly, my eyes hot with tears.

I can just see into the nurses' office, peering around

the corner. A woman sits at a desk, her back to me—
not Shauna but someone else, a large woman I've
never seen. Where's Shauna? This means there are
three people, not two; I don't know if I can hide from
them all. The footsteps behind me pause, and I look
back. Nothing. I hold my breath and slip forward,
my arm flailing through space, and walk right past
the open door. The nurse doesn't turn around.

Five more steps, soft as a whisper.

On the far side of the door I sink to my knees,
ducking below the open window to the office. The
computer monitor looms above me, buzzing softly.
My teeth move up and down, up and down. I reach
the gate. My right arm flexes.

How can I even enter the code?

I take my hand out of my mouth and grit my
teeth tightly, half of my jaw muscles fighting the
others. They make no noise. I use my left hand to
guide my flailing right down to the floor, where I
kneel on it to hold it in place.

The footsteps start again. He'll be at the corner
any moment. I reach out with my left hand toward
the keypad, and my fingers buzz when they get close.
Of course it's electronic! I curse silently. They'll
know I'm here the instant I touch it! I can't help it—
there's no other way. I force my hand forward and
type in the code: 685 . . . do I hit the 1 or the 2? The
footsteps behind grow louder.

Just do it!

2. The latch clicks softly, and the gate swings open.
I rise up from my knees and dart forward, my right

arm swinging wildly; it cracks against the gate and I grunt, trying to hold back the pain. There's a noise from the office, and I close the gate behind me. The latch clicks loudly.

"Who's there?"

The hallway beyond the gate stretches out on both sides, and I dive right to stay out of sight. I grab my arm to hold it still and stagger forward past a row of offices, each one dark and empty. At the first intersection I pause, thinking.

Should I just leave? Or should I try to learn something first?

There's something going on here; that much is obvious. If I run I can get away, and if I run fast I might get away for good—leave the city, disappear, and never come back. Maybe I could find a farm somewhere, far away from cell phones and TVs and anything else they could use to find me. But the thing is, what if I'm not the only one they're trying to find? A Plan this big, a conspiracy this ubiquitous, doesn't make any sense if it's all focused on me. I'm not that important—Vanek is right about that much. They must be planning something larger, and whatever it is, the key might be right here, in this hospital. If I can find out what it is, I might be able to figure out a way to stop them.

Click click click click. I'm losing control of my jaw again. I peek around the corner and feel a stab of fear—it's a cafeteria, buzzing with electricity from a sea of fluorescent lights, refrigerated counters, vending machines, microwaves. I pull back, panting and nodding, and lean against the wall. Where do I go from here?

I can't go forward. Even if the two doctors chatting at a table don't see me, the devices will—the Faceless Men will know I'm there the instant I step out past the wall. I turn back and move softly down the hall, looking at the names on each office door as I pass: Skarstedt. Beisinger. Zobell. I reach the turn-off to the secure wing and pause, listening.

"I swear I heard the gate."

"But we're the only ones here."

I don't recognize either voice. I peek around the corner, clenching my jaw as tight as I can. The heavy nurse is standing in the doorway of the office, talking to a black-clad security guard. Neither is looking in my direction.

"The janitor, maybe?"

"He knows he has to check in with me."

I take the chance and run past the gate, stepping lightly. There are more doors this way, and a dark corner at the end of the hall that might be a stairway.

"Wait, what was that?"

"I'm calling this in; something's going on."

The gate clangs behind me as someone comes through, and I race past more doors: Olsen. Layton. Little. I duck into Dr. Little's darkened office, clutching my arm tightly to keep it from swinging; my head nods so much I can barely see straight. I crouch against the wall as the security guard runs past me down the hall—the same loud, heavy steps I hear every night. I glance around the room, desperate for anything that could help me escape—

The office is covered with photographs: pinned to the walls, spread across the desk, spilling to the floor. Portraits too dim to see. My eyes focus and my pupils widen, adapting to the dark, and slowly I'm surrounded by faces—no, not faces. Heads. I choke down a cry, stifling my own terror: every photo is a corpse, mangled and bloody, the face torn off and bashed in. I stagger back and hit the wall, panting with terror. They're everywhere.

Information—I'm here for information. I step back to the table, jaw clenched, arms folded tightly around me, and look at the photos. Each one is marked with a date: two months ago. Three months ago. One. Ten victims, just like Kelly said, starting eight months ago and ending—for now—right in the middle of my two missing weeks. I stare at the most recent photo: a man in a brown jumpsuit, like a janitor. BRANDON WOODS, says the label. Chemcom Industrial Chemicals. Just like the FBI guy said. His face has been viciously destroyed, carved with a knife or bashed with a hammer or—I don't even want to think about what could have done it. JUNE 27, it says. Right in the middle of my missing memories.

I hear voices outside, but no one looks in. The door's still ajar, but I don't dare close it; I duck out of view, crouching by a filing cabinet. My files are probably in it. I wait for the voices to recede again and slowly press the button on the third drawer: N through S. I flip through the files, pull out my own, and scan through the notes:

My dosage of Loxitane isn't working and needs to be increased.

I resist treatment, but recently joined a social therapy session.

I display violent tendencies and need to be watched very closely.

Near the back is a half-filled report on Dr. Little's diagnosis:

Michael Shipman was treated for generalized anxiety disorder early last year, was deemed stable, and was released in early July with a prescription for Klonopin. During therapy and observation he showed no signs of active delusion. While his schizophrenia may have been present much earlier, we estimate that it did not become acute until approximately November, based on interviews with his father and employer. . . .

I stop reading. November was eight months ago, right about the time that I stopped going to therapy. Right about the time that I stopped taking Klonopin.

Right about the time that the Red Line started killing.

"Freeze!" shouts the security guard, and suddenly he's right there, filling the door, his Taser in my face. I step away and raise my hands, but as soon as my right arm gets free it flies out, flexing and twitching, and the security guard fires.

NINE

EVERY MUSCLE IN my body betrays me, some contracting into rigid bricks, others melting into loose, useless jelly. I fall against something and hit the floor in the flurry of papers and books.

"It's a patient! I think it's the one from 404—holy crap!"

My arm twitches again, flying across me in a wide arc. I try to get my bearings, but my eyes are still adjusting to the light, and my body is still too stunned to tell up from down. I can't seem to move anything on purpose.

"He's still moving!"

"You shocked him?" The second voice is softer, more feminine, and dripping with worry. Shauna. I manage to roll my head a few inches to the side. "What happened?"

"He swung at me. I couldn't even see who it was."

"How did he get out here?"

I try to speak, gurgle helplessly, and manage to raise my head. Almost instantly someone grabs me from behind, locking me in a security hold that keeps me fully immobile.

"Call Dr. Little—tell him one of his patients broke into his office." Footsteps cross the floor, a phone rattles in its housing.

My tongue is looser now, and my head is clearing up. "I need . . ."

"Easy, man," says the guard. "How's your legs, can you walk?"

"I need to get out of here." Click click click click. My teeth again.

"Just answer the question: can you walk? Can we stand up?"

"Hello, Dr. Little," says Shauna. "I'm sorry to call you at this hour but we have a situation." The guard pulls me to my knees, pauses a minute while I gain my balance, then pulls me to my feet. "One of the patients in lockdown escaped," says Shauna. "No, he didn't get far, but he went straight for your office. It's Michael Shipman."

I get to my feet and look at Shauna, but it's not Shauna—it's the other nurse, the heavy one from the office. She's older, mid-fifties maybe, with thick arms and permed, graying hair.

"Where's Shauna?"

The guard tightens his grip. "Who's Shauna?"

"The night nurse," I say. "She's here every night." I stare at the other nurse, confused. "Who are you?"

The nurse looks at me, but speaks into the phone. "He seems very disoriented, Doctor. Yes, we will. All right, we'll see you in a bit." She hangs up.

"Where's Shauna?" I'm scared now—a sick, vertiginous feeling in my gut, like I'm about to fall through the floor into a vast, bottomless nothing. "Why are these pictures in here? What's going on?"

"Easy, Michael," says the guard. "Let's get you back into your room, okay?"

"Maybe Shauna's that girl he keeps talking about," says the nurse.

"Shauna is the night nurse!" I shout. "What have you done with her?"

The nurse glances at the guard behind me, worry etched into her face. "I'm the night nurse, Michael. My name is Sharon. Do you remember me?"

I stare at her, remembering a face in the dark. Remembering peaches that didn't taste like peaches. "What's going on?"

"Let's get him back to his room."

THERE ARE MORE guards now, and they strap me into my bed with thick leather restraints, just like before, ignoring my cries for help and information. They stop acknowledging me altogether, speaking as if I wasn't even in the room.

"How do you think he got out?"

"Came straight at me with his fist—I had to stun him."

"We should never have let him out of these straps in the first place."

"Don't tell them anything."

I jerk my head up, looking at the door, but all I see are guards and nurses. The photos from the office flash through my mind like a gruesome slide show. The nervous speculation of the guards mirrors my own thoughts:

What if I really am a killer?

Someone is killing people I hate, turning them into the image I'm obsessed with. I feel my body shaking: a shiver, as if I was cold, but I'm sweating with heat.

What was I doing before they found me?

That day in the hospital, I bit a man on the arm trying to escape—I literally tore into him with my teeth. What kind of person does that? And if I'm willing to do that, how much further will I go? Is it possible that I, cornered by one of Them, would lash out fiercely enough to kill? Could I have done it so many times? It almost seems impossible—after I'd killed one or two they would have started coming after me with bigger numbers and stronger force.

Unless they weren't coming after me at all. Maybe it was me going after them.

Kelly said there were ten victims, maybe more. Nobody kills ten people in self-defense—not that messily, and never in such a specific, consistent way. There's nothing defensive about the way their faces were torn off. Those people had been executed, or punished. Maybe I'd gotten sick of running, and I took the fight to them.

How many did I kill?

Click click click click.

"How did you get through the gate?" The security guard is standing by my bed; other guards and nurses move through the background, both in my room and out in the hall, talking and searching and scurrying around. It's the middle of the night, but I've stirred up a beehive.

I look at the guard. "The gate was open."

"Did someone leave it open for you? Is it . . . what's her name . . . Shauna? Did she help you escape?"

"Nobody helped me."

"Who is Shauna?"

"That's what I'm trying to figure out," I say. "How many night nurses are there?"

The guard frowns. "We're checking the security cameras now, so if someone helped you we will find her. What were you looking for in Dr. Little's office?"

"I ducked in there to hide from you."

"Your own doctor's office," he says derisively, "with all of your files and information and everything—and you were there completely by accident."

"Listen," I say, "I don't know who's on Their side and who's not—I don't even know if I can trust you—but something is going on here, and we are all caught in the middle of it. Okay? There's something very big, and very weird, and if I can't figure it out I don't know what's going to happen—to any of us."

Dr. Little walks into the room, talking to another

security guard. He looks hastily dressed, and his thin hair floats over his head in an unkempt cloud. They probably woke him up. He's talking to another guard as he walks. "And no one else was in the hall-way?"

"No one," says the other guard. "Just Devon and Sharon and the patient. The night janitor hadn't even come yet."

"All right, thank you for showing me." Dr. Little turns to me, pastes that broad, patronizing smile across his face, and walks to the bed. "Good eve-ning, Michael. How are you feeling?"

"I didn't know it was your office," I say quickly. "I was just trying to get out. I didn't mean to do any-thing."

"He can't have been in your office long, Doctor," says the guard. "He's pretty confused."

"Yes, thank you," says Dr. Little, patting the guard on the arm. "I'll take it from here, thank you."

The guard looks at me, looks at my restraints, then nods. "Thank you, Doctor." He leaves the room, and Dr. Little pulls up the lone chair and sits.

"You were going through my files, Michael," he says. "What were you looking for?"

"Just stairs, that's all. A way out."

"You were headed for the stairs, but you turned around. They showed me the security footage."

"I . . ." And now I'm caught again. If I tell him what I was really looking for—a key to the conspiracy—he'll think I'm either crazy or too close to the truth. I waver back and forth; I have to trust somebody eventually, right? But not him. Why hasn't Lucy come back, or the reporter? I can't do this alone. I close my eyes and decide to say nothing. "I couldn't go that way."

"Were you worried about being seen?" he asks. "And yet by doubling back you had to pass by the two people who were already alert and suspicious. It makes no sense to . . ." He stops, cocks his head to the side, and smiles. "Aha. The cafeteria."

"What?"

"Your fear of electronics. You stopped and turned around when you got to the cafeteria—an entire room packed full of cords and transmitters and electromagnetic fields. You couldn't bring yourself to go past it."

I stay silent, cursing him in my head. How am I supposed to deceive the man being paid to psychoanalyze me? At least he still doesn't know what I'm looking for.

"That explains a lot," he says, rubbing his chin. "The security tape does, indeed, look like you ducked into my office to hide. I don't know how you got the gate code, but that's easy enough to fix. What I'm far more curious about, Michael, are the involuntary muscle movements: how long have they been that bad?"

My arm twitches against the restraint, and I shake my head and laugh; it sounds bitter and hollow. "Are you honestly going to tell me you don't know anything about that?"

"Of course I know about it, Michael, and I'll do

what I can, but I need to know how long it's been that bad."

"So you admit it?" I lean forward in disbelief. "You just admit, just like that, that you're a part of this?"

"A part of what?"

"You're controlling me! You and the Faceless Men—you're working for them, you're getting into my head and taking over my body." Click click click click click. "Dammit, I can barely talk!"

"Please, Michael," he says, reaching out with his hand, "please stay calm. I assure you that no one is trying to control your movements."

My arm twitches. "How can you say that? Look at me!"

"What you're experiencing is called tardive dyskinesia," he says, "and it's a common side effect of Loxitane. You're up to sixty milligrams a day, and a reaction like this is not unheard of, though it does seem to have developed awfully quickly."

"You're saying this is a drug reaction?"

"Precisely: involuntary movements, like the way you're nodding right now, and the way your arm was swinging so wildly on the tape. I apologize for not explaining the possible side effects earlier, but we didn't want to frighten you unnecessarily and we really had no idea that anything would develop this quickly. Your body may have a certain susceptibility to drugs. Anyway, dyskinesia is not debilitating, but it is bad, and I'm afraid we'll have to discontinue the Loxitane altogether."

"Well thank goodness for that."

"It's our only choice, really—your delusions and hallucinations are still fully present, so the Loxitane is clearly not working, and we obviously can't raise the dose."

"Wait!" I jerk forward as far as the restraints will let me. "I'm not hallucinating, Doctor; you have to believe me. If I was that messed up in the head, how could I have gotten out of here?"

"You're delusional, Michael, but you're not stupid. You're actually very intelligent—most schizophrenics are. But you are sick, and we are trying to cure you, and medication is the only way—"

"You're giving me more drugs?"

"We'll be starting you on Seroquel, which in some ways is—"

"Your drugs are making me lose control of my own body, so you're giving me more? What are you trying to do to me?"

"Loxitane worked on your brain's dopamine receptors," he says calmly. "The Seroquel will affect both dopamine and serotonin, so it should be more effective."

"Why didn't you just start with that one, then?"

"Because the side effects are potentially worse, so we don't like to use it if we don't have to. We tried Loxitane first to—"

"No," I say, shaking my head, "absolutely not. Do you have any idea what this is doing to my brain?"

"It's fixing it."

"It's frying it right in my skull! I won't even have

a brain left by the time you're done. I'll be a vegetable."

"The mechanism of this drug is completely different from the last one, so there will be no overlap in effect or risk; we'll start at the minimum dose and work up until we see a positive result."

"Or until it kills me."

"The potential side effects of Seroquel are annoying but completely nonlethal," he says, dismissing the idea with a wave of his hand. "There is some small risk of tardive dyskinesia again, but, as I said, the mechanism is different and they shouldn't overlap—plus, we'll be watching you much more closely now that we've seen how sensitive you can be. If there's the slightest hint of it, we'll discontinue treatment."

"And what else? You said it was worse than the first drug."

"Seroquel doubles as a powerful sedative," he says. "Some people even use it recreationally."

"And that's bad?"

"A *very* powerful sedative," he says. "You'll sleep like a rock, but you'll wake up with the worst hangover you've ever had. We can alleviate that somewhat with other drugs, but I want to observe you first to see precisely how it affects you."

"No," I say again, shaking my head. "I won't let you do it."

"I'm afraid you don't have a choice, Michael." He waves to the door, and three large male nurses come in. One of them hands Dr. Little a small plastic cup. "We're doing this for your own good, Michael."

They grab me, and I try to wriggle free, but the bed restraints hold me tightly in place. "We're only trying to help you." The nurses hold me down, forcing my head back until my face points up at the ceiling. Dr. Little sighs. "If you insist, we're perfectly prepared to do this the hard way."

I clamp my mouth shut, but he sets down the pill and picks up a syringe. The nurses hold me in place, my muscles rigid with the effort to break free. I feel a prick in my shoulder, a lance of solid pain that holds for five, six, seven seconds, and then fades to a dull ache. The nurses let go and I jerk forward, thrashing and coughing.

"No!"

Dr. Little smiles.

"Very good," he says. "I trust that in the future you'll be much more cooperative, but rest assured that we can do this every time if we have to." He smiles again, and they begin to file out. "The sedative will likely kick in very quickly—sleep well, and I'll see you again in the morning."

They turn out the lights, but I can see dim shapes and outlines from the faint illumination down the hall. I sit in bed, panting, trying to decide what to do, but there's nothing—I'm trapped, physically and mentally. I can already feel my head grow heavier as the sedative goes to work. I scream. The world dims.

There's a shuffling sound from the hall; a thick, wet slapping, like a mop. A snuffling, slurping sound. I fight the sedation and lift my head, forcing my eyes to focus on the door, and a low shadow coalesces into a solid form—slick white skin reflecting the distant lights from the end of the hall. It turns at the door, a translucent membrane stretched tight over grotesque muscles—a giant white worm, like a maggot or a grub, almost two feet thick and stretching far back into the hall. Its head is a horrid ring of teeth and slime, more of a hole than a mouth; it raises up, as if tasting the air; I hold my breath, still as stone, helpless in my restraints. Will it come in or move on? My eyes are dimming. The thing crawls into the room, wriggling horridly, and I fight to stay awake. Do I scream? I don't think I can; my throat feels thick and heavy.

The thing gets closer. My head buzzes and deforms; my eyes tear and burn and blacken. I can hear it inching closer, slick skin slapping the floor.

Then I hear nothing.

TEN

DARKNESS. SILENCE. ALL sense is gone, replaced with something else—some kind of deeper feeling, a knowing. The Earth shifts and groans; currents of energy ripple and flow. I am free and trapped at once. I am ancient and powerful, a thing beyond time. But I have nowhere to go, and nowhere left to hide.

Sound is the first to return, a deep, distant reverberation. I plunge into it like an ocean, hearing for the very first time, exploring each new sound, but too quickly the sounds grow harsh and violent—high shrieks, piercing cracks, unintelligible howls of mindless, braying beasts. Physical sensations come next, heat and cold and pressure, pokes and jabs and scrapes and scratches that threaten to tear me apart. What are they doing to me? Before the question has time to form I'm assaulted by sight—burning lights and waves of devastating color. I receive sight merely to be blinded. I blink at the pain and realize I have something to blink. Where am I? What am I doing?

I am being squeezed into a ball. The world bites me with jagged teeth. I have become . . .

I'm in a cave—a deep, dark pit. I will rise up and come into a world of . . . of empty houses. Long streets of nothing, of hollow homes where no one lives. I struggle to open my eyes, bracing myself for the shock of light, and through my tears a wall swims into view—gray and bare. That's not right. It should be wood. I'm in a room, tied to a bed. I'm in a . . . What's the word? Hospital. I'm in a hospital.

My name is Michael Shipman. I'm in Powell Psychiatric. I am hurt and tired and cold.

Dr. Little—I remember the name now—gave me some kind of drug. Sero . . . something. Serotonin? Somebody said that word. My own thoughts assault me, pushing through my brain like blood through swollen muscle. I try to grab my head, but my arms are tied. There was something in here, something I was afraid of—

I jerk back in a spasm of fear, remembering the giant maggot. I look desperately at my body, patting my legs and stomach where I can reach, searching for some sign of its passage; bite marks or slime trails or anything else. I look wildly around the room, but there's nothing there. Is it behind me? Under the bed? I strain at the straps on my arms, craning my neck to see around the edges of the bed, but there's nothing to see. It's gone. I have no idea what it did.

Was it real? I want it to be fake. I consider the doctor's diagnosis—that my brain is screwed up and sees things that aren't really there. I don't want that thing I saw to be real. I want it to be all in my head.

I shiver reflexively, the involuntary twitch you get when you touch something disgusting. The thought that the maggot could be in my head almost makes me gag with revulsion—and then I remember the faces of the Red Line victims, hollowed out and bloody. What if the maggots were in their heads, laid there like eggs, nestled up in their sinuses, and then ate their way out when they hatched? The thought makes me gag again, and I throw up; I'm still tied down, and the vomit covers my chest because there's no way to get it anywhere else.

It can't be true. It can't be. I feel a wriggle in my head, as if something's writhing against my brain, and I throw up again. I force myself to think about something else, about anything else, about the walls and the ceiling, about the nurses and the other patients, about Dr. Little and Dr. Vanek and everything I can possibly think of. They say that I'm crazy: what if they're right? Dr. Vanek said that my hallucinations are probably based on some kind of real experience; that my brain is constructing its artificial sights and sounds out of old memories and emotions, filtered through the lens of imagination and fantasy. If that's true, then the things I think are real could potentially be explained away, the same way you'd interpret a dream.

The maggot wouldn't have to be real.

But how can I possibly decide what is real and what's not? The mere thought of it hurts my already-throbbing brain. There's Shauna, the night nurse, who I thought at first was Lucy. Nobody else knows who I'm talking about. With no visits from my girlfriend, did I create a fake one?

And then there's the Faceless Men, and the pile of faceless corpses. I thought before that the corpses might be a result of my battle with Them, but what if it's the other way around? What if I saw a Red Line victim somewhere and was traumatized by the experience, and my brain created the Faceless Men as a way of dealing with it? That must be it—I saw them on the news, back when the very first body was found . . .

. . . except that I don't watch the news. I don't watch TV at all, and the people who do—my dad, my boss—don't ever talk to me. The only person I really talk to is Lucy, and of course Dr. Vanek, and something like a serial killer never comes up in those conversations. It's entirely possible that I saw those faceless corpses sometime in the past and simply blocked them all from my conscious mind, waiting for the day my subconscious dredged them up and created a delusion. My biggest block of lost memory is from that two-week period before I was put in the hospital, but my memory before that is anything but perfect. Does anyone remember 100 percent of everything? Can I account for myself every hour of every day?

But how and why would I ever come into contact with the Red Line's victims, unless I was the killer?

My head nods, and I think about the horror of my own body's rebellion. Someone was controlling me—no matter what excuse Dr. Little comes up with, I felt it. My body was not my own. What if someone really can control my body, fully and completely, and they're using it to kill people? What if I'm just a puppet, dancing on the end of a string, while a nameless, faceless killer sits in the dark and controls my every move?

Cell phones—that's got to be how They do it. Cell phones and computers and TVs.

Do I really have something in my brain? Do They control me through a chip in my skull? Or is it something worse—is there really some kind of grub inside me, drinking my blood, nestling against the motor functions of my cerebellum, picking up a signal and passing it on, wearing my body like a glove?

That maggot was real—I saw it, I heard it. I can't stay here, knowing it might come back.

A nurse comes into the room: Devon. He has a tray.

My throat hurts from disuse. "Breakfast already?"

"Yeah, but let's get you cleaned up first." He uses a towel to sop up my vomit. "You slept like a log, man."

I cough up phlegm, trying to clear my throat. "It's the drugs." Cough. "Dr. Little gave me something new last night."

"Seroquel," says Devon. "I hear it really kicks you

in the butt." He gives me a swallow of water through a straw, and my throat starts to clear a little. "I also hear you went AWOL on us last night."

"I have to get out." I close my eyes and fall back against the bed. "There's no point in hiding it anymore. I have to get out of here."

"Lunchtime," he says, holding out a spoonful of oatmeal. "They're going to unlock you again in a couple of hours."

"That soon?"

"You're not dangerous; once they figure out how you got through the gate they'll just patch up the hole and let you walk around again." He holds the spoon closer, and I take the bite. He scoops up some more while I chew. "How did you get through the gate, anyway?"

"I watched people enter the code."

"Really?" He laughs. "That's it?"

I nod, for real this time, though I feel guilty doing voluntarily what my puppeteer forces me to do against my will. There's no harm in telling them about the code—they're going to figure it out eventually, and at least this way I can get out of the restraints sooner. I take another bite, chew, and swallow. "I sat in Linda's social therapy class and watched people go in and out; after a couple of people I had a pretty good idea what the code was."

Devon grins. "You're kidding. I can't believe it was that easy."

I shake my head. "Most of the patients in here don't have the focus for something like that."

"Oh, they've got the focus all right—you've never seen people this focused. They just don't have the presence of mind." He feeds me another bite, frowns, and looks me in the eye. "You're different than most of our patients, Mike. You're . . . clearer. More clear-minded, like you know what you're doing."

"Not right now," I say. "Those drugs are killing me; I feel like I just drank a bathtub full of gin."

"You'll get used to it," he says. "You know Steve? He's on Seroquel and he's fine."

"Steve, the bookstore guy?"

"Yeah."

Steve's a little weird, but he's not a twitching mess. I take another bite and think, trying to find a way out. Devon's a lot more talkative than normal. I shake my head at the next proffered bite, and look at him carefully. I need to trust somebody. Why not him?

"You're not like the other nurses here, either," I say. "Why'd you become a nurse?"

"I . . . just like it, I guess." He laughs suddenly. "Plus there was this girl, Rebecca, who I went to high school with. She signed up for all these nursing classes in college, and I didn't really know what I wanted to do and she was really cute, so I signed up for some of the same ones." He smiles. "Then she ran off with an artist, like a sculptor I think, but by then I was hooked. I just . . . really liked nursing."

"You like helping people."

"Yeah."

"And you studied nursing in general, or psychiatry specifically?"

"There isn't really a psychiatric nursing specialty, at least there wasn't at my school. I—"

"So how much do you know about the patients here, and the diseases they say we have?"

He looks at me a moment, as if surprised by the question. He stirs the oatmeal in the bowl. "I've worked here almost two years, so I've picked up a lot, but I don't have a diagnostic background, if that's what you're asking."

"So you like helping us, the people, but you have no real connection to the—"

"Mike," he says, cutting me off firmly, "where are you going with this?"

I take a breath. "If I could convince you that I'm not crazy—that there really is a conspiracy here at the hospital, and I'm being held prisoner as part of it—what would you do?"

He stares at me.

"I know this is a very difficult question," I say, "and I'm sorry I have to ask it, but there's nothing else I can do right now. I'm sorry. You've got to tell me: what would you do?"

He laughs softly and shakes his head. "Looks like I never learn, do I?"

"Devon . . ."

"What is it you see again? Men without faces, or something like that?"

"Have you seen them?"

"And a woman too, right? An extra night nurse?"

"They are real—the men, at least. I don't know what to think about the nurse."

"Yeah," he says, nodding, "yeah, I do this sometimes." He holds up a bite of oatmeal—not offering it to me, just staring at it. "You're sharp, Mike, you really are, and sometimes I take that for granted."

"You don't believe me."

He sighs. "You're sick, and we're trying to make you better. Don't you think you'd be happier in a world where nobody's chasing you all the time, and you don't have to hide and scheme and run away? Don't you want that?"

"I want that more than anything," I hiss. "You think I like being chased, trapped in here with Faceless Men and phantom women and the damn clock radio watching everything I do? You know what came in here last night? A maggot—a giant maggot, bigger than you are, slithering right through that door. Of course I wish it wasn't real—I'd give anything to make it not real—but what if it is? What if there really is something sinister going on, with the government or aliens or . . . I don't know. Something. And what if we could do something to stop it? What would you do?"

He stirs the oatmeal, back and forth, watching it fold and curve. He scoops up a bite and holds it out to me. "Come on Mike, let's just eat your lunch, okay?"

"This is serious!"

He holds out the bite. "Let's just eat."

"I don't want any."

"That's okay," he says. "Sorry it's just oatmeal— that's pretty much the only food we have for, uh, restrained patients. Anyone that has to be fed by hand." He stands up. "I'll see you at dinner."

"I don't want dinner!"

He turns and walks out.

"I want to get out of here!"

DINNER IS MORE oatmeal, and this time an extra nurse comes to back up the first and make sure I eat. I fight them for the first few bites but they hold me down and force it in, and eventually I give up and eat it all.

I try to imagine I'm eating peaches, but it doesn't work.

ELEVEN

EVERY NIGHT DR. LITTLE arrives with another pill and a gang of guards and orderlies to help force it down my throat. I fight him every time, and after a few minutes they inevitably resort to the shot, but they never stop trying. I sleep every night like a corpse, and I awake each morning from a vast, primordial void.

Dr. Little takes me into the hall, flanked by the biggest orderly I've ever seen. "I want to show you something, Michael." We walk toward the gate and I stop just shy of the office door. The window in the wall, formerly home to the top half of a monitor, is now adorned with a larger monitor, computer speakers, a clock radio, and a phone. The gate looks the same as ever, but I don't dare get any closer.

Dr. Little turns, smiles, and beckons with his hand. "Come closer."

"No thank you."

He clasps his hands together and stands there, smug and satisfied. "That is precisely my point," he says. "As you can see, we've upgraded our security: the gate code is now changed daily, and the office nurse and I are the only ones, in general, who know it. Anyone passing through the gate will have to ask for assistance, which not only reduces the number of leaks but has the helpful side effect of putting at least one extra person in the hall every time the gate is opened; this will help block your view of the keypad." He gestures at the shelf of electric devices. "These, of course, pose no threat to anyone at all, but we have the feeling they'll serve to keep our primary security risk—namely, you—well away from the gate altogether. With time, medication, and therapy, we of course hope that your fear of electronics will go away, but by then we imagine you'll be much less of an escape risk anyway." He smiles, his eyes buggy and massive behind his glasses.

I reach toward the row of devices, tentatively, testing them. My hand buzzes as it gets close, a tiny tremor. I pull it back quickly. "Is the code posted anywhere?"

"Obviously we're not going to tell you that."

"But if it's outside the gate somewhere, it doesn't matter if I know or not, right?"

"You're a very resourceful man, Michael; even the scant details I've just given you are tools you're probably already using to plan another breakout. Assuming, of course, that the details I've given you are true." He smiles.

I watch him, trying to read something from his face besides that maddening smile. Is he really layering lies and half-lies just to confuse me? Am I really that dangerous? I escaped once, yes, but I didn't get far, I didn't do anything, I didn't hurt anyone—

But what if he thinks I did?

If the Faceless Men truly aren't real—if that really is just a delusion—then Dr. Little is worried about something else altogether. Abnormally worried. I turn to face him directly. "Tell me about the Red Line Killer."

His eyes narrow and his brow creases, though the smile never leaves his lips. "Why?"

"People keep talking about him," I say, "and your desk was covered with pictures of his victims."

"I'm afraid there's nothing to tell, beyond the facts already available."

"What does he have to do with me?"

"With you?"

I step closer, one wary eye on the wall of electronics. "Do you think it's me? That I killed all those people? Is that why you're keeping me in here?"

He smiles and shakes his head. "Michael, you're far from my only case. Anything you happened to see on my desk is not automatically related to you."

"But their faces are missing!" I say. "Of course that's related to me—I made that connection immediately, surely it must have crossed your mind as well."

"There are some superficial connections, yes, but it's nothing. The FBI has asked me to look over their files; I have no experience in criminal profiling, but I have more experience with the . . . local psychiatric community than anyone else, and they thought something might stand out." He smiles. "So far nothing has."

"Nothing but me."

"Perhaps."

I step forward again. "There's something you're not telling me."

He opens his mouth to answer, but in that moment the computer speakers chirp loudly and my head explodes in pain. I clutch my ears, trying not to fall over, and somewhere nearby a cell phone rings. Arms grab me, supporting my weight, and my entire body is a knot of agony. Someone drags me down the hall to the commons room and the pain lessens instantly; by the time someone props me in a chair my head is already beginning to clear—at least as clear as it can get with the lingering fuzziness of the Seroquel. I look up and see Dr. Little on one side, the large orderly on the other. The room dances madly.

"Are you okay?" asks the orderly.

"What did you do to me?"

"We didn't do anything," says Dr. Little. "My cell phone rang and you had an acute phobic reaction."

"The headache hit before the phone rang," I say, closing my eyes and breathing deep to slow my pounding heart. "It wasn't the phone that did it, it was that chirp from the speaker—it was like a sonic attack. You deliberately incapacitated me!"

"That chirp was the phone," says the orderly. I open my eyes to look at him in surprise, and I see Dr. Little doing the same.

"You're sure?" asks the doctor.

"Speakers like that produce sound with a magnetic field," says the orderly. "A cell phone signal that crosses the field warps it enough to change the sound. It happens to my home computer all the time."

Dr. Little looks at him, then at me. He pulls out his phone and I shy back.

"Stay here, Michael. Carter, come over here." He nods toward the hallway, twenty or thirty feet away, and the orderly follows him over. "You have a cell on you?"

The orderly nods and pulls it out. Dr. Little gives him his number. "Dial that in, but don't call yet." He walks back toward the nurse's station, and I stand up to get a better view—keeping well clear of the orderly and his phone. Steve and a couple of other patients wander over to watch as well. We've never seen Dr. Little this concerned.

"All right," says the doctor, standing next to the speakers, "call me." He holds his phone up to the speakers, and the orderly hits a button on his phone. I take another step back, just in case. A few seconds later the speakers chirp—a loud, syncopated rhythm. A second after that the doctor's phone starts to ring. Dr. Little stares at it a moment, then presses a button to stop the call. The ringing stops, and with it the chirp. "Well," he says. He takes a step, glancing up at the speakers. "Well."

A nurse steps out from the office. "The monitor image flickered too, not just the speaker. What did you do?"

Dr. Little puts his phone away, takes a few steps, and stops. He pauses, turns, and stops again. "It could still be a psychosomatic reaction."

I stare, incredulous. "What?"

"If you knew about the speaker effect, even sub-consciously, your mind could produce the same re-action to that chirp that it does to a cell phone ring."

"It's not mental," I say, "it's a real, physical reac-tion. That signal is screwing with something in my head, the same way it screws with the speakers—it's a microchip or a transmitter or one of those damn alien bugs!"

"Of course it's a physical reaction," he says, walk-ing toward me. "Your brain is a physical thing—even your hallucinations are physical reactions, produced by real, physical impulses and chemicals. There's no implant in your head, just regular ears; they hear a sound and tell your brain, which consults your delu-sion and creates a psychosomatic pain response."

"But you can't be sure!" I shout. "You're just guessing now—you're brushing this off like you ig-nore everything else I say!" I step closer and the orderly reaches for me, but suddenly Dr. Little pulls his phone back out of his pocket and I shy back, cringing at the memory of pain. He holds it up like a cross and I step back again.

The doctor stands silent, watching me. "It's nothing," he says at last. "Nothing at all. I'm ignoring your ideas because they are patently ridiculous: you do not have an electrical signal or some kind of alien being locked inside your head." He looks around at the gathered patients. "Back to your . . . We're done here." He turns and walks away, the massive orderly flanking him protectively.

I HAVE A tracking device. It's the only explanation. In one of my episodes of lost time I was abducted, by who or what I do not know, and they planted something in my brain that reacts to electronic fields— that's how they track me, that's how they control me, that's how they do everything. Dr. Little either doesn't believe it, or he's deliberately lying. But is he lying to me or to himself? Is he ignoring the ramifications, or covering them up?

"Hey Mike."

I look up; Devon is standing in my doorway. He grins.

"Someone's here to see you, man."

Lucy! I stand up quickly and step to the door. "Finally!"

"It's your father."

I stop short. My father. We've been apart so long— nearly a month in here, plus the two weeks before that I still can't remember. My father. My face falls, and I step back. "What does he want?"

"Well he wants to see you, man," says Devon. "He's

your dad, of course he wants to see you." I don't move, and he reaches for my shoulder. "Come on, Mike, you've been in here five weeks and this is only your third visit. Come say 'hi' to the guy. Come on."

I hesitate a moment, but Devon grabs my shoulder and pulls me to the door, and I let him lead me through the hall and into the commons room. My father is there, standing stiffly by the wall, his hat in his hands. He wears a wool hat every time he goes anywhere.

He straightens when he sees me, but his face is hard. I keep my face impassive and walk toward him. I stop a few feet away.

"Dr. Little told me to come," he says brusquely. I wait for more, but he says nothing.

I look at the floor. "He probably thinks it will help me."

My father grunts. "Doesn't know us very well, then."

"Do you want to sit down?"

"I won't be here that long."

I nod. It figures. I don't want to spend much time with him anyway. I stare at the wall, not sure what else to say. "Was the traffic bad getting here?"

"Bad as ever."

"Ah." I nod again. Am I nodding too much? Is it the . . . the tar-something? Dyskinetics? I worry a lot these days, maybe too much. I fix my eyes on the wall and try to hold still.

"Doctor's been asking about your mother," he says, a hint of anger entering his voice. It's subtle, but I've learned to identify it before it gets out of hand. "Medical history and such; wants to know if she was crazy like you. What are you telling these people about your mother?"

"Nothing," I say quickly. "They've never asked me about her."

"I didn't ask what they asked about her, I asked what you told them." His voice is rising now. I feel like a child again, standing in a corner, listening to him yell about breaking something or playing too far away. He never liked me to go far. I think he was scared they'd come after me again.

I shake my head, looking at the floor. "I haven't said anything, sir. Not about Mom. She has nothing to do with this."

"You're damn right she has nothing to do with this," he says. "I don't like you running around crazy and stupid, but I like you making your mom look crazy and stupid even less. You hear me, boy? She doesn't deserve this."

"Excuse me, sir," says Devon, stepping forward, but my father cuts him off fiercely.

"You keep your nose out of our business, you got that?"

Devon pauses a moment, then walks around us, headed for the gate.

Something about this doesn't make sense. Dr. Little got a full medical history on me and my parents last time I was in here, years ago; there's no reason to be asking more questions now. Dead medical histories don't change.

"What kinds of questions was he asking?"

"What do you care what kinds of questions he was asking?"

I shift my feet, trying to summon more courage. I keep my eyes on the floor. "I just want to know what they're asking," I say calmly. "I need to figure out what they . . . what they think is wrong with me."

"What's wrong with you is you're weak," he says. "You always have been. I don't have time to come running down to the loony bin every time you can't deal with whatever stupid thing sends you over the edge. Your mother deserves better."

My mother. It always comes back to her.

Dr. Little steps up behind my father; Devon is a few paces behind him, looking stern. "Excuse me, sir," the doctor says, taking my father by the shoulder. "If you don't mind, I have a few more questions for you."

"Of course," my father says gruffly. He turns and walks with Dr. Little to the gate, never saying goodbye or even giving me a final glance. I watch him go, relieved.

My mother deserved better than him.

TWELVE

"VERY GOOD," SAYS Linda, smiling, "that's excellent, Gordon."

Gordon looks up with a grin, his hands still moving the broom: back and forth, back and forth, a full six inches off the commons room floor.

"Remember to keep it on the ground," says Linda, and Gordon's eyes grow wide with despair. The broom slows, but doesn't lower, and Linda steps in looking as gentle and loving as she can. "It's okay, Gordon, you're doing a great job!" She guides his hands down, lowering the broom until it touches the floor. "There you go—you did it! Now keep going back and forth, just like that."

Gordon smiles again.

"This is stupid," says Steve. "We shouldn't have

to sweep the floor—they have janitors who do that for us. This is like a hotel. I need to order room service."

"This is your home," says Linda. "Don't you think you should help to take care of your home?"

"They have janitors for that," says Steve. "I've seen them. There's one who comes at night."

"They do have janitors," says Linda, "but it's important to learn how to do it for yourself. Are you going to live here forever?"

"I'm leaving soon. Jerry and I are leaving next week."

"I don't think you're leaving us that soon," says Linda, "but you will be leaving eventually. Our job is to make sure you know how to act when you go."

"I already know how to sweep," says Steve. "See? Gimme that broom, Gordon, gimme that broom so I can show them." He wrestles with Gordon for a moment, Gordon still struggling mutely to move the broom back and forth across the floor. Linda steps in and separates them.

"You don't need to show me, Steve, I believe you. Would you like to try something else? Job skills?"

"I worked in a bookstore."

"We have a cash register right over here," she says, leading him over to a lunch table. "You come too, Michael, you can be the customer." I follow her a few steps, then stop. The register squats like a dull metal toad on the table. "We have a bag of plastic groceries right here," says Linda, pointing to a pile on the table. "All you have to do is . . ." She turns and sees that I didn't follow. "It's okay, Michael, it's fun. You can help Steve."

I don't say anything.

"He's afraid of the register," says Steve. "He thinks it's going to kill him."

"It's not going to kill me," I say.

"He thinks it's going to read his mind, or write on it, or do something else like that. He's kind of crazy."

I don't say anything. What's the point?

"We have some kind of weird people in here," says Steve, leaning close to Linda and whispering, "but I think there's something wrong with Michael. He should probably see a psychiatrist."

"Why don't you see if you can figure out the register," says Linda, "and I'll have a talk with Michael alone." She leaves him by the table and comes to me, smiling faintly. "Are you okay today, Michael?"

"It doesn't matter."

"Why not?"

I shake my head. "I'm never getting out of here. Not alive."

"Do you think your life is in danger?"

I look away. I don't want to tell her what a waste I am; she'll just give me a pep talk about sunshine or happiness or some dumb thing.

"Come with me, Michael, I need to show you something."

I follow her; we walk through the commons room, past patients wiping down tables and reading books to each other and playing all kinds of weird little games. I've been in here two months now. What's the point? I'm never getting out alive.

How much longer can I last?

"I have a treat for you today," says Linda, stopping by the couches. "This is the best therapy session you've ever had." She pauses, waiting for me to talk, but I say nothing. After a moment she continues. "We're doing social therapy today, like I was telling Steve. We're helping to give you the skills you need to live out in the real world again. For most of these guys that means cleaning up, but everyone's different. Steve's getting pretty good at cleaning, so he's moved on to job skills. It seems simple, I know, but playing with an old cash register and some toy food is going to help him get ready to move back outside and have a real job. He's probably pretty close."

I stay silent, staring at the floor, listening to a train whistle howling in the distance. There are other voices, whispering angrily, but I ignore them. They never say anything good.

"What would you like to do?" asks Linda.

I shake my head. "I don't want to clean anything."

"That's good; I wasn't going to ask you to. Sometimes social therapy is even simpler than that. Sometimes social therapy is just learning how to fit in. How to stop being scared."

I look up, wary, but it doesn't matter what she asks me to do. Nothing matters anymore.

"I want you to sit right here," she says, leading me around to the front of the couch, "and watch TV."

I step back firmly, yanking my hand away. "I can't."

"All you have to do is sit here," she says, smiling. "For everyone else TV is leisure time—it's like a reward. I'm giving it to you for therapy, how lucky is that?"

"I can't do it." I'm shaking my head. "I can't sit here, and I can't turn it on, I can't watch it—"

"I thought you said nothing mattered?"

"This does!"

"Listen," says Linda, planting herself between me and the TV. "This is important. Nothing is going to happen."

"You don't understand—"

"I do understand," she says calmly, "that's why I'm doing this. TVs and cell phones and computers and everything else—they're not out to get you. No one is reading your mind. No one is altering it."

"I can't do it," I pant, "I can't do it . . ."

"You're going to get out of here," she says. "You don't believe me right now, but you will—one day you'll be happy, and healthy, and free. You'll have a home and a job and friends. Do you want to spend that time terrified of TVs?"

My eyes are closed; my head is shaking.

"Look at me," she says. She holds my head with her hands, holding it still. "Look at me, Michael." I open my eyes slowly. "There we go. Now listen. You've been scared of electronics for too long, and even when the drugs kick in and the hallucinations go away, you'll still be scared of them out of pure habit. But there is nothing wrong. Can you say that?"

"No," I whisper.

"Let's start simple," she says. She pushes me down into the couch, and I try to move but she holds me in place and I'm sitting on the couch and I can see the TV behind her, black and silent and staring. "We're going to start very simply," she says, "as simple as possible. We're going to sit here, together, and just look at it, okay? We won't turn it on, we can even unplug it if you want, but we're going to sit here and get used to it. We're going to pretend like there's nothing wrong in the whole world."

My voice is a quiet rasp. "Why do you want me to be here? What is it going to do to me?"

"It's not going to do anything," she says. "That's why we're here—so you can see that it's not going to do anything. Alright?"

I look at the TV. It looks back. I grit my teeth.

I don't want to be scared.

"Alright." There are tears in my eyes. "Let's do it."

IT'S NOT LIKE a switch in my head; it's not like the drugs just pulled a magic lever and suddenly all the crazy is gone. But the drugs are working. Slowly but surely, the Seroquel is changing the way I see the world.

Imagine that you're looking through a pane of glass, thick with dirt, and someone's washing it clean. It's still smudged and dirty, covered with smears and grime and residue, but it's better than it was. Light is peeking through, and certain images are coming clear. I'm getting better.

And that means I was sick.

I'm pretty sure the maggot was a hallucination. I mean, how could it be real? Things like that don't exist, and if they did I definitely wouldn't be the only one who knew about it. It would have left some tracks—a slime trail, or spoor, or bite marks, or something to show that it had been here. Someone would have seen something, and questions would have been asked, and the whole hospital would have gone into high alert. You can't hide something like that. It can't have been real.

I spend my days watching things—watching everything. There's a patient in the commons room that no one ever talks to: is he real? He sits in the corner, talking to himself, and people pass by without saying anything. He might exist solely inside my head. At dinner one of the nurses talks to him, puts a hand on his shoulder; does that mean he's real, or that she's imaginary too? I watch her as she moves on, talking to other patients, asking about their day or their food or their anything. Maybe I'm imagining it all, making the patients move and respond in my head while in real life they sit still and say nothing because the nurse isn't there. Can I do that? How real are my dreams? How deeply is my false reality blended with the real one? If Dr. Vanek is right, I have no way of knowing.

One thing I know for sure—the footsteps at night,

the soft ones I thought were Shauna's, are completely gone. There is no nurse who checks on us at
night, only the night guard who wanders the halls
and peeks in our windows. I think Shauna must be
imaginary too, like the maggot: a hallucination created by a desperate mind. My subconscious mind
created the quiet nurse, soft and beautiful and kind,
because I'm lonely.

Why did my mind create the maggot?

I shudder again, seized by the fleeting thought of
it shrunk down and burrowing through my head.

Dr. Little, I'm fairly sure, is real, and so are Devon
and Linda and Vanek. Too many people have seen
them, talked to them, reacted to them. They're either all hallucinations or all real, and if my hallucinations can be that widespread then nothing's real
at all. What about my father? It almost makes sense
that he's fake—that my schizophrenic mind, left to
raise itself as a young orphan, would create a father
and, not knowing how a father should behave, pat-
tern his behavior after the cruel realities of the world
around me. The voice of the Earth, telling me I was
no good and nobody loved me. As a child I fed myself, bathed myself, walked myself to school; is that
because my father was negligent, or because he didn't
exist?

But he came in, he talked to me, he yelled at me
and he yelled at Devon, and then Devon and Dr. Little
both talked to him, both touched him. I don't know
where the real world begins and ends.

It's wishful thinking, I guess, to hope that my father isn't real. I'm not that lucky.

What about the reporter, Kelly Fischer? She made me promise not to tell anyone she existed; she made me swear it. When she hid in the bathroom so the nurse didn't see her—was she really in there, was she really hiding, or was it just my mind making excuses for why the nurse couldn't see her? When she came in that day to the commons room she sat with me, right over there, but she didn't talk to Linda, and Linda didn't say anything to her.

There's a knock on the door, but I don't look up. I never do anymore. It's never anyone I want to talk to. The handle turns and the door cracks open, and I smell her before she even speaks: the soft scent of flowers. Lucy.

"Michael?"

I look up and there she is, back again, back at last, peeking through the door. She sees my face and recognition lights up her eyes, and suddenly she's running in again, holding me in her arms, crying into my neck. I hold her too, a long, warm bear hug. We sit that way for a minute, for two minutes, just holding each other. It's been over a month since she was here, and I never want to let her go again.

"I'm so sorry," she whispers. "I tried everything I could do, but I couldn't get you out."

"How did you get in here?"

"I bribed the night janitor," she says. "He's not part of it—you can trust him."

"Part of what?" I take her by the hands and whisper darkly. "I'm sick—I really am. What is there to be part of?"

She frowns. "How can you be sick?"

"The drugs are working," I say. "I think I might actually be schizophrenic."

"But I've found so much," she says. "You told me to look it up—the Red Line and the hospital and everything. There's really something going on—"

"But I don't want it to be true," I say. "I've seen things that *can't* be true—monsters, real monsters, and they have to be hallucinations. And there's another girl—"

"Another girl?" asks Lucy, her voice loud and jealous. I quiet her with my hands, looking nervously at the door. She puts her hands on her hips. "What other girl?"

"A reporter," I whisper, "from the *Sun*—but she's completely fake. The last time you came to visit me, so did she, and I didn't think anything about it because Dr. Little told me I was going to have a visitor, but he was talking about you—he said it was a girl, and that was you. The reporter was another hallucination trying to pull me deeper into the killer and the conspiracy and everything that isn't real. Don't you get it, Lucy? All of that is fake! Maybe it's everything—the killer and the Faceless Men and everything. Don't you see what this means? If it's not real then I don't have to be afraid anymore. I don't have to hide."

Loud footsteps echo in the hall, slowly coming

closer, and I pull away from her. "The guard," I say. "Close the door, quick—"

But it's already closed.

I look back at her, confused. "Did you close the door?"

"I think so."

"You just ran straight to me—the doors here don't close by themselves, there's no springs. Who closed the door?"

"I'm sure I closed it. I must have."

The footsteps are almost here. "It doesn't matter—get down."

She rolls off the bed on the far side, away from the door, and ducks down behind it. I fall back, pretending to sleep, and watch through a slim crack in my eyelids as the night guard stops, looks in my window, and moves on. I wait longer, counting his steps as he moves away. He pauses again at the next door and I hold my breath. At last the footsteps continue, and I roll over to look at Lucy. She peeks up from the edge of the bed.

"This isn't a hospital," she says, "it's a prison."

"You said you'd found something," I say, still staring at the door. "What did you find?"

"They're really out to get you," she says. "The whole hospital. The janitor is the only one you can trust—his name is Nick, and he's going to help us escape."

"What do they want?"

"I don't know what they want," she says, "but it doesn't matter anymore—we can leave. We can leave right now and never come back, and you'll never see them again, and then it won't matter what they want because you'll be free."

I stare at her, breathing heavily, thinking about the outside. "The drugs are working," I whisper. "Even if some of it's real, some of it's not, and I don't want to go back to the way I was."

"We can get you other drugs, but you have to come with me! Nick let me in, and he's going to let us out, but we . . ." She stops. She stares at the door, then at me; her face is streaked with confusion. "We can't."

I stare back, feeling worry grow through me like a weed. "We can't what?"

"We can't leave."

"But you bribed the janitor, right?"

She looks confused, like she's struggling to remember something. "Well, yeah . . ."

"And he's going to let you back out again, right?"

"Of course, but . . ." she shakes her head. "This doesn't make sense."

I step toward her. "What doesn't make sense?"

"I remember bribing the janitor, and I remember coming in to get you out, but we can't leave."

"*We* can't or *I* can't?"

She looks at me, disoriented, her mouth open. "It's not that specific, it's just . . . I know it. It's a fact in the back of my mind: we're going to go to the gate, just like my plan, but the janitor's not going to be there, and we're going to be trapped. There's no way we can get out."

"You think he's betrayed you?"

"It's not like that, Michael, it's—it's not a hunch, it's a fact. I know it as clearly as I know my own name." She pauses. "Lucy Briggs." Her voice is tentative; probing.

I nod, slowly. "Lucy Briggs." Her eyes are wide with fear. I realize that she's wearing the same clothes she had on last time—a black T-shirt and black jeans. I try to remember her wearing something else, but . . . I can't.

"What's going on?"

And then I think it, and the instant I think it I know it's true, and she knows it too, and I see it on her face and I know that she thinks my thoughts and that means that I'm right, and I don't dare say it out loud.

Her voice is a puff of wind. "I'm not real."

My heart breaks in half.

"I'm a hallucination, Michael."

"No."

She steps toward me. "The night janitor didn't let me in here, you just imagined me here, and the janitor was the explanation you made up to explain how it happened, but it doesn't hold up because now we can't get back out."

I grit my teeth. "You're real."

"You knew it—in the back of your mind you knew it was all a fake, so I knew it too, because everything I am is a part of you."

My eyes are hot with tears, and I shout with rage. "You're real!"

She comes closer, catching my wrist with her hand, and I feel the touch and the warmth and the pressure but no texture, and I look in her eyes and my reflection is wrong—a younger me, well-dressed and handsome and half-remembered. A distorted reflection from my own memory; an idealized me in the eyes of my ideal woman.

"Michael, I'm so sorry."

"How can you be sorry if you don't exist?" I'm crying; I twist away from her grip and grab her arm, but it doesn't feel right—the heft is there, the solidity, but I can tell it isn't real. There should be more give—and suddenly there is. I think that I should feel her heartbeat in her wrist and suddenly I can, in the same instant I think of it. My mind is filling in the details in a desperate bid to hold on to the fantasy.

"This can't be real," I say, then instantly contradict myself. "You have to be real."

"I wish I was."

"You have to be real!" I shout. She flinches, pulling away from my grasp. "I can see you, I can feel you, I can smell you."

"I'm all in your head."

"You're smarter than me," I say, throwing up my hands. "You have a bigger vocabulary than me; you talk about people I haven't met. How could I possibly have made you up?"

"You've heard things," she says, stepping toward me. "You've seen things, you've read things, and you've absorbed it all like a sponge and now it's locked in your subconscious, and when you talk to me it all just . . . comes out. You don't know it—conscious Michael Shipman doesn't know it—but it's all in there and your brain decided, for whatever reason, that Lucy Briggs can remember it even if you can't."

I sit down on the bed. Lucy puts her hand on my shoulder and I know it's there, but I also know it's not. I stare into her face—perfectly beautiful, delicate and strong at the same time. The girl next door who's also a supermodel. I laugh.

"I guess I should have known it was too good to be true, huh?" I take her hand—I hold it in my own, soft and warm and alive. "The perfect woman, smart and funny and gorgeous, who just happened to fall madly in love with a nobody."

"You're not a nobody."

"I'm a homeless mental patient with a high school equivalency and a dead-end job found for me by a social worker. If you were real you'd have a rich boyfriend and a penthouse in the middle of downtown."

"I do have a penthouse in the middle of downtown."

"Because I imagined it for you! Because I'm such a lonely, pathetic loser that I made myself the most perfect girlfriend I could think of."

"Listen, Michael, I can help you."

"Go away!"

"If I'm really inside your head, and I really can remember things you don't, maybe I can remember other things too."

I turn to the wall. "Just leave me alone—"

"Dr. Vanek said your hallucinations might be based on real experiences that you can't remember because you can't get inside your own head." She pushes herself in front of me, and I turn away again. "Michael, I'm already inside of your head. If they're in here, maybe I can find them!"

"Dammit, Lucy, you're not real!"

"Of course I'm real!" she shouts. "I don't exist for anyone else but I exist for you. I can think, right? Therefore I am."

"You think what I tell you to think—you have no will of your own."

"Is that your perfect girlfriend?"

"What?" I look at her again and her eyes glisten with tears, soft and sad and deep as endless holes.

"If this is true," she says, "if you created your perfect girlfriend, would you really make her that weak? Would she really have no will? No power? No thoughts of her own?"

I feel my heart breaking again. "Of course not."

"I love you," she says. "Who tells you to stick with your job every time you want to quit? Who convinced you to join that reading skills class? I have my own will because you know you couldn't love me without one—because you understand that love is not about accepting people, it's about making them better. We make each other better, Michael." Tears form in her eyes—tiny drops of water, glistening like diamonds. "At least let me try."

"Michael, you okay in here?"

I look up, over Lucy's shoulder, and I see the night guard coming in. "I heard shouting," he says. "You all right, buddy?" He steps forward, directly toward Lucy, and she steps out of his way.

"Why did you step out of his way?" I ask, ignoring the guard and staring her down. "If you're just a hallucination, you could just stand there and he could walk right through you."

"Who are you talking to?" the guard asks.

"Your brain won't let me do anything it considers impossible," says Lucy, shrugging. "Technically, I shouldn't even be here with him, because it will only underline the fact that he can't see me."

"Can you see her?" I ask, looking at the guard.

He answers without looking. "There's no one here but you and me, Michael."

"She's standing right there, can you see her?" He doesn't move. "Can you just turn and look?"

"He thinks you're trying to trick him," says Lucy, walking behind him. "You're not the only schizophrenic in lockdown, you know—he's seen this trick a hundred times."

"Hit him," I tell her.

"Just calm down," says the guard, holding up his hand.

"Come on," I say, "you're right behind him—hit him! We can run, and the janitor can let us out like he promised, and we can be together again, forever."

"I'm not real, Michael."

"Yes you are! Hit him!"

"Easy, there, Michael," says the guard, putting a

hand on my shoulder. I shrug him off violently and he pops like a spring, grabbing me in a tight wrestling hold so suddenly I barely even see him move. "Easy, Michael," he says again, "just calm down. Everything's going to be okay."

"Help me!"

She waves, a tear rolling down her cheek, and then she's gone. I struggle against the guard but he holds me tightly in place, calling for the nurse. I try to kick him and suddenly we're down on the floor and he has my whole body pinned.

"Lucy!"

There is no answer.

THIRTEEN

IN THE MORNING they raise my dose of Seroquel, and a few days later they raise it again. Dr. Little says my confrontation with Lucy was a good thing—that even though I still saw her, my knowledge that she wasn't real was a big step forward. It means the drugs are working. Bit by bit, the glass is becoming clearer.

Dr. Vanek comes to visit on the weekend, shooing off a handful of other patients to clear us a private space in the corner of the commons room. I ignore him.

"Michael," he says, lowering himself into a chair. "You become more and more interesting almost every day, don't you?"

"I don't want to talk." My head nods, all by itself. Did he see that?

"Why?" he asks. "Because your girlfriend's not real? You're not the only man in the world with a fake girlfriend, I assure you. Look at our beauty industry—it's amazing anyone's satisfied with real women anymore."

"I said I don't want to talk."

"But you recognize your illness now," he says, leaning in. "You've admitted that you see hallucinations, which puts you in that glorious middle ground where we can really get some work done: you're crazy enough to see them, but sane enough to discuss them openly. I hate trying to psychoanalyze by memory."

I turn on him angrily. "It's not about being crazy, it's about being alone. What good does it do me to get better now that I don't have anyone to be better with? I was going to get out—I was going to get better and get out and live in a great big house in the country with . . ." I turn away.

"Are you content, then, simply to play with your imaginary friends?"

"Shut up." My arm twitches, but I hold it still.

"Don't get angry with me," he says, "you're the one acting like a child. Besides, if you didn't want to get better you wouldn't be talking to Dr. Jones."

"Dr. Jones?"

"Linda," he says with distaste, as if the name itself is unpleasant in his mouth. "She's the queen of the psychiatric hippies and a purveyor of feel-good claptrap, but she's apparently been having some success with you. Regular sessions, individual and group, where you've apparently delved quite deep into your hopeless Freudian wasteland."

"She's helping me."

"Helping you what? Kill your girlfriend?"

"Shut up!"

"Do you want to lose her or not? Have I misunderstood our entire conversation up to this point?"

"Look," I say, turning to face him and locking his eyes in a murderous gaze. "Lucy was one of the only things I loved in this entire world, and now she's gone, and I think I have the right to be sad about that. But losing her is the price I pay for losing a whole horde of monsters and aliens and God only knows what else I have crawling around in my head. I've been running away from a worldwide conspiracy of omnipotent Faceless Men for almost a year, and now for the first time I can stop running because I know there's nothing to run from. No Faceless Men, no giant maggots, no phantom noises in the hall. For the . . . I can't even watch TV, Vanek. I could barely stand to ride in a car, for fear that the stereo was trying to read my mind. It breaks my heart to lose Lucy, but if that's the trade-off—if I get to have a real life now, with a real job and maybe even, someday, a real girlfriend—then who are you to accuse me of anything?" I sit back and turn away, nodding, and when he starts to speak again I dive straight back into my rant. "If you'd been half the psychiatrist Linda Jones is, I might have gotten to this point years ago and saved myself a lot of trouble."

I stare at him, breathing heavily, daring him to speak. I'm so tired—worn out and beat up and full of rusted holes, like an old car in a junkyard. The light hurts my eyes and the sound hurts my ears and every movement makes my muscles burn—the dull, lactic acid smolder of fatigue and hard exercise. My Seroquel dose is almost maxed out, and my body can't take much more.

Dr. Vanek watches me calmly, saying nothing, until finally I turn away in exhaustion.

"You're going to go to prison," he says. "As soon as you're better. They're curing you so they can put you on trial."

I keep my eyes on the floor.

"Every word you say convinces them you're a killer. You fit the profile too perfectly: an angry young man, friendless and with no family to speak of; paranoid and persecuted; convinced that the source of your troubles is a band of nameless, faceless men who haunt your every move. Who are the victims, Michael? Neighbors who teased you? Teachers who got in your way? How easy it must have been to convince yourself they were part of this "plan" to destroy you, and how easy then, their humanity erased, to take their lives and cut off their faces and show the world what they really were."

"It's not true."

"I know it's not true!" he shouts, shocking me with his anger, "but what are you doing to prove it? Where were you when you lost your memory?"

"I don't remember."

"You have to remember! You have to give them an alibi or they'll lock you away for the rest of your life. Or they might just kill you: we do have the death penalty in this state, you know."

"I don't remember anything," I say, "just patches, maybe, that might not even be real—I was at home, I was at work, I was . . . I was somewhere empty."

"'Empty?'"

"Just houses with nobody in them, a whole city of them."

He pauses. "Tell me more."

"I don't know any more!" People are starting to look at us now. "I remember waking up in the hospital, and everything before that is a blur, like a big black hole in my head. I already told you, it was the MRI that did it—they got in and screwed up my whole head—"

"Who got in, Michael, if the Faceless Men are a delusion?"

"I . . ." I stare at him, not knowing what to say. There are no Faceless Men, no mysterious Plan, no one controlling my thoughts through every passing cell phone. If electronics are safe then the MRI is safe. I can't answer my problems with a conspiracy anymore.

"Michael?"

"What if you're right?" I whisper. "What if I am the Red Line Killer?"

"You're not."

"You don't know that." I look around, suddenly worried that someone is listening. A few patients are watching us, but they're all on the far side of the room; the space around us is clear. I lean in closer. "I do fit the profile, like you said, and I have two weeks I can't account for. Maybe more. If I'm capable of schizophrenia, who knows what I'm capable of?"

"Schizophrenia isn't something you're 'capable of,'" he says, "it's a disease. You don't commit it, it happens to you. Now try to think back to those weeks you lost—"

"I'm twenty years old," I say, cutting him off. "It's not just two weeks. Can I account for all that time? Can you account for every moment of the last twenty years?"

"I think you'd remember killing someone and flaying his face."

"Maybe I would, or maybe I'd block it out—selective memory . . ." I struggle for the word. "Repressed memory . . ."

"Dissociative amnesia," says Vanek. "You're suggesting that the act of killing was so traumatic that your mind repressed the memories to save you from them."

"It's possible."

"It's idiotic. Repressed memory, as a neurological function, is designed to protect you from things that happen to you; things you do willingly are, by nature, not foreign enough to shock your psyche that profoundly."

Foreign enough to shock you . . . Something about his words remind me of Lucy, and the last thing she said: that my brain wouldn't allow her to do anything impossible, like pass through a security guard. Once the mind creates an illusion, it won't let itself be shocked by anything that might break it. But there is a gap in the system, a gray area where an illusion can progress to the point where reality can't help but intrude. Like when Lucy broke in, and our inability to break back out brought the whole charade crashing down.

"What if," I say slowly, "I thought that the killing was a good thing—maybe even a moral thing—and only realized the mistake when the deed was done?"

Vanek raises an eyebrow. "You're determined to incriminate yourself in this."

"I don't want to be a killer, but think about it. What if my brain, thinking the Faceless Men were real, decided that it was my responsibility to save the world by stamping them out. So I'd go out and do it, and then when I tried to unmask them I realized it was all false, and the illusion shattered and the trauma forced the memory to repress."

"And this happened twelve separate times?"

"It's possible, isn't it?"

"It's scientifically possible that I could burst into flame at any moment, but it's not exactly probable. Nor is it believably probable that your messed-up psychology managed to turn you into a first-time serial killer on twelve separate occasions. When I scared you with that bit about being the Red Line Killer, Michael, I was trying to force you into some semblance of self-preservation—to make you come up with an alibi. I need you to remember where you were in those lost weeks, but now you're desperate to prove yourself guilty."

"I'm just trying to follow the facts."

"Then follow them down reasonable pathways. Your obsession with the Red Line victims is just one more example of your delusional narcissism—that if there's a mystery somewhere in the world, you must be at the heart of it."

Click click click click.

Vanek frowns. "Is that what I think it is?"

Dammit. "What?"

"You were clicking your teeth again," says Vanek.

"On purpose." It's all I can do to keep them from clicking again.

"Then do it again."

"What?"

"If you were clicking your teeth on purpose, do it again. I want to hear it."

"No."

"Should I call Dr. Little, then? Or Dr. Jones—you'd do it for her, I bet."

"Fine." Click. Click. Click. Click. I can't do it as fast on purpose; can he tell the difference?

He pauses, thinking silently.

"It's nothing," I say again. "It's not the drugs."

"Tardive dyskinesia is very serious," he says. "If it goes too far it can be irreversible, even without the drugs."

"Why do you care so much all of a sudden?"

"Because you're . . . you're an interesting puzzle, and I don't want you broken before you're solved."

"You're as loving as ever."

He stands up. "I'm serious, Michael. You have to break through to your lost memories—it could be crucial to the case as well as to your own mental health."

"But the case comes first."

"I don't care what comes first," he says, checking his watch. "Just remember." He turns and walks away.

I scan the room, looking for the patient I think is a hallucination, and I watch him, willing him to walk through a wall or a nurse or another patient. He sits dumbly, staring at the TV.

Why is Vanek so concerned about the lost time?

What does he know that I don't?

THE MOVEMENTS ARE getting worse.

I've learned to control the teeth click by tearing up a sock and keeping a ball of the rolled up fabric in the back of my mouth, wedged between my teeth; it doesn't stop the movement, but it stops the noise, and if I'm careful around the nurses no one can tell. My arm is harder to hide, but all I really have to do is keep my hand in my pocket, clutching tightly to the fabric of my pants. It keeps my arm stiff, but that's better than letting it fly all over the place. It's just my left arm, and I'm right-handed, so I can still go around and do everything I used to do.

My head movements are the worst, nodding up and down almost constantly, but I've learned I can control it, at least in part, by flexing my neck muscles as hard as I can. When no one's watching I hold my head with my right hand, or brace it against the wall, or slouch down in a chair and press my head against the back. It works well enough. Nobody's noticed it yet.

I suppose they think I'm weird, keeping my hand shoved into my pocket all day and slouching down in chairs and corners, but that doesn't bother me. They already think I'm crazy, right? As long as they don't take away the drugs.

I'm a little worried about Dr. Vanek's warning— that the dyskinesia becomes permanent after too long—but the drugs are worth the risk. I'm cured now: literally cured of all my hallucinations. I haven't seen any maggots or Faceless Men; I haven't heard any weird sounds or phantom footsteps. All of the terrors I've lived with for year after year are completely false—nightmares I thought I could never wake up from. I know that now. And I never want to lose that again.

I don't know how to explain what it's like—to suddenly wake up one morning and not feel psychotic anymore. To be free of the buzzing in my ears, the voices in my head, the twitching shadows on the edge of my vision. Some of my secondary symptoms are still there, of course—you can't just turn off a lifelong phobia of cell phones just because the false cause of the phobia has finally been removed. I still feel paranoid sometimes, and scared, and worried that as soon as I let my guard down, something—I don't know what—is going to jump out of the darkness. I never realized just how scared I used to be, all the time, thinking about running and hiding and all the ways the monsters were trying to kill me. Losing that is like learning to breathe for the first time. The dirty window I've been looking through is finally clean, and the view to the other side is glorious.

If I can hold my head still long enough to look through it.

Meals are the hardest part. I can't hold my head because I need my hand to feed myself, and I can't muffle my teeth because the wadded fabric in my mouth stops me from chewing. I have to take it out, and grit my teeth as long as I can, and flex my neck until it feels like my head is going to burst. One bite at a time: pick up a piece of food, raise it to my mouth, open wide, and hold still and try to get it in without knocking the food and the fork and the whole tray across the room. Chew slowly; carefully. Pick up another piece of food and do it again. Every meal is as long as a lifetime, and when I finish eating I hide in my room and lie on my bed exhausted, twitching and shaking until I feel my brain rattling in my skull.

Today is meatloaf and mashed potatoes; easy to cut, easy to swallow. I barely even have to chew, though that's hardly a problem with my jaw clattering like a wind-up monkey. Halfway through the meal I see Dr. Little watching me from across the room, and I flex my neck even harder, feeling my face go red with the effort, doing everything I can to stay still. Raise the fork, open the mouth, chew. Dr. Little comes toward me, and my heart sinks. Please don't notice me.

"That's remarkable," he says.

I smile, forcing my lips to move and my chin to stay still. "Thank you." The words are a grueling effort. "What's. Remarkable?"

"Your self-control," he says. "You hide it so well I don't think I would have noticed if Linda hadn't raised the suspicion in her last report."

My words are slow and measured. "I haven't done. Anything wrong." I set down my fork and rest my hand in my chin, hoping it looks natural.

"Oh," he says quickly. "Oh no, of course you haven't done anything wrong; we're trying to help you, not punish you. But your tardive dyskinesia is back, the involuntary movements we talked about before. You hide it well, but it's simply not safe. Your drugs will have to be switched."

"No." I shake my head, my control slipping. "Please don't take. Me off Seroquel. It works. It. Clears up everything. I've never felt like this. Before."

"You're trading a mental prison for a physical one," he says, shaking his head. "It's not worth it. We'll start you on Clozaril tomorrow morning."

Starting over from scratch—a low dose of a brand-new drug. I feel my eyes grow hot, and my voice is a ragged whisper. "It will all. Come back."

"Probably," he says. His plastic smile is gone; he looks at me impassively, the closest Dr. Little ever gets to sympathy. "Your hallucinations will likely return, for a time, but Clozaril is very effective and you should be back in shape again soon."

"Please don't—"

"I'm sorry, Michael. It's for your own good." He walks away, summoning Devon and pulling out his prescription pad, and I feel my life crumbling around me.

FOURTEEN

I GET NO Seroquel that evening, and all night long I lie awake in bed while the world around me warps and curdles. My room is full of noises; the hall and the hospital and the whole city beyond it echo with shouts and horns and scrapes and howls. I have no way of knowing if they're real. Should the drugs wear off this quickly?

It's nearly one in the morning when I see a light in the corner of my clock radio display—a tiny red dot I don't remember seeing before. Is it watching me? Was I a fool this whole time, eating up their psychobabble and believing it was all a delusion and letting down my guard? But I'm just freaking out; it's probably completely innocent. But then why is that dot there? I lie still just in case, showing them nothing.

Click click click click.

In the morning Dr. Little arrives with a new nurse—not one of the regular care nurses but a clinical tech I've never seen before. She carries a tray of needles and tubes. There's a guard behind them, large and somber.

"Good morning, Michael!" Dr. Little has his smile pasted on again, broad and delighted, his eyes wide and slightly buggy under his glasses. "Sleep well?"

I glance at the clock radio, just barely, and he follows my gaze and his smile never falters.

"As I told you yesterday," he says, "we're starting you this morning on a drug called Clozaril."

I glance at the nurse, setting her tray of needles on my dresser. "It's an injection?"

"It doesn't have to be," he says, holding up a small plastic cup with a tiny yellow pill; I look closer and see that it's been clipped in half. "Twelve point five milligrams," he says, "so small you don't even need water, though of course we brought you some." He smiles again, and the nurse sits me up in the bed. "Either way, though, we need to draw a little of your blood. Nothing frightening, just a test."

I hold out my arm while the nurse ties a plastic tube around my bicep. "Is there something you can do with my blood? Something about the dyskinesia?" If they can, maybe I won't need a new drug after all.

"I'm afraid not, Michael; the dyskinesia will have to go away on its own or not at all, and we sincerely hope that we've discontinued treatment early enough to be rid of it. The good news is, Clozaril bears an extremely low risk of tardive dyskinesia, a mere fraction of the other neuroleptics you've tried. It's not even a concern, really, though naturally we'll keep an eye on you just in case." The nurse swabs my arm with disinfectant, on the inside of the elbow, and preps a syringe. She pricks me in a bulging vein and begins to draw out blood while Dr. Little continues. "On top of that, Clozaril is happily the most effective drug we have for the treatment of schizophrenia, and now that you're on it—"

"Wait," I say, "it's the most effective, and it has no side effects? Why didn't you just start with it, then?"

"I didn't say it had no side effects, Michael, I said that tardive dyskinesia is not one of them. Clozaril runs a very high risk of blood and heart disorders, hence the blood test—we'll be testing your blood again every four days to see what kind of effect the drug is having, and we need a healthy baseline of comparison."

"What?"

The nurse slides the needle out of my arm, pressing down on the hole with a wad of cotton and bending my elbow closed to hold it in place. I put pressure on the cotton and stand up angrily. "This is going to give me a heart disorder?"

"Not with regular blood tests, no. You'll be perfectly safe. Without regular blood tests . . . yes. The risk is actually quite high, which is why we only use Clozaril for cases like yours that prove highly resistant to treatment."

"That doesn't sound 'perfectly safe' to me."

"I apologize for the word choice, Michael." He offers me the cup with the pill, but I don't take it. "Nothing is 'perfectly' safe. But you're in a hospital, Michael—you're surrounded by doctors and nurses every hour of the day, with medical facilities close at hand if there's ever an emergency."

"Is there going to be an emergency?"

"We're doing everything we can to prevent one."

"You need my consent for something like this."

"We have your father's consent." He smiles. "He signed last night."

I stare at him for a moment, then turn away. I'm a mental patient; I don't get to make my own choices anymore. I take a deep breath and run my hand through my hair, trying to think.

"Look, Michael," says Dr. Little, stepping closer. "The Seroquel was working, and you knew it—you loved it. You were finally free. I want to help you get back to that point but this is the only thing I can give you. There are risks, I admit, but everything else has more risks." He holds out the cup. "The symptoms and the hallucinations are all going to start coming back—slowly at first, but then more and more as the Seroquel washes out of your system. It will take awhile for the Clozaril to build you back up to the same point, but the sooner you start it, the sooner your problems will all go away again."

I close my eyes. He's right—heart disorder or not, I don't want to be like I was. I can't live like that again, and this drug's either going to cure me or kill me, and aren't those the only options anyway? I turn back, darting a quick glance at his eyes, then at the radio. The red dot is still there, an unblinking eye. The nurse has my blood in a vial on her tray, all ready to go.

Dr. Little pushes the cup closer. I take it from his hand.

Half a tablet. A pale crescent moon no wider than a nail.

I drop it in my mouth and swallow. I don't even feel it going down.

"MICHAEL."

There's no one in the room. I go back to my jigsaw puzzle.

"Michael, it's me. The one who's trying to help you."

"You're not real."

"Of course I'm real, I'm as real as you are."

"You're a voice in my head."

"Don't believe their lies, Michael, you're not crazy—they're studying you. You're a rat in a maze."

I look up. "If you're real, where are you?"

"I'm in the vent."

"That's impossible."

"My voice is in the vent; my body's in the next room."

"Should I go there and look?"

"You can't let them see—you can't let them know we're working together."

"We're not working together."

"We have to kill Dr. Little, Michael—he's the one keeping you here. It's your only way out."

I stand up abruptly, storming to the door and running to the next room: Gordon's room. There's no one there. I look under the bed, behind the chairs; I even open the dresser drawers. No one. I go back to my room and do the same, searching under and behind everything I can find, but there's no one hiding anywhere. I push the heavy chair in front of the air vent and go back to my puzzle.

The voice is muffled. "You're such an idiot, Michael; you're a useless, worthless, brainless idiot! Kill Dr. Little and get out of here! Are you a coward?"

I scrape the puzzle pieces back into their box and take them to the commons room. The voice keeps shouting at me, and I count out loud to drown it out.

I SLEEP IN my chair, the blankets piled on top of the clock on the dresser. In four days I get another blood test, and when the results come back Dr. Little approves a raise in my dose. The voice in the air vent goes away, but Shauna tells me that patient was transferred anyway. I eat by myself; I talk to Linda about my father. In four more days I have another blood test, and now I'm getting twenty-five milligrams of Clozaril twice a day, and of course Shauna isn't real. I know that.

After a while I don't cover the clock anymore, but

I still don't go near it. It's a lifelong habit, and habits are hard to break. Linda says the little things, like being scared of phones and stuff like that, are the last to go because they're learned behaviors, not psychiatric disorders, and it will take time to un-learn them. They're a sane reaction to false data, and now that I'm perceiving real data, more or less, the therapy will help my reactions shift to match. I can watch TV now, plugged in and turned on and everything.

Dr. Little says I get better every day, but I still have symptoms and he's raising my dose. Dr. Vanek is still working on my memory, doing everything from drugs to hypnosis, but the holes are still there. I don't mind so much. Why would I want to remem-ber being crazy?

By the time the FBI comes back, I haven't had a hallucination in nearly two weeks. I figure that means the agents are probably real.

Devon takes me in to the small therapy room. There's only one this time, the taller one. He smiles and holds out his hand to shake.

"Good afternoon, Mr. Shipman, I'm Agent Jon Leonard with the FBI. Do you remember me?"

"Were there two of you last time?"

"Yeah, my partner, Agent Chu."

"Just making sure."

He gestures to the chair opposite his, and I nod politely. It's a real nod this time, though they aren't always; the dyskinesia hasn't fully gone away. I don't mind so much, since I got my whole life in exchange. Devon leaves us, shutting the door behind him, and Agent Leonard sits down.

I sit as well, watching him. "Did you find the man I saw?"

"We did."

"And?"

"Nothing. His name is Nick; he was applying for a job here. He wasn't faceless, he wasn't an authority figure, he wasn't anything to be afraid of."

"I figured as much." I sit back, sighing in relief. "You have no idea how great it is to hear that."

He raises an eyebrow. "You don't believe in the conspiracy anymore?"

"I have schizophrenia, Agent Leonard. The conspiracy was all in my head."

He nods, eyeing me from across the table. "What do you know about the Red Line killings?"

"Not much," I say honestly, trying to gauge his reactions as I talk. Does he still think I'm a part of them? "I had a, uh, longtime phobia of TVs and radios, so I never really heard about the killings until I got in here." I laugh nervously. "To tell you the truth, I was kind of hoping it would all turn out to be just one of my hallucinations, and not be real at all."

Leonard laughs as well, a shallow chuckle. "No, Michael, I'm sorry to say that the Red Line murders are very real. What else do you know about them?"

He's fishing for something he can pin on me, I think, and then immediately I tell myself I'm wrong. I'm just being paranoid—no one's out to get me. He probably just thinks I'm a witness. Just calm down and everything will be fine.

I shake my head. "I don't know anything else. I don't even know why they call him the Red Line."

He chuckles again. "Mostly just a sick joke, really. The first detective on the case—a local guy, not a fed—was a big Blackhawks fan."

"Hockey?"

He nods. "You watch hockey?"

I shake my head. "TV phobia."

"Oh yeah. Well, this guy was a big fan, and he called the crime scene the 'Red Line' because that's where you have a face-off."

I grimace. "Seriously?"

"I told you it was kind of sick."

I fidget in my chair, suddenly anxious again at the mention of missing faces. "But they don't have anything to do with me, right?" I'm too nervous now for subtlety. "I mean, just because I saw Faceless Men and, and stuff like that, doesn't mean I'm the killer, right?" My arm twitches; the movements get worse when I'm nervous.

"Do you still see them?" he asks. "The Faceless Men?"

I freeze, too nervous to answer. He waits, then raises an eyebrow.

"Michael?"

"No," I say, shaking my head. "I haven't seen them in weeks."

"Excellent," he says, smiling. "You have no idea how long we've waited for the chance to talk to you, but your doctor wouldn't let us back in until today."

"Because I'm cured?"

"Because you're lucid."

I nod. He still didn't answer my question. I feel cold and small.

"You're aware," he says, pulling his briefcase up from the floor, "of who the Red Line Killer seems to be targeting?"

I nod again. "The Children of the Earth."

"Precisely," he says, opening the briefcase with a sharp *click*. "And what do you know about that organization?"

"It's not an organization," I say darkly, "it's a cult."

"Fair enough," he says, "but as cults go this one is remarkably well organized. They own a farm; they sell fruit and cheese in stands by the highway; they're almost fully self-sufficient. The only thing they buy from the state is water."

"No power?"

"They've refused electrical power for nearly two decades," he says. "They even tore down the power lines that used to connect them. They're practically Luddites—they make the Amish look high tech."

I swallow nervously. Why does that make me so scared? I rub my hands together, trying to warm them. "What does this have to do with me?"

"Two things." He reaches into the briefcase and holds up a piece of paper with a long list of names. "One: of the thirteen Red Line victims, nine have been members of the Children of the Earth. The other four were connected indirectly, friends and family and so on." He sets down the paper and picks up what looks like a legal document. "Two: at present day the cult resides in a farming commune outside of Chicago, centered around the former home of Milos Cerny."

That catches my attention. "*The* Milos Cerny? The kidnapper?"

"I'm afraid so. But that's not even the weird part." He sets down the document and holds up another list of names, shorter than the first. "Of the five children recovered from the house of Milos Cerny twenty years ago, four of them ran away from home to join the Children of the Earth, at ages ranging from fourteen to seventeen. They were found by the police, of course, and were returned to their parents, but as soon as they came of age and their parents couldn't hold them, boom, straight back to the cult. Every one of them." He pauses. "Except you."

I frown, not sure what to say. I'm not even sure what to think. "Were they . . ." I feel faint, like my heart is beating too fast. "The cultists—did they help Cerny abduct the women? Did they help kill them? Why aren't they in jail?"

"Some of them were," he says, trying to calm me, "but only as accessories, and all of them have completed their sentences or been released on parole."

I sit back in my chair. "You can't be serious."

"I'm afraid it's all true. Now you see why I came to talk to you."

"You think they're going to try to contact me?"

"Frankly, I'm astonished that they haven't already done so. Once the other four children started drifting back to the cult, we contacted your father to ask about you; we got in touch with your school. Your name's been flagged in the system for virtually as long as we've had a system, but there's never been any sign, that we could see, that you'd been contacted. We were hoping that you might be able to tell us more."

"Wait," I say, pushing my chair back from the table. "You mean to tell me that I really have been under government surveillance? All this time I thought I was paranoid, or crazy, and now I'm in this damn madhouse taking drugs like they're candy, and you're telling me it's true?"

"Michael—"

"Is it the clocks? Are you the ones watching in there? And what about the—"

"Michael," he says, more forcefully this time, "please calm down. You have not been 'under surveillance,' you've been flagged in the system. That's very different—it just means that if you ever show up on a police report, or a medical report, or anything like that, I get a little email and I read it. That's all it is."

"You've been watching me."

"I've been protecting you. Listen, Michael, the people that kidnapped you and your mother are out there, and they're tied up in another string of murders, and I am doing everything I can to figure it out. Our best theory right now is that they're killing dissenters; anyone who leaves or speaks out against the cult. I need to know if they've contacted you, because that might give me some kind of lead—"

"How did they contact the others?"

"We have no idea. One day the kids just got up and left; nobody called them, nobody drove them, by all appearances they did it completely on their own."

"That doesn't make sense."

"You're telling me. Listen, there's got to be something, somewhere, that you can tell me. A letter shoved under a door, a stranger on the street, something."

I laugh, frustrated and confused. "I've had imaginary men chasing me for years. Maybe they were the contact."

He starts to speak, but suddenly I'm flat in my chair, writhing in pain, and Agent Leonard's pocket rings loudly.

"Shut it off!" I force myself to sit back up, clutching my head with one hand and reaching for him with the other. My arm pulses with the same syncopated rasp as the computer speakers in Dr. Little's experiment.

"Are you okay?"

"Turn off the cell phone!"

He pulls out the phone, brow furrowed in confusion, then clicks a button. The ringing stops, and my headache starts to fade. He stares at the phone in shock.

I rub my temples, groaning in pain. "That's not supposed to happen anymore."

He looks up, and his eyes get wider. "Your nose is bleeding."

I touch my lip and he's right; my fingers come away slick and red, and I can feel the blood dribbling down my lips. I shake my head. "That's not supposed to happen."

"What's going on?"

"Get Dr. Little."

"Are you okay?"

"I need him now!" I shout, and go to the door myself. "Get Dr. Little in here!" The headache explodes again, sudden and devastating, and I fall against the wall in a cringe. I turn around to see Agent Leonard holding his phone to his ear. "Are you calling someone, you idiot?" I stagger back and snatch the phone from his hand, throwing it against the wall. The signal stops, the headache calms, and I let out a long, exhausted breath.

"What the hell?" shouts Agent Leonard.

Dr. Little rushes in. "What's wrong?"

I gesture at the broken phone. "I had another headache from a cell signal. Two, thanks to him."

"Hey," says Leonard, picking up the phone; the back has come off, and he collects the batteries.

"You can't have had another cell phone attack," says Dr. Little. "That's a psychosomatic delusion and your medication prevents those."

"Yeah, well, apparently not," I say. "It's not a psychosomatic . . . whatever. It's a physical thing—I've been telling you that since I got here. There's something in my head!"

Dr. Little shakes his head. "There is nothing in your head, Michael—"

"Wait," says Agent Leonard slowly. "What if there is?"

Dr. Little narrows his eyes. "Excuse me?"

"I've seen this reaction before," he says, "on the security camera at ChemCom. Right before the Red Line killed the janitor, the janitor had some kind of sudden migraine, just like what you just had. It almost looked like the headache warned him of the attack, but we didn't understand how—but if he reacted to cell phone signals, like you do, then that could be what tipped him off."

Dr. Little frowns. "You think the Red Line had a cell phone?"

"Everyone has a cell phone."

I shake my head. "I don't. I guess that means I'm not the killer."

"But you are a potential victim," says Agent Leonard, "just like Brandon Woods and the other cultists."

"I'm not a cultist," I hissed.

"But there might be something in your head," says Leonard, "like a chip or a beacon or . . . I don't know. Something. If Cerny implanted something in the babies he kidnapped, like a communicator, that could be how the other children were contacted and brought back into the cult. Maybe they all have one." He shrugs. "Maybe yours is faulty, and that's why you never went back."

"I told him something just like that almost two

months ago," I say, jerking my head toward Dr. Little, "but I'm the crazy guy so no one listens to me."

Dr. Little shakes his head. "Now you both sound insane."

Agent Leonard looks at Dr. Little. "I know, and I agree, but there are . . . other factors at play here. We saw certain things on that tape, which I am not at liberty to discuss, but which lead our agency to believe that this investigation goes well beyond what we typically consider to be normal. A tracking implant would be one of the least insane explanations we've come up with."

Dr. Little purses his lips. "Two months later, all things considered, the theory doesn't seem entirely out of the question."

"So if there's really something in his head," says Leonard, "how would we go about finding it?"

Dr. Little pastes his broad smile back across his face. "This is a mental hospital, Agent Leonard. Finding things in people's heads is our specialty. I'll schedule an MRI first thing tomorrow morning."

FIFTEEN

DR. VANEK STORMS INTO my room in a fury. "You can't let them give you an MRI! It's out of the question."

"Calm down," I say, closing my eyes. "This is hard enough for me to deal with without you in here stirring up all my old twitches."

"You're going through with it?"

I open one eye, looking up from my chair as he storms through the room in directionless agitation. "Yes, I'm going through with it, it's the smartest thing to do."

"It's an MRI," he says.

"Which is completely harmless, as you told me yourself the last time I got one."

"Am I not allowed to be wrong on occasion?" He stops pacing and points at me with a thick finger.

"We still don't know why you lost your memory, and I've been going over the evidence for weeks and the only good lead is the MRI."

"I fell out of a window; I probably hit my head."

"The MRI confirmed that you didn't."

"Because that's what an MRI does," I say. "It looks at your brain and tells you if there's a problem. Now we're going to use it again to confirm that I do or do not have a foreign object inside of my skull."

"And if you do," he says, "the MRI will interact with it again, just like it did before, and frankly we'll be lucky if two weeks of memory is all you lose. Assuming there's actually an electronic device in your head, and knowing absolutely nothing about what it is or how it works, it's unconscionably stupid to bombard it with radiation."

"I am trying to get better!" I shout. "I'm trying to get rid of my delusions and work through all my phobias, and nothing you are saying is helping!"

"It's not helping because you're not listening!"

"I don't have any say in it anyway," I say, shaking my head. "You people haven't let me decide anything for myself since you put me in here, so stop yelling at me and talk to Dr. Little."

"I've already talked to him, and he's more stubborn about it than you are."

"Then talk to my father."

He shakes his head. "An MRI is not considered a dangerous test, so they don't need your father's approval."

"He could refuse treatment, though, right?" I

shift in the chair, suddenly not sure which side I'm arguing for. I don't want to be afraid of the MRI, but I am. "I mean, if my father demanded that you not do the test, you'd have to stop, right? Like those religious groups that refuse medical treatment—dangerous or not, you still have to follow the wishes of the patient or the patient's guardian."

"It's a possibility," says Vanek thinly, "but depending on your father's parental concern has never gotten us anywhere before."

"Then . . . ," I throw up my hands. "Then just forget it, and I'll get the MRI, and we'll be fine." My pulse quickens at the thought of it—the giant tube, the whirr of magnets and motors, the invisible menace of a thick magnetic field slamming through my body. I close my eyes again and fight off the wave of panic. "It's all in my head; nothing's going to hurt me."

Dr. Vanek grunts, a deep growl of anger. "The fact that it's all in your head is precisely the problem." He looks at me sternly. "We still haven't figured out what happened during the two weeks you lost."

"We never will," I say. "It's all gone."

"Memories don't disappear, Michael, only our access to them. Whatever you saw, or did, during those two weeks is still in your head. You just need a way to get it out."

I nod. "Lucy said the same thing."

"Lucy is a dream," Vanek snarls. "Focus on reality. Can you remember anything?"

"I remember an empty city," I say. "And a . . . a

pit. Like a deep black hole. That's the root of it all—it has to be."

"Ignore the hole for now," says Vanek. "Focus on the empty city. Remember every little detail you can think of."

"Why does this even matter?"

"Because your mind is important," he says, "to me at least, if not to you. Because you need to prove you're not a killer, now more than ever. Because . . . because we don't know. You are surrounded by mysteries, Michael. Those two weeks might be able to answer some of them, maybe all of them. If you're going to risk erasing even more of your own mind, the least you can do is recover it first. Write it down so it doesn't just . . . disappear."

"I . . ." He's right. If I can remember where I was—what I saw, what I did—then I can know for sure that none of it is real. "I'll do it. I'll remember— I'll try as hard as I can." I look up. "What are you going to do?"

"I'm going to stop this idiocy." He stalks to the door. "I'm going to talk to your father."

I REPEAT THE phrase over and over, all evening, trying to keep myself calm: It's all in my head; nothing's going to hurt me. My delusions are gone, my hallucinations are gone, and I'm back to the way I was at the end of the Seroquel—I'm better, actually, because I don't have any of the other side effects like fatigue and muscle aches. Even the dyskinesia is almost completely gone. There's nothing to be afraid of. The test won't hurt me because the reasons I'm afraid of it are all based on stupid, crazy things I don't even believe anymore. It's just habit. I'm fine.

It's all in my head.

I'm too restless to stay in bed, so I get up and pace around the floor, watching the clock, wishing I had a window. I realize I haven't seen the stars in two months—we have outside windows in the commons room, but we're only in there during the day. The impulse seizes me, and before I know what I'm doing I'm opening my door, listening for the night guard, and slipping down the hall in bare feet. The commons room is vast and dark, faintly lit by moonlight from the windows and harsh yellow light from the nurses' station down the hall. The sound of a TV drifts through the air. We're not allowed out of our rooms at night, but if I'm quiet she won't even know I'm here.

I trace a path through the tables and chairs and come to the window, leaning against the metal grate and peering up into the sky. The bars are cold against my cheek. The city lights are bright, turning the dark sky pale, but the clouds are thin and the brightest stars shine through. I can count maybe a dozen. Half the sky is blocked by the neighboring building, and I move to the next window, then the next, looking for a better view. The stars are tiny, barely visible from the heart of the city. I press my face against the grate and stare.

The sky is a geometric puzzle, cut apart and pieced together by cold metal bars.

I hear footsteps behind me. I turn quickly, not wanting to get caught, but the noise is still somewhere down the hall; I haven't been seen yet, but I can't get back to my room. Moving from window to window has brought me to the far end of the room, to the TV area, so I slip behind a couch and lay down. The footsteps come closer, but there's another sound with them—a high-pitched squeak, loose and intermittent. It seems vaguely familiar. I creep to the edge of the couch and look out just in time to see a dark figure come out of the hallway, pushing a mop and a rolling bucket. The janitor. I've heard his wheels before, but I've never seen him. Like the stars, he only comes out at night.

I pull back behind the couch, waiting for him to continue to the gate and leave, but instead the squeaking stops. I peek out again and see him standing in the dark—not mopping, not moving, just standing. I think he has something in his hands, something wide and flat, but I don't know how he could see it in this light. I hide again.

This is stupid. He's just a janitor—he doesn't care if I'm out of my room. I should go back now, before the guard shows up, and everything will be fine.

I need to stop being so paranoid.

I shake my head and take a deep breath. I've been in here for two months; I feel better than I ever have. I'm practically cured. If the last few things I need to

deal with are these stupid, lingering fears then the
best thing to do is to face them head-on. I stand up.
The janitor's mopping the floor, backing slowly toward me as he goes: I weave around a long table
and call out softly.

"Excuse me, I just need to get back to my room—"

And then he turns around, and the world stops,
and my heart freezes in my chest.

He has no face.

"Um. Um." My mouth is babbling by itself, my
brain too shocked to do anything. The man lowers
his mop and takes a step toward me. His voice is a
thin whisper.

"Michael."

I can't talk. He drops the mop with a loud clatter
and comes toward me, slow steps at first, but as I
back away he breaks into a run. My eyes go wide
and I stumble, tripping over a metal chair. He's almost on top of me now, his face a dark blur of nothing, and suddenly panic takes over—a pure animal
instinct—and I pick up the metal chair, swing it
around in a full arc, and slam it into his blank, horrifying face right as he lunges the last few feet to
tackle me. He flies to the side and I stagger backward, carried by the chair's momentum. He hits the
floor with a heavy smash, scattering two more chairs
as he lands. I fall to my knees, clutching my make-
shift weapon, waiting for the guard or the night
nurse to come running, but nobody comes. The TV
from the nurse's station drones in the background.

Did nobody hear me?

I watch the fallen body, a shapeless black shadow, but it doesn't move. Slowly I stand up, creeping forward, nodding compulsively; I'm too distracted to bother trying to stop it. The man lies completely still. He's not breathing.

I killed him.

SIXTEEN

I GLANCE UP again, looking for the guard, but no one's coming. I walk around the table and creep closer to the fallen body, pausing as I get within arm's reach. Nothing. I pick up a fallen chair and set it aside, moving closer. The janitor lies on his stomach, his face—if he has one—to the floor. I prod him cautiously, getting no response, then jab him harder in the stomach. When he still doesn't move I stand up, glancing around again, and grab him by the arm, hauling him over onto his back. He rolls heavily. In the dim moonlight I can see him more clearly, and it's true—stunningly, shockingly true. He has no face. I move my head and the air around his face seems to ripple and fold. I reach toward him, my breath catching in my throat, irrationally convinced he's going to lunge up and grab me. He stays still. I reach closer, simultaneously thrilled and horrified by the blank blur, morbidly desperate to touch it. A foot away my fingers start to buzz and I jerk my hand back in surprise. It's the same electric resonance I feel from a clock or a TV. I reach out again, probing the air to be sure, and there it is again. I've known that feeling all my life.

Drugs or no drugs, it terrifies me.

The Faceless Men are real. I feel my pulse rushing through my chest and arms, searing my skin with a violent inner heat. He's real. I stagger away to sit on the floor and put my head between my knees. I've had 100 milligrams of Clozaril in the last twelve hours; I haven't seen or heard or smelled a hallucination in weeks. I live a life dedicated to snuffing out every conceivable psychotic element. I can't see anything unreal because it's physically, medically impossible.

And yet here he is. A Faceless Man.

I push myself farther back, scooting away from the horror in the dark. He knew my name; he tried to attack me. Why? Why is he here?

It doesn't matter why he's here. He is, and that means there's more, and that means I need to get out—I need to get out now. I climb to my feet, crouching lightly, ready to run. Where? I should be safe in here; there are people watching and protecting me. I shake my head. Watching me, yes, but protecting me? I have no idea.

The world seems to shift around me, spinning

wildly, and I grip a table for support. He's real, an actual Faceless Man, but does that mean the rest is real? The clocks and the maggots and the cyanide in the hot water and all the things I thought and feared and ran from—is that all true too? What about Lucy? Reality shifts around me so fast I can't keep up. What if I'm hallucinating again? What if I've killed an innocent man? I shiver and gasp for air, trying not to retch.

He was looking at something. I creep across the floor in the dark, the tables turned flat and jagged in the dim moonlight filtering through the windows. My hand rakes across a shadow and I pull it back quickly; something cut my finger. I probe the darkness carefully and find a clipboard, and when I pull it into the moonlight my breath catches in my throat: clipped to the board is a page with my name and photo, plus a short dossier. I hold my breath, reading in shock through a full list of all my symptoms, my full police history, a record of every place I've lived. The information runs onto the back of the page. Behind it, stuck to the wooden face of the clipboard, is a Post-it note with a four-digit number: 4089. I glance at the keypad on the gate; is that what I think it is?

The guard's been gone too long; he'll be here any minute. I stand up and take a step, then stop myself: what can I even do? If I'm right then my nightmares are true—the whole hospital could be infiltrated—and if I'm wrong then I've killed an innocent man. Either way I need to leave. I look back at the clipboard, tapping the gate code with my finger. If I hide the body they might not find it until morning; I could be long gone by the time they even know I'm missing.

But only if I work quickly.

I take the papers off the clipboard and shove them down my shirt, then grab the janitor by the feet and pull him around the chairs and down the hall to my room. I pause, look at the clock, then toss a blanket over it just in case. I check the janitor's wrist, hoping against hope. He's still dead.

I'll never get out of the hospital wearing patient's pajamas so I pull off the janitor's dark blue jumpsuit and pull it on over my clothes. Aside from his face, the man's body looks completely normal. I heave his body up into the bed, in case the guard looks in the window, and position him as best I can without touching his head. I listen for footsteps, but there's still nothing.

I need drugs; I can't leave without drugs. If I start hallucinating again I'm as good as caught.

I slip into the hall and grab the mop handle, pushing the bucket in front of me and trying to look like a janitor. I pause at the nurses' station, eyeing the gauntlet of electronics Dr. Little still keeps in the window. The gate's right there, less than fifteen feet away. There's no other way. I just have to deal with it. I push forward, glancing through the door into the bright nurses' station. Sharon the night nurse is slumped forward in her chair, her head on the desk, the colored lights from the TV dancing across her hair.

What's going on?

I slip into the room quickly, searching for medicine cabinets, but there's nothing. They must store them somewhere else. I slip back out of the office, gasping, realizing I had held my breath the whole time I was in the office. *Calm down,* I tell myself, *you're not getting out of here if you don't calm down.* I can't risk any more time wandering through the hospital; I'll have to get medicine somewhere else.

The hallway buzzes with electrical fields, and my head buzzes back. I press forward, gritting my teeth, and type in the code from the Post-it. It works. I push the bucket through and let out a gasp of breath as the gate closes behind me. I lower my eyes, push through the double doors, and go. I find the stairs; I find the lobby.

I'm outside.

I'm free. I can feel wind on my face, and soft rain on my hair, and when I look up I can see the sky— not a piece of it, half-glimpsed through a grated window, but the whole thing, vast and dark and endless. I walk slowly, through the hospital parking lot and out to the street, never looking back, never hurrying, trying to look like a normal guy leaving a normal job in the most normal way possible. It's just after three in the morning.

The janitor had some change in his pocket, but no identification. A small ring of unidentified keys. I assume he left his wallet and car keys in a locker somewhere, but I don't dare go back to look for it. The change is enough for a bus, if I decide where

I'm going, and maybe a cheap breakfast or a burger. I could take the train, but they have cameras; once they know I'm gone, they'll start checking around and they'd see me on the train cameras. Do buses have cameras too?

I can't risk public transit; I need to find the nearest freeway and hitch a ride out of town. Get out, get gone, and never look back. The farther I go the better. The Faceless Men are real—I'm still reeling from the discovery. I have to go as far and as fast as I can. Whatever they were trying to do to me, I've escaped, and I can't ever let them find me again.

I come to an intersection and wait, turning up my collar against the rain. The street is full of cars, even in the middle of the night; dark blurs and streaks of reflected light. The city is alive with light, teeming with light, neon and halogen and phosphorus screaming electrified photons in every direction. Even the pavement glows, gleaming back colored lights from puddles and gutters. The traffic lights snap from red to green; the flow of traffic shifts and I move with it across the street. There's a camera hanging over each traffic light, and I keep my eyes down. They'll have access to those too. I need to get somewhere safe.

Powell Psychiatric Hospital is in a relatively expensive part of town, a business district with office buildings and trees and storefronts. I walk another couple of blocks and the taller buildings fade away into gas stations and car dealerships, shorter and brighter. The sky is sectioned by tall poles and skeins of wire. I'm not the only person out in the rain, and

I wonder what the others are running from. I keep going, moving away from the traffic cameras into the back-streets of an industrial district: block walls and barbed wire and long, lonely warehouses. I pass security gates with more cameras. My clothes are wet and my legs are tired and sluggish. I wipe rain from my eyes and keep walking.

The freeway, and then out of town. It's my only chance.

I walk past old dry cleaners and pawn shops, through slums and alleys and business parks, until at last I reach a freeway ramp. I stand and rub my hands together, stamping with cold. A car passes, and I stick out my thumb. Nothing. A minute later another; traffic out of the city is practically nothing this time of night. I hold out my thumb to ask for a ride and the car drives past without slowing. Minutes pass, and the sky grows slowly lighter. Three more cars, then four more, then nothing.

The tenth car stops.

"Need a ride?"

I shuffle closer. "Where you going?"

"Manteno. That far enough?"

"Sure." I reach for the door. I stop.

The man gestures at the door. "Hop in."

I don't move. For the second time, faced with an open escape, I know that I can't take it. There are too many others—other victims, other children. Other corpses. The Faceless Men are real, and it's not enough to free myself when there are so many people still trapped in the Plan.

I still don't know what the Plan is.

"Hey buddy, you coming?"

I look up and catch his eyes. "Do you have a newspaper?"

"What?"

Dr. Little told me there was a girl there to see me, and then I was visited by two. Lucy turned out to be a hallucination . . . which means the reporter was real. "The *Sun-Times*," I say. "Do you have a copy?"

"No I don't. You want a ride or not?"

"No thank you. I have to find a paper."

"Whatever, man." He rolls up his window and drives away. I walk back the way I came and find a garbage can on the sidewalk, dark and hooded and bolted to a streetlight. I walk forward slowly, conscious of the stark yellow glow above me, and pull back the hinged metal lid. The can stinks like old food and overflows with trash. I root through it gingerly, avoiding the worst of the sludge, and pull out a folded newspaper. The morning is brighter now, weak sunlight filtering through the night's gray. I find Kelly's name on the seventh page of the paper, on a story about an accidental shooting. *Kelly Fischer.* She's real. She's a crime reporter, just like she said. I refold the paper and look for a number in the masthead—some contact info of any kind—and find a tip line. I walk another block to find a pay phone— the only safe kind, with the signals curled into shielded cords instead of buzzing sharply through the air. Still frightening, but not as painful. I drop in a quarter and dial.

Ring.

A machine answers with a list of business hours; I hang up in a rush, breathing heavily. Machines are bad enough when they don't try to talk to me.

I look at the slowly graying sky. It's still early; I can rest now and call again when she gets there for work. I find a place to curl up out of the rain—the entrance to a parking garage. I drape the paper over my head and try to sleep.

I dream of a hollow city, filled with hollow, shambling people.

RING.

"*Sun-Times.*"

"I need to talk to one of your reporters," I say. "Kelly Fischer."

"Who's calling?"

I hesitate. I don't want to give them my name. "Ambrose Vanek."

"One moment."

The phone clicks, dead, and I wait. The phone clicks again and I hear the reporter's voice.

"This is Kelly Fischer."

"Hi, it's me."

"Mr. . . . Vanek? I'm afraid I don't recall the name."

"No," I say, looking around, "it's me." I pause, waiting, but she doesn't speak. "Michael."

"Michael," she says slowly, then abruptly her voice changes. "Michael Shipman? I didn't know they let you use the phone in there."

"I'm not in there anymore. Can I meet you somewhere?"

"Congratulations on being released, that's great. There's no need to meet, though. That story . . . took a different direction. Thank you, though."

"This is important. There are things I didn't tell you before."

"I don't doubt it, but really, we don't need to meet. Thank you—"

"Don't hang up!" I shout, desperate to keep her on the line. "Listen, this is very important, but we can't discuss it over the phone—I don't know if They're listening or not. You have to believe me—"

The line goes dead.

I shake my head—I've got to get Kelly to believe me. Something's going on here, not just with Powell and the Faceless Men but with the Red Line Killer and the Children of the Earth and who knows what else. They're all connected, and Kelly is the only one I can talk to—the only one who's done all the research to figure it out. I need her information. I need her.

I pull out my change: nine quarters left. I think about dialing her again, but I know she won't answer. I dial Vanek's number instead.

Ring.

"Ambrose Vanek."

"It's me."

"Bloody idiot," he curses, "what on Earth possessed you to run? And to kill someone!"

"They've already told you?"

"Of course they already told me—I was the first one they called, because they knew I'd be the first person *you* called."

"So they're listening," I say. "I'll be careful—"

"Of course they're not listening," says Vanek, "there hasn't been time for anything like that—"

"Not for the normal police, no, but the Faceless Men have resources you haven't dreamed of."

"They're not real, Michael. Has your medicine worn off this quickly?"

Medicine—dammit, I need that too, I forgot. There's too much to do, and I feel myself slipping under.

"They are real, Vanek, I've seen them—one of them, the janitor I killed. I was fully dosed on Clozaril and I saw him anyway. He had a paper—I still have it." I unzipped my janitor coverall and pulled out the crumpled paper. I held it close to my body, shielded from the rain. "It's still here, Vanek—a full dossier on who I am, where I've lived, what I've done, everything. Why would a janitor have this?"

"It could be another hallucination," said Vanek. "Your mind remembered what it created last night and it's reproducing it now to protect you from the realization that it's false."

"I have it right here," I say. "You can see it for yourself."

"Oh no," he says, "I can't get anywhere near you, Michael—you're a wanted man, and I could go to jail just for talking to you. The last thing I want to do is meet you in person."

"There's something going on," I say. "I know you don't believe me, but there's a real conspiracy and they are trying to . . . I don't know yet. One of the Children of the Earth was working in a chemical company—why? The FBI said the cult is completely self-sufficient, so he didn't need the money, so why was he there?"

"Why does it matter?"

"Because he also said they're like Luddites, completely antitechnology, so why leave the farm at all? Why go into a huge city full of technology you hate to get a job you don't need? It has to mean something."

"The cult hates technology?"

"That's what Agent Leonard said."

"As much as you do?"

"I don't—" I freeze, catching his meaning. "It's not like that. It's completely different."

"You don't know that," he says. "Dr. Little told me about the man who died at ChemCom—Agent Leonard said he had the same sudden headache attack that you have. Maybe they avoid technology because it hurts them, the same way it hurts you."

"Because there's something in my head."

"You need to find them."

"I'm not going to find them," I snarl. "They're evil—they have some kind of Plan, some horrible thing they're doing, and I've got to stop them. Maybe that's . . . maybe that's what the Red Line Killer is doing too. He knows about the Plan and he's trying to stop them."

"Are you sympathizing with the murderer now? Because this conversation is already about as dangerous as it can possibly be. Doctor-patient confidentiality is completely out the window now."

"Then tell the police," I say, "but I need medicine first."

He growls, scoffing.

"I'm serious," I tell him. "I can't fight them with my brain screwed up. I need to stay lucid, and you're the only one I know who can help me."

"I'm not going to buy you drugs."

"Just a prescription! Just a piece of paper with your office and your name so I can go somewhere and buy them myself."

"I could get arrested, Michael. I could lose my license and go to jail."

My voice is desperate and ragged. "You have to help me."

"I've helped you too much already, Michael. I . . ." He stops. "You need to go back."

"I'm never going back."

"Not to the hospital," he whispers, his voice growing soft and urgent, "but to wherever you were before that. Maybe something there will trigger your memory, and you'll remember the time you lost."

"Will that help?"

"I'm going to tell the police that you contacted me," he says, "because I don't want to be an accessory to murder or drug trafficking, but I won't tell them where you're going. That's all I can give you. Don't call me again." He hangs up.

I swallow, nodding, and put the phone back on the hook. Go back to where I was? I don't know where I was—all I remember is an empty city, and I don't even know what that means. An empty city and a deep, black pit. How do I know if they're even real?

I need Kelly Fischer. Maybe if I . . . I look at the paper in my hands, then carefully tuck it back into my coverall. Maybe if I show her the paper she'll believe me. It proves someone's after me—even if she won't believe anything else, the paper will show her that. Then with all the information she's collected, maybe some small shred of it can lead me to the next step. I have to try.

But Vanek was right about my medicine wearing off—it hasn't happened yet, but it will, and when it does my brain will crumble back into nothing and the hallucinations will return and I'll be a useless wreck again. I can't risk losing my lucidity. I don't dare go to a pharmacy or a hospital; I need to find drugs somewhere else. On the street, I guess. Dr. Little said that Seroquel was a recreational drug, so I know it's out there.

I start walking.

SEVENTEEN

I DON'T KNOW where I am. I walk to the nearest corner and look at the street signs, but I don't recognize either of the names. I jog to the next street, much bigger than the last, but there's still not a name I recognize. I turn slowly, examining the skyline, trying to find a fix for my location—where's north?—but I find nothing. The morning is light enough that I know the sun has risen, but it's too overcast to actually see it; instead of sky and sunbeams I see only mist and clouds, infused from behind with a soft, directionless light. I watch the traffic, nearly even in both directions; I can't even guess a direction by watching the flow. I pick a direction at random and start walking.

I fall easily back into the patterns of homelessness, always watching for cops and dogs and any scrap of food or money. I pass a train stop and keep my eyes down, my face obscured from the cameras. My hair is thick and wet, plastered to my skull with grease and old rain. I pass a man in a suit, hurrying past me to the train station, and before I'm aware of it I ask him for change. The words leave my mouth like a reflex. He ignores me, just as naturally, and we pass and are gone. I keep walking.

I try to piece together the little I know of the Faceless Men—so little because I don't know how much of it I know for sure, and how much is the lingering delusions of a broken mind. They have chased me forever, I think, but Dr. Little says my schizophrenia is only eight months old. Before that I had depression and anxiety, which the Klonopin was intended to help. If I'd taken it then, would the schizophrenia have developed anyway? If I don't treat the schizophrenia now, will something worse come tomorrow?

The Faceless Men—try to remember the Faceless Men. How long have they been watching me? More than a year, I'm sure of it. The man from the FBI, Agent Leonard, said the government had been keeping tabs on me since early adolescence. Are they connected to the Faceless Men? Could the hospital be under Their control *without* the government's help? But no, I don't know that for sure: I don't know if Powell was under Their control or not. That was the paranoia talking. Let me look at the facts.

One: Nick, the night janitor, was a Faceless Man.

I confirmed this by sight and by touch, while firmly under the influence of antipsychotic medicine. He had a paper with my information, and I still have it, and it still says today what it said last night. My hallucinations are rarely ever that consistent.

Two: Before the janitor, I saw more Faceless Men, watching me from a distance, though no one else ever seemed to see Them. Either the hospital was part of the conspiracy and helping to cover it up, or I was the only one who saw Them. I was still hallucinating back then; they probably weren't even real.

I stop walking, gripped with a sudden realization. The hospital found the janitor and told Vanek, but they didn't say anything about his face. They could be hiding it, true, but what if they just didn't see it? What if I see Faceless Men not because I'm crazy, but because somehow I can see Them as they really are? Somehow everyone else sees normal, everyday people, and I see their true nature.

But no—that's the schizophrenic narcissism again, telling me I'm different and better and more important than everyone else. It makes more sense to say I'm hallucinating than to say I have some kind of superhuman awareness. And yet . . . I have the proof. I have the janitor's paper. I get it out again, desperate to see it, to touch it, to know that I'm not crazy. It's still there; it's still my dossier. I touch it reverently and tuck it back inside.

There's one more fact I haven't considered: the nurse was unconscious. If the Faceless janitor was coming for me, and if the hospital was in on it, why was the nurse unconscious? And where was the guard? It makes more sense that the janitor was acting alone, observing me for months and then finally, when the time came, incapacitating the nearby witnesses to hide his actions. But what was he going to do? I searched his clothes and his equipment—he didn't have any drugs or surgical tools or anything else suspicious. Only the paper and the gate code. Was he going to talk to me?

Was he going to take me?

I hear a siren in the distance, short and clipped. A cop just pulled someone over. The sky is brighter now, and I realize I need to get off the street. If the cops are looking for me I should keep to the back roads and out of sight. I'm too conspicuous in this coverall. I turn down the next alley, hiding in the narrow space between two fat brick buildings.

I need new clothes. Drugs and clothes and money. I could go home, I guess; there're clothes there, and the old Klonopin I never took, but it's too risky. The police are sure to be watching it. Even if they're not, my father would sell me out in a heartbeat. I can't go home. But then where?

Where can you even buy drugs on the street? High schools, probably, but I couldn't get in to one of those looking like this. Maybe the parking lot behind one? I see a bank with a large electric sign. Eight in the morning; school's already started. Is the sign watching me? I shake my head and keep walking.

It feels like I walk for hours before I find a school. It's a brown brick high-rise, set in among a forest of smaller buildings; the block across the street is a fenced-in field covered with dying yellow grass. The parking lot is small, and the swarm of parked cars spills out to fill the curbs in every direction. I don't see any cops, but I assume they're close by; my own high school was always filled with them, and this one's just as ghetto. I've seen drugs, and drug deals, but I've never bought them myself before. I don't know what to do. I walk down the street slowly, taking in every detail. There are people here and there in the shadows, some in the cars and some on the front steps of the neighboring houses; some are kids, some are adults. I'm too scared to approach them. What will I even pay with? Maybe I can just find out the price, and come back later. What if I get arrested, or shot? What am I doing here?

I walk around the block, trudging slowly, running through my approaches in my mind. Do I want to look confident, or will that make me look too aggressive? If I try to stay quiet and nonthreatening, will I come off as too weak? It doesn't matter if they try to rob me—I don't have anything to steal. I should leave. I circle the block again, slowly, watching the people as I pass but never making eye contact. The dealers I saw in high school were usually older, sometimes much older—thirties or forties. Old pros who've been doing this for years. I walk past without talking to anyone. I feel the anxiety rise in my chest, fluttering like a trapped, angry bird. I can't do this.

I'm hungry; I haven't eaten breakfast. I walk until I find a diner and carefully count out my change.

"What can I get for $2.25?"

"Cup of soup."

"Thanks." The waitress brings me clam chowder and I sip it slowly, trying not to burn my tongue. There are a handful of other patrons in the diner, but none of them look like cops or drug dealers. Are any of them Faceless Men? If they can hide from others, can they hide from me? Could anyone I see be one of them, wearing a face like an insidious mask? I'd have no way of knowing. I leave the diner and walk back to the school, always moving, always watching. There's an old man in a window; there's a little girl on the steps. Who's watching me?

The school is surrounded by students, talking and eating and smoking through the eleven o'clock lunch break. Half of them are talking or texting, and I turn down a side street, away from their phones.

The city is alive with energy, sharp fields of electromagnetics crossing back and forth through the air—TVs, radios, cell phones, wireless modems, buzzing and humming and prickling at the edges of my consciousness. They are formless pain. They are barbed tentacles of thought. They are voices from beyond the world.

It is nearly three o'clock when I return to the school, bone tired and sweating from exertion and heat. The clouds have cleared and the sun is hot and bright. School hasn't let out yet. I walk in a slow circuit around the edge of the school.

"You looking for something?"

I stop; it's not an old man like I'd hoped, but a

young kid, maybe fifteen at the most. I recognize him from my walks this morning, still in the same car.

I look back, not sure what to say. *I want to buy drugs* is too simple, too forward. He could be a narc, or there could be one nearby. I shrug. "Yeah."

"You homeless?"

"Yeah."

"You can't walk around a high school like this, man, people think you're a perv. You got money?"

I hesitate. He'll turn me away if I say no. I nod. "Yeah."

He smiles. "Then what you need, my man, is some soup. I know a great soup kitchen, get you fixed right up, maybe find you a place to sleep and get you out of those stank-bag clothes. Get in."

"I'm not really looking for soup—"

"Get in, dammit." His face is hard. I nod, catching on too late to his pretense; I'm more tired and hungry than I think. I open the back door and sit down.

"Geez, Brody, this guy smells like a urinal!" There's a young man in the backseat next to me. "What'd you go bringing him in here for?" I don't remember seeing him before—is he actually there? Have the drugs worn off that much? He leans closer and sniffs. "You sleep outside last night?"

I don't dare answer him; the other kid will throw me out if he thinks I'm crazy.

The driver, Brody, starts his car and pulls away from the curb. "You don't want no soup, huh? You think I care if you want any damn soup? When I say get in the car you get in the car."

"I'm in the car now."

"What you looking for?" asks the man in the backseat. I look at Brody, still too scared to answer the other man out loud.

"Answer him, trashman—what are you looking for?"

I sigh softly, relieved to have the man confirmed by a third party. I swallow. "I need neuroleptics," I say carefully. "Clozaril works best, but Seroquel can do in a pinch—"

"You want some Suzy Q?" asks Brody. "We can do that. How much?" He's driving slowly, aimlessly, cruising the streets while we make our deal.

I frown and swallow again, nervous and scared. "How much does it cost?"

"That's not how this works," says the kid in the backseat. "You tell us how much you want to pay, and we tell you how much that'll get you."

"I . . ." I stop. "Can I get a . . . sample, first?"

Brody laughs. "You hear that, Jimmy? He wants a free sample."

Brody's voice is hard. "This ain't no ice cream shop, junkie. You addicted to this stuff?"

"I need it for a medical condition."

"He's addicted," Jimmy laughs.

"How much do you want?" Brody asks again.

I have nothing—no money, not even the $2.25 I spent on lunch. My pockets are completely empty, except for the paper and—

—and a small ring of keys. The janitor's.

I touch my pocket, feeling the keys through the

fabric. "I need to make kind of an unorthodox deal with you guys," I say. "I don't have any money."

Jimmy and Brody curse in unison. Brody pulls over and swears again. "Get out."

"Listen to me—"

"No," shouts Brody, "you listen to me! You don't come into our place of business and waste our time, and I don't care what kind of deal you're trying to make because if it doesn't involve money I am not interested, end of story. Now get out of this car while that's still the worst thing that's going to happen to you."

"I work in a hospital," I say desperately. "See this logo on my coverall? It says Powell Psychiatric, I'm a janitor there. Half of the drugs you sell, that's where they come from."

"Then why are you buying them from us?"

"Because I lost my job, and I can't get back in, but I can get you in and you can take all the drugs you want."

The car is silent.

Brody shakes his head. "These places change the pass codes every time they fire someone."

"I have metal keys," I say quickly. "They change the pass codes but not the locks."

Silence.

"It could work," says Jimmy.

"It's dumb as hell," says Brody.

"Look," I say, "if you get me a change of clothes I'll even throw in the uniform. Clean it up and you can walk all through the halls without batting an eyelash. They know my face but they don't know yours."

Brody stares at me, eyes narrow. "Show me the keys."

I try to look firm. "Drugs first."

Suddenly Jimmy is holding a gun. "You want to do business, you follow our rules."

I nod, my eyes never leaving the gun, and slowly pull out the ring of keys. "They're all right here: exterior doors, service hallways, medical cabinets, everything." I don't actually know what any of the keys do, but I try to sound convincing.

"Now we're talking," says Jimmy. He looks at Brody. "This could work."

A train whistles nearby, shrill and piercing.

Brody starts driving. "Take off the uniform."

"And you'll give me the Seroquel?"

"He said take off the uniform," Jimmy snarls, gesturing with the gun.

"We had a deal."

"Money is a deal," says Brody. "All you have is a handful of keys. How do we know they even work?"

"Why would I lie to a man with a gun?"

"Because you're a junkie," says Jimmy, "and junkies are stupid."

The train whistles again. I look at the gun, then at Jimmy's face. We're in a residential neighborhood now, the houses grim and cracked. I need the drugs—I can't leave here without them. I lick my teeth, feeling my chest grow cold and hollow. I hold up the keys.

And toss them straight into Jimmy's eyes.

"What the—"

He flinches and raises his hands to cover his face, and as soon as the gun isn't pointed at me I lunge forward, grabbing his wrist with one hand and pounding him in the face with the other.

"Holy—!" Brody shouts. The car swerves wildly as he first looks back and then overcorrects to regain control. "Shoot him, you idiot!"

Jimmy tries to point the gun at me but I'm too strong—strong enough to attack a whole room full of doctors; strong enough to accidentally kill a man with a chair. He fires one panicked shot into the roof, and I punch him again, feeling the crunch as his nose breaks and sprays us both with blood. The car lurches awkwardly to a stop as Brody slams on the brakes and stumbles out of the car, sprinting for the nearest side street. Jimmy and I lose our balance, nearly falling into the foot well, and I wrench the gun from his hand as he clutches feebly at his face.

I have the gun. The car is moving slowly again, drifting diagonally toward the side of the road. The train whistles loudly again, deafening and painful. I thrust the gun into Jimmy's face.

"Give me the Seroquel."

"Are you crazy, man?"

"I didn't want to do this," I say, "but there are bigger things I have to deal with. I am helping you, but I need Seroquel to do it."

"We're going to kill you, you know. Me and Brody and everyone else—we're going to hunt you down and kill you."

"Brody ran away," I say. "You're alone." The train whistles again, a jagged blade of sound, and I grimace and cover my ears. "Why is that train so loud?"

"What train?"

It whistles again. "That train!"

"What are you talking about, man?"

I look up: there is no train. We're in a tiny residential neighborhood, old houses and old cars, without a railroad for miles. I look back at Jimmy and he has no face, and I scream along with the blare of the train.

"We're going to kill you," says the Faceless Man. "All of us. You're a dead man and you don't even know it—"

The gun goes off.

Jimmy gasps, falling back against the door, a puckered hole in his chest spilling deep red blood. He grits his teeth and wheezes, eyes screwed shut in pain, his entire face a clenched, rigid mask.

His entire . . . face. He has a face.

I fumble the car door open and run.

EIGHTEEN

A WOMAN IS screaming. I look down and see the gun in my hand, black and inert. Can anyone else see it? Brody's car is still moving, creeping slowly toward the side of the street until it bumps a car with a soft metallic crunch. A woman screams again, not in terror or anger but simply a scream. Inarticulate.

I look at the gun again. I shot a man—he had no face, and I shot him, and then his face was back, just like that. Was it real? Is he hiding his true nature, or did I kill an innocent man?

I run as fast as I can, arms and legs pumping like a cartoon. My chest is cold in the wind. The gun is in my right hand, and I don't know where to put my finger. Will it go off? How should I hold it? I reach up with my other hand, slowly, awkwardly, and flip the gun down so I'm holding the barrel. I wrap my fingers around the outside of the trigger guard. Everyone can see it, up and down, up and down, waving like a flag as I run. I need to hide it. I need to run.

I need to get hold of myself.

I'm in a wide street, with short, dirty houses stretching endlessly in every direction. Two men on a porch stare at me as I go by. A little girl on a bike pedals fearfully away around the corner. I drop to the curb in the shadow of a garbage can, crouching in the gutter. What do I do? I should throw the gun away, tip it into this can and be gone . . . but those men, that girl, who knows how many people peeking through their windows—they all saw me. They'll know where I dropped it, and when they tell the police they'll find it and they'll catch me. I can't leave it here.

And what if Brody comes looking for me? Or more Faceless Men?

I shake my head, struggling to breathe evenly. Was Jimmy really one of Them? I saw him, not two feet away, as faceless as the man from the hospital. But in the hospital, the drugs were still working—now it's been too long, and I don't know if the hallucinations are coming back or not. There was a train whistle that only I could hear: is that because it was fake, or because he was too terrified to notice it? And why did his face come back when the janitor's didn't?

Focus. Whatever Jimmy was, he's not coming after me now. Brody's the immediate threat, and the cops.

They'll come for me—I can't throw away my only defense. I look at the gun, hefting it, then glance around at the neighborhood. The men I saw earlier are gone, probably hiding inside, probably calling the police. I look down at myself, filthy with dirt and dust, my jumpsuit crusted with dried rainwater. I run my fingers through my hair, greasy and wild. I can't stay out here like this. I have to find clothes, and I have to hide the gun.

The gun is small enough to fit in my pocket, but I don't know if I trust it. What if it goes off? I already fired it, so that should mean the safety's off, right? Unless I bumped it while I was shifting it around in my hands. I find what I think is a safety switch, but it's not labeled. I flick it, then flick it again, off and on—or on and off. Back and forth. I pick one and leave it there, placing the gun gingerly in my pocket.

I glance around again. Someone's watching me through a gap in the drapes of the nearest house; I recoil not from the person, but from the TV glaring brightly behind her. Is it watching me? I suppress a shiver, duck my head, and run.

The light is fading, and I hear a distant siren—coming for me? Coming for Jimmy? I reach a major street, wait anxiously for a gap in the traffic, then dart across into a cluster of commercial buildings beyond. A mechanic's garage. A hair salon with window ads in a language I don't recognize. A pawn shop; a butcher shop; a sex shop. The buildings grow taller as the light fades, and I run past the long wall of a storage center. At the far end is a small office building, just two stories high, the windows dark. I duck behind it and find a small parking lot sandwiched between the offices and the back of another building, really more of an alley, the narrow space almost completely filled by three dented Dumpsters. I slip between two of them and lean against the wall, covering my nose against the smell.

When Jimmy got shot his face reappeared, but the janitor's last night didn't. Does that mean Jimmy wasn't really a Faceless Man, or that the janitor, somehow, didn't actually die? Did I check his breathing, or was the electric buzz around his face too strong? Did I check his pulse? I don't remember.

If the janitor didn't die, the police might not be looking for me—the hospital will have told them to keep an eye out for me, but that doesn't mean there's an active search. And Brody almost certainly didn't call 911—the car and Jimmy's body are probably both filled with drugs—

Drugs. I didn't get the Seroquel. That was the whole point of finding dealers in the first place, but I got so scared I ran away. I need to find more somewhere, especially if the hallucinations are already coming back.

So I might be okay, at least for now. I still look like a criminal, though, and this jumpsuit only makes me easier to identify, especially if the people on the street called in a report about a dangerous, gun-waving lunatic. I need new clothes. I have my patient pajamas under the jumpsuit, but that's even more recognizable. Where am I going, anyway? What's my plan? I take a deep breath and try to calm myself down. I'm smarter than this—I'm just spooked by the shooting. Calm down.

I need clothes, and I need medicine, and I can get both at home. If Dad hasn't thrown it away I have some Klonopin in my room—whole bottles of it, maybe hundreds of pills that I picked up and never took. They're not as strong as the Seroquel, but they'll help. If I can find a train station I can look at a map—just enough to see where I am, and where I need to go.

Home, and then . . . to wherever I was before. Like Vanek said.

Something shifts in the alley and I leap to my feet; it sounds like garbage, I think, a bag of it knocked over and spilled across the ground. I pull out the gun.

A wet, smacking sound, like a mouth. Chewing, maybe, or drinking.

I peer at the gun in the near-dark, fumbling with the safety switch. Which is on and which is off? The garbage shifts again, an erratic rhythm of scrapes and thuds and the sound of fallen bottles skittering and clinking across the asphalt. A low screech of metal. A wet, heavy slap. I grip the pistol tightly and step to the edge of the Dumpsters.

There's no light in the alley, just the distant blue-white glow from a streetlight beyond the wall.

More sounds, closer this time, and I step out from the Dumpsters and turn to face them. A soda can falls from a pile of garbage bags, half-crushed, and then a low, wet shape appears behind it—a giant maggot, skin rippling and slick, inching toward me through the pile of trash. My breath catches and I stagger back three steps, my hands trembling on the gun.

I struggle to breathe. "What do you want?"

It snorts and whiffles, nosing at garbage with its ringed, toothy mouth.

My hands are shaking. "What do you want?"

Its body contracts, a single thick muscle under a thin white membrane, and it pulls itself closer. The gun is right here, right in my hand, already pointed at the monster just seven feet away. All I have to do is move my finger. Will that be enough? Is the safety really off?

Is it really a monster?

I shot Jimmy, not because he was a drug dealer, not because he wanted to kill me, and not because I had to defend myself. He could barely move. I shot him because I thought he was one of the monsters in my head, and then he wasn't, but it was too late. Can I do the same thing again? The maggot shuffles closer, swelling and lengthening, its mouth opening and closing, tasting the air.

"Say something." It might be a bum, or a homeless mother looking for food. It might be a lost child, or a sick man, or a dog. My eyes feel wet. "Tell me who you are."

Five feet away. I stumble backward, the gun still trained on the nightmare before me. I scream in frustration—I don't know what to do! I can't trust my own head! I know the Faceless Men are real, but

I know at least some of them are fake; I have to fight back, but I have no way of knowing if the visions I'm fighting are real. I roar again, gritting my teeth.

"Say something!"

I can't take the chance. I wheel around, drop the gun in the Dumpster, and sprint out of the alley. I glance back when I reach the street, watching the maggot shuffle slowly toward me. A horn blares from the intersection, a blur of head- and taillights, and I turn and run.

I reach a bigger street and I slow to a jog, trying not to look like I'm running from something. The street here is crowded, full of shops and restaurants and people.

"Why did you pick this direction?"

I swallow and keep jogging. "Brody's car is back that way."

"You think there's a train station this way?"

"I hope there is. Eventually there's got to be, if I go far enough."

She nods. "A train station will have maps, but it'll also have security cameras."

I stop and close my eyes, panting. "I don't need the ride, I need the map. I need to know where I am."

"Keep going," she says, urging me forward. "It's not safe to stop yet."

"Keep going where?"

"To my place—I can hide you there."

"Lucy." I turn to face her, and she's gone. I close my eyes again, straining at my mind as if it were a muscle I could flex. Lucy isn't real. Stop hearing her.

A train station will have a map and a name, and I'll get a better fix on where I am. I start jogging again, and then I hear a siren and I dive against the wall.

Nothing here but shops and lights—I can't go in. I need an alley. I look for the police car, see nothing, and take off at a run again. Lucy sees the gap in the wall just as I do.

"In there!"

I follow her, sprinting the last few seconds, barely registering the surprised faces of the people on the street as we run past them. We dive into a big, black opening and find it to be the driveway of a private garage, probably an office building; the path extends up a short ramp, maybe ten feet deep, and stops at a wide metal door. I press up into the corner, my back to the bricks, and take a few deep breaths. Lucy crouches next to me, scanning the street with dark eyes.

"You think they're looking for us?"

I shake my head. "For me, yes. You're not real."

NINETEEN

"OF COURSE I'M real," says Lucy. She glances up at me and raises an eyebrow. "I'm a real hallucination."

"That's the same thing as not being real."

"You've got bigger problems to deal with right now, Michael." She turns back to the street, watching intently. "How are you going to get home?"

"How do you know I'm going home?"

"I live in your head, Michael. If you think it, I know it."

"Then why are you asking me anything? Just . . . read my mind."

"I'm trying to get you to think, Michael—I'm trying to help, and that's pretty much all I can do. It's easier to sort through a problem when you have someone to talk to, so here I am: talk to me."

"I'm trying to overcome my delusions, Lucy, not feed them."

"You're trying to survive," she insists. "Your delusions aren't going to matter if you get arrested for murder. Get home, get the drugs, and then we can talk about what is and isn't real."

I pause, watching the street, then slide down against the wall and sit on the pavement. It's cool and dry, though the air around us is still hot. "I don't know how to get home. Give me time to think."

"You've been running for too long," she says, "you're stressed out. Just take a minute to breathe; I'll keep watch."

I close my eyes and crane my neck back, stretching it. Thank goodness Lucy's here to watch—

I snap my eyes open and look back at the street. "You're not really here, Lucy, how are you going to watch the street?"

She pauses, saying nothing, then shakes her head. "I don't know. Subconscious cues? Drawing attention to sights and sounds you sense in your periphery without immediately flagging them as dangerous?"

I frown. "Is that possible?"

"I told you, I don't know."

"Then let me keep watch. You think."

"I thought I wasn't real."

"All my thoughts are your thoughts—anything I can think, you can think. And probably better, since you're apparently the fabrication of an idealized woman."

She smiles. "That's sweet of you, Michael." She stands. "We need a way home. . . ."

"We need to know where we are first."

"So where are we?"

I shake my head, still watching the street. "I don't know." Cars and people pass the mouth of the garage in a constant stream, occasionally glancing in at us, but no one stops or points. It's a normal night, just a crazy guy talking to himself in the city. Nothing to see here. "I don't think we're downtown, but that's all I've got."

"We're definitely not downtown," says Lucy, "I live there. The only time I ever come out this far is to visit . . . you." She grabs my shoulder, and though I can't feel it I'm aware of it, the knowledge of her touch completely replacing the evidence against it. "I've passed this street before, on my way to visit you! I know this neighborhood!"

"You can't know it unless I know it."

"That's what I'm saying," she says. "You've been here before, at least long enough to figure out that this is a major road into the heart of the city; your subconscious mind knows where this street goes, and now I know it."

"Great," I say, "so which way do we go from here?"

She walks to the edge of the garage, looks around, then gestures impatiently for me to join her. "I can't actually look around without you, you know."

I stand and join her, glancing furtively up and down the street. She smiles and pats me on the shoulder; her fingers are soft and cool.

"This way." She heads out onto the sidewalk, going back the way we came.

"That's getting closer to . . ." I stop, not wanting to say *the place where I shot a guy* in a crowded street. I lower my voice. "You know."

"We're only backtracking a couple of blocks," she says, "and then we'll be pulling away again."

"You're sure?"

"Of course I am, and that means you are too. Come on."

I adjust my dirty jumpsuit, feeling self-conscious, but I step into the crowd and start walking. Lucy picks up her speed, weaving effortlessly through the press of people, and I hurry to catch up. After several blocks the crowd thins as we leave the entertainment district behind; restaurants and specialty shops give way to pawn shops and locksmiths and liquor stores. As the pedestrian traffic dwindles, the car traffic picks up, and soon the road becomes a major thoroughfare. I jog from shadow to shadow, my eyes jumping back and forth between the buildings and the cars and the lampposts, streetlights buzzing with angry electrons. We come to a major intersection, traffic lights blazing like lidless eyes, and Lucy runs ahead to the corner.

"We cross here, and go right."

I hang back, in the shadow of a dark building.

"Come on, Michael, let's go."

I shake my head. "The traffic lights are watching."

"What?" She sighs. "Nothing is watching you, Michael, wake up. Snap out of it."

"I can't just snap out of it, Lucy—there are traffic cameras over the lights. I'll be on them. They will be watching."

"The police aren't watching for you on the traffic cameras."

"Not the police. Lucy, the . . ." We're the only people on foot, but I hesitate to say it out loud. She cocks her head, stepping closer to hear.

"The what?"

"The Faceless Men!" I grab her arm and pull her into the shadow with me. "They're watching me— that's what we're running away from."

"I thought we were running from the police?"

My brain feels thick, like sludge. "We're running from both . . . listen, Lucy, I don't know why I didn't think about it before, but all of these traffic lights are just one more opportunity for Them to see me. I don't know how many we've already passed, but—"

"You didn't think about it because it is a *delusion*," she says, enunciating the final word with gripping finality. "Your drugs are wearing off—that's why I'm here, right? It's getting worse, and all of your old symptoms are coming back, but you have to trust me: none of it is real." She tries to pull me toward the street, but I hold her back.

"No," I say, "the Faceless Men are real. I saw one in the hospital, under full effect of the drugs, and it was real."

"You thought Jimmy was real too, and look what happened to him."

"I know!" I shout, then pause and try to calm myself. Every headlight from the street feels like a searching eye, and I pull back farther into the shadows. "Listen, you have to trust me. You say that anything I know, you know, so you have to know this."

"You are hallucinating," she says slowly. "You are trying to explain your reality to a hallucination. Do you see how crazy that sounds? How can you even trust yourself? Jimmy is the proof that—"

"Jimmy proves nothing," I say harshly. "Look, Lucy, I know you're not real—you were the perfect girlfriend, but I created you in my head, and I know that now. But that doesn't mean every girlfriend is fake, right? One imaginary girlfriend does not invalidate the entire concept of girlfriends—they exist, they are everywhere." I clench my fingers, trying to keep my breathing steady. "The Faceless Men are the same way—just because Jimmy was a fake doesn't mean they're all fake. I thought he was one of Them, and I was wrong, but that doesn't mean They don't exist."

Lucy rubs her forehead. "I am your subconscious mind telling you that they're not real—"

"You are my subconscious fears telling me that I'm wrong, just like the entire world has trained me to think I'm wrong for my entire life. But I'm right this time, Lucy. You've got to believe me."

"But—"

"If you love me," I say, gripping her hands, "you will trust me."

She stares at me, gripping me back—solid and reassuring, her eyes reflecting tiny points of light. She nods.

"I trust you."

"Thank you."

"And if you love me, you'll cross this street."

"What?"

She pulls me out from the shadow, her grip stronger than I expected. "You have to cross this street," she says. "We're about six blocks away from the bakery where you work—I met you there for lunch a few times, remember? From there it's only a mile or two to your house. But first you have to cross the street."

I pull back, intensely afraid—irrationally afraid—of the cameras on the traffic lights. Of the traffic lights themselves. Every headlight, every car, every faceless driver; in my mind the street is a raging torrent of steel predators, howling past at breakneck speed, all searching for me, all ready to swerve and crush me like a hail of meteors, car after car after car slamming into a massive pile with me at the bottom. I miss a step, losing my balance, and Lucy catches me, steadies me with her firm, gentle hands.

"Look at me, Michael."

"I can't go out there. . . ."

"Look at me," she repeats. "Look at me. Look at my eyes."

I look up slowly, see the curve of her cheek, the dark wave of her hair, the faint reflection of her eyes. I stare into her eyes—eyes I've stared into so many times before, eyes that I've loved since before I even saw them. I start to cry.

"You're just a dream, Lucy."

"Do you love me?"

I sob again. "Yes."

"Then it doesn't matter. We are going to cross this street, and we are going to be fine, and we are going to be together. Nothing will happen."

"They'll see me—" I say, looking toward the traffic lights, but she turns my face back to hers.

"Look at me," she says softly, "only at me." She steps backward, pulling me with her hands, and I follow slowly, focusing on her eyes. We leave the shadow; we approach the curb; we wait on the edge of the street. On the edges of my vision I see the lights change, and I start to shake in fear at the sight of them, my chest seizing up, but Lucy pulls my eyes back to hers and we step into the street. Left foot, right foot. Inch by inch. Cars rush past us and I push them out of my mind, pushing out everything but Lucy's deep brown eyes.

Halfway.

Three more lanes of cars, lined up at the intersection like a swarm of bright, crystalline beetles. Their headlights watch us like eyes, anxious soldiers in rumbling formation. They're too close and I start to falter, taking small side steps away toward the perpendicular traffic. Lucy pulls me back.

"Look at me, Michael. Don't look at anything but me."

The green glare on the pavement turns red, and in the corner of my eye a red light turns green, and now the rumbling beetles begin shrieking and blaring in anger. I try to hurry, but my nervousness slows me down even further. I pass the second lane, and the cars roar to life behind me, leaping past me with a snarl. I feel like I can't breathe.

"I'm right here, Michael. Stay with me."

I step onto the curb and the dam breaks behind me, a thousand cars tumbling past in a furious blur. I clutch Lucy's arm and she walks beside me now, hurrying me away from the intersection, but a car behind us turns at the corner and pulls up next to us, driving slowly. Police. My heart beats harder, and I can feel sweat dripping down my back.

"Stay calm," says Lucy.

A window rolls down. "Is there a problem, sir?"

"Just keep walking," Lucy whispers. "Tell them you're fine."

"I'm too scared."

She turns to the cops. "I'm fine, thanks. Just out for a walk."

I glance at her through the corner of my eye. "You can't talk to people."

"I just did."

"Did he hear you?"

"He heard you," she says, "now be quiet, he's still watching us."

"Are you alright, sir? Have you been drinking?"

"They're here because you're walking unsteadily," says Lucy, "not because they recognize you. They don't know who you are."

"I'm just . . ." I swallow, keeping my face forward. The back of my mind is screaming *Look at them—they have no faces!* But I refuse to look; I refuse to let my hallucinations take over. "I'm just going home. I'll be fine."

"You look a little unsteady," says the officer.

"See?" says Lucy.

"Have you been drinking?" he asks again. "Are you in pain?"

"He thinks you're on drugs," says Lucy.

I laugh hollowly, still shuffling forward. "I wish."

We turn at the next corner, and the police car turns to follow us. It's a smaller street, just two lanes, and another car approaches slowly on the far side. The policeman leans farther out of his window, trying to get a better view. "Where's the jumpsuit from?"

"They know," I hiss.

"Just keep going," says Lucy, letting go of my arm. "I'll take care of them."

"Let's take a look at you, sir," says the policeman, and they pull forward a few feet, preparing to stop and head me off. Lucy moves away suddenly, running behind them and into the street. I lunge a few steps after her, then scream as I realize what she's doing.

She's charging straight at the oncoming car.

I wave my hands wildly, diving off the curb to chase her. "Lucy, no!" The officer driving the police car sees me run, sees Lucy just as the oncoming driver does; the second driver swerves and the policeman loses control for a split second—just long enough to swerve left. The two cars crunch lightly into each other, headlights shattering, and I scream again.

"Lucy!" She's right in the middle of them—

She's nowhere.

I spin around, looking for Lucy in the shadows. "Lucy, where are you?" Lucy's gone, like she never existed.

Lucy never existed.

The cars slam on their brakes, and the driver of the police car leaps out angrily.

"Watch where you're going!"

"There was something in the road!"

They saw her—she isn't real but they saw her, they swerved to miss her. What's going on?

"I . . ." The policeman stops, staring at the road and pointing. "He was shouting at someone right here."

The other officer gets out of the car, slamming the door angrily. "What kind of idiot rams a parked police car?"

No one's watching me; they're too caught up in their argument. I run for the side of the road and dash down a narrow driveway, vaulting the wooden fence at the end and sprinting through a parking lot to the next street. How long before they notice I'm gone? Lucy was right about the neighborhood—I do recognize it now. I can find my way home from here. How could she know that?

What is real?

TWENTY

I RUN THROUGH back alleys and side streets, hiding from every car and listening for sirens. I hear a train whistle, though I know there are still no tracks nearby. At least I thought I knew it. Maybe the sound is real, and my memories are the delusion.

There's the bakery where I used to work, closed and dark. Mr. Mueller closes early so he can get up early and start baking—four in the morning most days, earlier when he has a special order. Now the ovens are off, cold and dead and empty.

I remember something empty—an empty city. What does it mean?

A helicopter passes overhead, a dark, thundering hole in the sky. I'm in a residential neighborhood now, and I cling to the trunk of a tree. Is the helicopter looking for me? It flies away and I run for the next street, hiding under a carport. A dog barks, first distant, then closer. I run to the next house on the street, pelting across the lawn at top speed, the helicopter searchlight just inches behind me the whole way. It doesn't see me.

More dogs. I peek around the car in the driveway and look at the backyard—no gate, and no dog; the dogs must be somewhere else. Search dogs? I run into the backyard, leap at the wooden fence, and pull myself over it. The dogs are getting louder, but they're still behind me. I run out to the street and race the full length of the block. A police car crosses, two blocks ahead, and is gone. The searchlight plays over the houses behind me, and I run to the far side of the street.

I can smell the dogs now—heavy, sweaty animals growling at the air and straining against their leashes. If I can smell them, the wind is in my favor; they won't be able to smell me until it shifts. There's a golf course near here, with a small stream; I might be able to hide my scent in there. I run another block to the right, ducking under the latched metal bar that blocks off the parking lot and slipping past the tiny pro shop to the greens beyond. The air is sweeter here, though the musk of the dogs is still thick in my nose. I pause at the edge of a tree line, wait for the noise of the helicopter to pass, and sprint across the open ground. The stream isn't much, but I slog through it desperately, watching over my shoulder for pursuers. No one's seen me yet. I follow the stream until it meets the far fence, then run along it until I find a gap. The houses on the other side are run-down and small; I'm only half a mile from home now.

I can't smell the dogs anymore, which makes me worried that the wind has changed, but I can't hear them either—maybe I actually lost them in the stream. I watch from a bush as a police car drives down the next street, and when it passes I run in the other direction. I hear footsteps and shouting from behind a high wall, and I pick up speed. I'm almost there.

If the police are searching my neighborhood, they must know I'm heading home. They'll be waiting for me. How am I going to get past them? The air explodes in a rush of wind and noise, and suddenly the helicopter is right above me, searchlight jerking back and forth across the lawns. I run for a shed in the nearest yard; it's dark and cluttered inside, but it hides me from the light. The helicopter moves on, and the deafening roar of the rotors gives way to the baying of dogs. They've found me. I scramble with my hands on the floor of the shed, looking for anything I can use as a weapon, and come up with a heavy jack—too heavy, I think. I set it back down and keep looking, discarding a short shovel, a pair of garden shears, and a wobbly saw blade before finally finding a thick metal pipe; it's about eighteen inches long, solid and heavy in my hands. I peek out of the shed, watching a black silhouette walk past on the far side of the street. It goes, and I creep out and around into the backyard. I'm very close now—if I hop a few fences I can come up behind my house, maybe sneak in the back without anyone knowing. Only a few houses away.

I climb the first fence, pipe clenched awkwardly in my hand. I drop down into the next yard—nothing. The noise of the dogs gets louder, and I can hear the helicopter coming closer above us. I run across the grass and hop the next fence, struggling with the pipe before finally throwing it over and climbing up after it. Another empty yard. I pick up the pipe and run for the last fence, freezing at the sound of voices. More police.

"You sure he's coming here?"

They're already here. They're in my own driveway.

"That's what the chief says." A second voice. At least two of them. I walk slowly across the last few feet of lawn, leaning as close to the wooden fence as I can without touching it. A radio squawks.

"Suspect has been spotted by two officers off of Damen Street, say again Michael Shipman has been spotted. Suspect fled the scene, may be headed home. Suspect is not armed, say again not armed; whereabouts of the gun are unknown."

I heft the pipe in my hand: if they think I'm not armed, that gives me an advantage. How many are waiting in my driveway? Could I take them out before they called for help? Before they drew a gun?

I think about Jimmy, and the maggot in the alley. Do I dare attack anyone at all?

"Can you believe what he did to that guy?" asks

one of the cops. "Point-blank in the chest, boom! No provocation at all. Kid was just sitting there, trying to talk him down, and suddenly he shoots him out of nowhere, like it was nothing."

"It's kind of weird," says the other cop. "Don't you think?"

I creep closer, headed for the edge of the fence to get a closer look.

"Weird?"

"I mean, yeah, it's cold-blooded and everything, but it's nothing like the rest of his attacks."

I freeze again, listening. I hit the janitor, but he said "attacks," plural. What attacks is he talking about?

"Thank goodness," says the other cop.

"Yeah," says the first, "but I mean, why? Why do you cut off ten faces and then all of a sudden you just shoot someone? And then leave?"

They think I'm the Red Line Killer—but I can't be, because Agent Leonard said there was a cell phone. But no, he said he *thought* there was a cell phone. It was all conjecture. I clutch the pipe tightly, my knuckles white. What do I do now?

"Do you remember that one in the warehouse?" the cop continues, "where he hung it from those hooks?"

"Come on," says the other cop, "why are you talking about this? Waiting here for him is spooky enough as it is."

"That's why I'm talking about it," says the first cop, "because it is scary—this is a knock-down, drag-out, scary dude. I've trained with my gun for hours on the range, but I've never actually shot anyone, let alone killed anyone—he's killed a couple dozen. What if he comes here? He has all the advantage. Do you want to end up scalped and flayed and hanging on a hook?"

"Kill them," whispers a voice in my ear. I turn in shock, but nobody's there. "Go now, while they're alone and distracted. Kill them now before they kill you."

I scream silently: You're not real!

"You know how he gets the faces off?" says the cop. "He uses a scalpel—takes him hours, inch by inch, millimeter by millimeter, peeling it away from your head. It's like he's looking for something. Felix says they're still alive when he does it—alive and awake."

"Bash in their brains," says the voice, louder now. Can they hear it? "Use the pipe and cave in their skulls—it's as easy as crushing an egg."

I come around the fence and I can see them now, two cops, alone in the dark, faces lost in shadow.

"He cuts it away bit by bit," says one, "slicing the membranes under the skin so it all comes off in one bloody piece."

"It feels so good to crush a skull, just banging and banging until there's nothing left."

"All your troubles go away and there's nobody left to bother you—"

"No!" I stand up, plugging my ears and screaming. "Stop talking!"

"Holy—!" The policemen spin around, facing me with their guns drawn. "Michael Shipman, drop your weapon!"

"Hit them! Kill them!"

"Stop talking!"

"Michael, drop it now!"

"Kill them!"

I drop the pipe and it clangs loudly against the cement.

"Now put your hands in the air!"

"Everyone just back off for a second," I say, stepping backward. The cops step forward in unison, their guns never wavering. "Just give me a minute to think."

"Put your hands in the air!"

I look up, waving my hand to silence the voice shouting *Kill!* Something's wrong—where are all the other cops? Where's the helicopter and the dogs? Why aren't they calling for backup?

One of the cops puts a hand on the radio clipped to his shirt. "Dispatch, this is Officer Kopecky, we have found Michael Shipman; repeat, we have found Michael Shipman at his residence. Request immediate backup."

"Put your hands in the air," says the other cop.

"Kill them . . . ," the voice whispers.

I shake my head. "Where's the helicopter?"

"It's on its way," says the cop, but I hear nothing. "Put your hands in the air!"

"Why do you keep saying that?"

"I'll ask the questions, Michael! Tell me why you killed Jimmy."

I raise my arms. Is this what cops are really like? I've met some, but this is the first time I've ever been arrested—I didn't expect it to be so . . . clichéd. They've done everything but read me my rights.

"You have the right to remain silent," says the cop. "Anything you say can and will be used against you in a court of law. You have the right to an attorney—"

"You're not real, are you?" I stare at the cops in shock. They're doing everything I think a cop would, as soon as I think of it—the radio, the rights, even the way they're standing. "You're just in my head."

"You have the right to an attorney."

"Then what comes next!" I shout. "If you're a real cop, then what comes next? I don't know, so you can't know either!"

"If you do not . . ." He stops, glancing in confusion at his companion. "If you choose to . . . to waive this right, an attorney will be . . . provided for you."

"Is that it?" I ask.

"Yes that's it, now get down on the ground!"

I look at them, back and forth between the policemen, between their guns. Are they real? Do I risk it?

I remember Lucy's hands, strong and solid only when I'd accepted the illusion; when she'd first arrived tonight they'd felt wrong, intangible, like I could pass right through them. She was only real when I let her be real. I don't have to let these cops be real.

I lower my arms. This is it.

"Get out of my way."

"Get your hands back up and turn around," says the cop.

"I'm going inside now," I say, swallowing nervously. "If you think you can stop me, go ahead and try." I take a step forward.

"Stay where you are."

I step forward again.

"I'm warning you, Michael, we will shoot. Turn around and put your hands in the air."

I stare at the guns, cold metal gleaming in the moonlight, black barrels like soulless eyes. They could be real. They could kill me right here. I step forward again.

They step aside.

"Don't go in there, Michael. You're not going to like it."

"Go away," I say, taking another step past them. "I'm done with you."

They shout behind me. "We're going to report this!"

I stop, staring nervously ahead. "To who?"

Their voices are hollow. "You know who."

I pause a moment, trembling, then continue walking. It doesn't mean anything—they're just trying to scare me. When I reach the back of the house, I turn to see them, but they're gone.

I climb the few steps to the back door and try the

handle; it's unlocked. I open the door and walk in. My father stands in the hall, a shotgun in his hands.

"They told me you might be coming back here." He cocks the shotgun. "I told them you were just stupid enough to try it."

TWENTY-ONE

I STAND IN the doorway, staring at my father. He levels the shotgun calmly, almost casually, as if the fact that it's inches from my chest is the most normal thing in the world.

He scratches his head. "I was kind of thinking I'd never see you again."

I shift nervously, eyes glued to the shotgun. "Thinking or hoping?"

"Your doctor told me you were nuts," he says. "Said you needed some kind of new medicine that would either cure you or kill you. I said, 'Go for it. Gets him out of my life either way.'"

I nod. "I'm leaving."

His grip tightens, just slightly. "You didn't come here just to say good-bye."

"I need my pills."

"You need your . . ." He stops, staring at me, then shakes his head and snarls. "You need your damn pills—that's all you ever care about." He raises the shotgun abruptly, sighting it straight into my face. "I told you before, I don't want a homeless crackhead son running around here."

"It's not crack," I say, "it's medicine. I have a prescription—it's going to make me better."

"You can't get better!" he barks. "You've been screwed up since you were born, since before you were born for all I know. I've been paying for your medicine and your doctors and your everything else for your whole life, Michael, and it's never done anything! You're twenty years old and you can't hold a job; you live here with me; you flunked out of school, now you've flunked out of the nuthouse. You give me one good reason not to pull this trigger and flunk you out of the whole damn world."

I stare at the gun, too terrified to speak, too certain that anything I say—anything at all—will set off any one of a hundred different triggers in his mind. I've lived here too long, spent too much time listening to him and hiding from him and nursing the bruises he gave me. If I cry, I'm a disgrace; if I agree, I'm weak; if I fight back, I'm an ungrateful, disrespectful punk. If I say I need the pills, it means I'm a crazy retard and a shame to my mother; if I say I don't, it means I'm a liar and a waste of money and a shame to my mother again. I can't win. I've never won.

I stare down the shotgun, dark and deep and ter-
rifyingly real. My father's never pulled a gun on me
before—does he really want me dead? Is he going to
call the hospital, or maybe the police? I can't think
clearly—I can't sort through my thoughts and come
up with anything remotely useful. Why is he doing
this? Why am I here? I know why I came, but now it
doesn't make sense anymore and all I want to do is
run. I need my pills; I can't think without my pills.

I try to force myself to be calm, reciting mantras
and numbers and anything I can think of to clear
my head. He wants to get rid of me—I can help him
with that. Better I leave on my own than make him
clean up a dead body, right? He doesn't want to
shoot me—or at least I hope he doesn't; maybe he
does. But he doesn't want the hassles that come with
it, that I know for sure. He hates anything that disrupts his routine.

I look my father in the face, not quite meeting his
eyes. "I'm leaving," I say again. "I'm going away,
and you'll never see me again."

He snorts. "I've heard that one before."

"I'm serious," I say, trying to keep calm. Do I dare
to tell him why I'm here? If I ask him for help—for
anything at all—will I die before I even finish the
sentence? "I . . ." Just ask him! "I need some clothes."
I grit my teeth, bracing myself for the shotgun blast
in my face. "And I need my pills."

He doesn't shoot. I watch his eyes, deep and
brown, laced with a web of bloodshot red. After a
moment he speaks. "Where you going?"

"Away. Nowhere. Out of state somewhere."

He pauses again, shifting his hands on the shotgun. Finally he nods, gesturing at me in derision. "How you gonna live? You never held a job more than five months."

"I'll get by."

"You gonna steal?" He steps closer, dropping the shotgun slightly to reveal a furious scowl. "You gonna sell those drugs, Michael?"

"I'll get a job," I say quickly. "I'll do . . . something. But I'm not going to sell the drugs or break the law. I just need my pills; I can't do this without them."

"You're a disgrace."

I say nothing.

He pauses a moment longer, then lowers the shotgun a little farther. "How you gonna get there?"

"Where?"

"Wherever the hell you're going—how am I supposed to know?"

I shake my head. "I don't know."

He watches me a moment longer, then drops the shotgun to his side, dangling it by his leg. He raises his chin.

"You promise you're never coming back?"

"Yeah."

"Then take the car." He pauses, then shouts angrily. "Well go on, then, dammit! Go get your clothes!"

"You're giving me your car?"

"I said get your clothes and your pills and get out of my house."

"I . . ." I nod. "Thank you."

"Don't thank me, just go!" He waves his arm brusquely and turns around. "And I don't want to ever see you again, you hear me?" I nod again and walk down the hall to my room.

The Klonopin is under my bed, in a shoebox half-full of empty bottles. I have five bottles, about a year's worth of mental clarity—if they work. I open one with shaking hands and swallow two pills without waiting for water. It will take a while before I feel an effect, but I feel safer just having them in my hand, just knowing that I have some in my system. I scrounge through the bottom of the box, looking for more, and when I find nothing I go through every drawer of my nightstand, looking for every loose pill I can find. It seems so stupid that I used to hate these—that I ever refused to take them. Didn't I know what they meant to me? Didn't I know what it was like to live without them? That's the problem with depression—it discourages its own treatment. It's like a virus, almost, perfectly adapted against its only natural predator.

I look at the pile of pills on my bed, counting them over and over in my head. Why is my father giving me his car? He doesn't like me—he was ready to kill me just a few minutes ago. He's never done a nice thing for me in my life. I guess he gave me this room. I look around at the bare walls and the half-empty closet. Why did—

My room has been searched. It hasn't been ransacked—nothing's tipped over or torn apart—but I can see some things that are definitely moved. A lamp, a comb, a book on my nightstand. Was Dad looking for something, or was it someone else—the police, maybe, or the hospital, or Them? The only thing I have worth stealing is the Klonopin, and it's still here. What were they searching for? I imagine Agent Leonard of the FBI, looking for secret messages from the Children of the Earth; maybe other agents too, scouring my room for evidence of the Red Line killings.

"Your father's going to betray you," said a voice. "You need to kill him now, while his guard is down."

I ignore the voice and open my dresser, talking out loud to drown it out: "It doesn't matter why they searched my room. I'm leaving. I'm going to take off these clothes and put on some new ones, and I'm . . ." I pull on a clean shirt and the feel of it stops me: deliciously clean, like an embrace. When was the last time anyone embraced me, or gave me any kind of friendly human contact? I hug myself, pressing the shirt against my skin, closing my eyes and trying to conjure Lucy from the depths of my brain. She's gone. I wipe my eyes. "No time. Keep moving." I shove a handful of shirts and socks and underwear into a backpack, then cram in the five bottles of pills.

Only one thing left to do. I walk back down the hall; my father is outside, doing something with the car. Taking his stuff out, I guess. I find the phone book and flip it open: Fillmore, Finch, Fischer. There's a Kelly Fischer on Holiday Street. I write down the address and put the phone book away.

My father comes in the back door, the shotgun replaced by a single key held tightly in his fingers. He holds it out. "You never come back."

I nod. "I never come back."

"You never call, you never write, I never hear *from* you or *about* you ever again."

"I'll even change my name."

He drops the key in my hand. "Take Highway 34. It's your quickest shot out of the city, and from there you're on your own."

I stare at him, not knowing what to say. The words are out before I can stop them. "Why are you doing this for me?"

"I'm not doing it for you."

I nod. For my mother. Always my mother.

"Now leave, before I call the police."

I pause, saying nothing, then turn and push open the door. He doesn't follow me out. I throw my bag and the old clothes into the car and climb in after them, staring at the dashboard like a sleeping enemy. When I turn it on I'll feel it—it doesn't send a signal, the way a phone does, but it does create an electric field. I'll feel it vibrating through me like a seizure. But it's the quickest way to Kelly, and to the answers she's got to have.

I put the key in the ignition. If I leave the radio off I should be fine—a little pain, maybe, but nothing terrible. I hope.

I turn the key, and the engine roars to life, and I feel my feet prickle like a wave of static electricity. It stings, but it doesn't cripple me. I shift into drive, whispering a silent thanks that my father only drives automatics; I haven't driven a car in almost three years, and I don't think I could get a stick shift out of the driveway. I pull onto the street, glancing back one last time at the house. My father is watching from the window.

He closes the curtains. I drive away.

I drive slowly, scanning the streets for cops. I don't know how many of the ones I saw before are even real, if any were real at all, but—

There's one. I turn my head, trying to look inconspicuous, and he drives past.

Holiday is on the far side of town. I turn at the next intersection, weaving through narrow residential streets, then turn again. It's not until I get to the first big cross street that I realize how terrified I am to drive in real traffic. I wait for a gap in the cars and pull onto the big street, keeping in the right lane and driving slowly. Speeding trucks honk and pull around me, rocking my car with bursts of wind as they speed past. The noise and the lights are too much, and I pull back off on the next street. It feels safer on the smaller roads, but I can't just hide like this—I need to keep moving. I wander through the back streets for a while, psyching myself up, and stop at the corner of another big street. This one's calmer than the other, with fewer cars and slower traffic. I take a deep breath, and duck my head as another cop drives past. My head is down, nearly on the seat.

There's a red blink in the passenger's foot well.

I lean down further and see a small, rectangular outline—a little plastic brick. The light blinks again, and I recognize it as a cell phone. I recoil in terror, like I'd just seen a snake; my foot comes off the brake and the car rolls forward, then lurches to a stop when I get my foot back down. A cell phone! Is someone tracking me? Did my father forget it? If I hadn't been looking in just the right place, at just the right time, I wouldn't have even seen it—if my father had dropped it during the day, when the red light wasn't as visible, he might never have seen it either.

I can't just leave it there. I put the car in park and lean over slowly, reaching out gingerly. What if it chirps or buzzes? What if it shocks me or attacks me? I feel like I'm reaching for a bomb. I have to pick it up—it's better to do it now, when I'm thinking about it, than have it go off while I'm driving. I pause, my hand hovering over it. It blinks again. I growl and pick it up, yanking it back to my seat and flipping it open as fast as I can. The screen blinds me as it lights up, and I squint against pain as I search for an off switch. I don't see one; I've never used a cell phone, I don't even know how they work. I jam the buttons, careful not to push anything that might start a call, all the while terrified that a call will come in at any second. Nothing's working—why isn't there an off switch? I flip the phone over and look at the back: the batteries. I pop open the door and yank out what looks like a little black battery pack. The screen goes blank and the red light stops blinking.

I slump back in my seat, breathing heavily. It's dead now. I roll down the window and throw out the phone—but wait. What if they find it—what if they use it to trace my path? They might know that I left home, but they won't know where I went; finding the cell phone would tell them my direction and help them follow me. I don't know if I can dare throw anything away—the phone, my old clothes, not anything—until I can destroy them completely. I get out, collect the phone and the battery pack, and drop them into the cup holder. As long as I keep the battery out, they can't use it to trace me. I put the car back into drive and stare at the busy street. Linda covered a lot of life skills in my therapy, but driving wasn't one of them; the controls feel loose and alien, like it's designed for a different body. I can't do this.

I have to do this. The tingling in my feet and legs feels strange and painful, but it's not debilitating, and I'm getting better at ignoring it. The traffic is faster than I'd like, but I can drive in it. I can even see a highway sign—it's 88, not 34, but it will get me to Holiday Street. I merge over, trying to keep up with traffic, and pull up onto the highway. It's easier on a highway—faster, but with no stops or turns or cross traffic. I grip the wheel with hard, white knuckles. Head- and taillights pass me like beams of solid color. I find the exit; I find the street; I find the building.

It's an apartment, but not the kind with a gate or a doorman. I park and walk in, climbing stairs and looking for the number. 17A. There's a light in the window.

Will she turn me in? Is she one of Them? I knock softly.

She opens the door, recognizes me, and screams. I grab her face in panic and shove her back inside.

TWENTY-TWO

SHE STRUGGLES, FIGHTING and backing away. I keep a firm grip on her jaw with one hand, wrapping my other arm around her shoulders. I knock the door closed with my foot; she kicks and flails her fists.

"Don't scream," I say. "I'm not here to hurt you, I just don't want you to scream."

She bites my hand, and I try not to howl. My grip goes loose and she stumbles away from me, falling; she goes for her purse, leaping across the couch.

"They told me this would happen; they told me not to talk to crazy people."

I dive after her, knocking the purse from her hand; a can of mace goes spinning across the floor. She kicks me again, a solid blow to the chest, knocking away my breath. I choke on the sudden void and she runs to a small counter separating her living room and kitchen. She's unfolding a cell phone.

How does she know?

I gasp for air, sucking in a sudden burst, and run forward just in time to slam my hands down on hers. She shrieks and drops the phone, her fingers red from the impact. I snatch up the cell phone and bend it backward, moving it too far, snapping it in half. She cries and runs for the door but I grab her arm and yank her back. She falls, sobbing. I let go gingerly and block the door with my body.

"I'm not here to hurt you," I say again. She's crying. "I didn't come here to attack you, or hurt you, or anything, I just want to talk."

"I think you broke my fingers, you bastard."

"I'm sorry—you scared me, I didn't know what to do. I couldn't let you shock me."

"Shock you?"

"The phone," I say, gesturing toward the fragments. "You were trying to attack me with your phone."

"I was calling the police, you idiot." Her face is a mask of hurt and fear.

I've ruined everything.

"They said you weren't likely to come after me in person," she says, rubbing tears from her eye with the palm of her hand. "I guess they can tell that to my raped and mutilated corpse, now, huh?"

"I already told you I'm not going to hurt you."

"You attacked me!"

"You screamed!" I say. "I panicked! There's a lot

of people looking for me, and I can't afford to attract any more attention."

"Then why did you come here?"

"Because I need help." I crouch down, still guarding the door but getting closer to her eye-line. "I can't do this on my own. There's something big going on, and I have some of the pieces and you have others, and together we might be able to learn enough to stop it."

"You're talking about the killings."

"I'm talking about everything: the Red Line, the Faceless Men, the Children of the Earth—they're all connected somehow, they're all part of a bigger picture—"

"You *are* crazy." She rubs her eyes. "What have I gotten myself into?"

"Look," I say, pulling out the paper, "I can prove it to you. The janitor at Powell attacked me last night, all alone, when everyone else was asleep. He even knocked out the night nurse. He was carrying this."

I hold out the paper. She looks at it cautiously, as if I were handing her a snake.

"What is it?"

"Look at it."

She doesn't move. "Drop it, and back away."

"Whatever you want." I toss the paper gently toward her, then raise my hands and press back into the door. She picks up the paper.

I'm holding my breath. Some part of me is still terrified the paper isn't real—that it's blank, or a cleaning schedule, or something else that has nothing to do with me. She looks at it carefully, pursing her lips.

"What is this?"

"You tell me."

She stares at it, eyes flicking back and forth. She's reading it.

What is she reading?

"It's your whole life," she says, looking up at me. "It's everywhere you've ever lived or worked or went to school."

I collapse against the corner, clutching my face in relief, gasping and sobbing. "It's real," I say, "it's real. This is actually happening."

"You say the janitor had this?"

"It's real," I mumble again. I sink to the floor, leaning on the door in exhaustion. "I'm not crazy."

"Did he have anything else? Anything on the other patients?"

I shake my head. "Nothing—just that and a ring of keys. And a Post-it note with the gate code."

"And you're sure it was the night janitor?" she asks. "You're sure it wasn't some other guy who'd snuck in?"

"I'm positive."

She raises herself to her knees. "Could you recognize his face if I showed you some pictures?"

"He didn't have a face."

She stops, mouth open, then shakes her head. "Not this again."

"It's true," I say, "or maybe he had a face, but I

couldn't see it—it was like there was a . . . field or something, like a blur around his head. His hair was there, but his face was just a . . . nothing."

"You're hallucinating."

"No," I say firmly. "I mean, sometimes yes, but this was real. I promise it was real. I was still on my drugs."

"Are you still on them now?"

"Yes. Different ones, I mean, but they still work."

She sighs. "Listen to yourself, Michael. How can you recognize the janitor if you couldn't even see his face?"

"But I . . ." I stop, and I realize that I've never seen the janitor's face—I'd never seen him at all before last night, but I'd heard him, and I'd . . . felt him. Somehow I'd always known who he was, and where he was, and I'd known it even through the wall and the closed door. "I just knew," I say. "It's like I had a . . . another sense, like sight or scent or something, but different, like a new one that was totally . . . natural."

She rubs her eyes, pulling herself up to sit in a chair. "Do you hear how crazy you sound? Can you understand how *wrong* this all sounds? You're living in a fantasy world, Michael—none of this is real."

"I know it sounds crazy," I say. "I know it sounds stupid and ridiculous and . . . and . . . listen, I'm not good at talking. I never do it, not with anyone real. So I don't know how to make you believe me, but I know that you have to. Okay? The Faceless Men are real, and they have a plan, and we have to stop them."

"Then what's their plan?"

"I . . . don't know yet."

She closes her eyes and falls back in the chair. "I can't believe this."

"But it's real," I say, "I swear it's real. It has something to do with ChemCom. You have to trust me."

"But I can't trust you," she says. "You are sick; you are delusional. I don't know how you can even trust yourself."

I shake my head, trying to control my breathing. *Don't get nervous. Don't freak out.* "You saw the paper," I say. I hold my forehead, sucking in a long, slow draught of air. "What about the paper?"

"I don't know about the paper," she says. "It could be anything."

"What could it be that isn't horribly suspicious?"

She stares at me, jaw clenched, then throws up her hands. "I don't know! I'm not a psychiatrist, I'm not a . . . I don't know why you came here in the first place."

"Because you've studied them," I say. "The Red Line Killer and the Children of the Earth; I came because you know what they're doing, and who they are, and everything."

"I don't know anything," she says, "nobody does. I'm not even on that story anymore."

"You gave up?"

"My editor killed it."

"And that doesn't sound like a cover-up to you?"

"He pulled the story because there was nothing to it," she says, "no leads, no witnesses, no evidence. If the police have more info about the killings they're not sharing it, and the Children of the Earth are a black hole: they won't talk to anyone, no one *ever* defects, and the last reporter to go into their commune never came out." She stiffens, her eyes tearing up again. "She was a friend of mine."

"Has anyone gone in after her?" I ask. "Her family, the police, anyone?"

"She had to join the cult, officially, or they wouldn't let her in," says Kelly. "She signed a hundred waivers and legal papers and who knows what else, just to get through the door, and now no one can touch her." She sits back, tired and defeated. "I guess she thought she could handle it, but . . . she's been brainwashed, I know it."

I nod, trying to sort through the facts. It's just like Agent Leonard said about the other kidnapped children—they went straight to the cult, fully converted, and nothing anyone said could convince them to leave. It sounds like brainwashing, sure, but those kids were brainwashed before they even joined the cult. They did it when we were infants—implants, maybe, though that doesn't make any sense for an anti-technology cult. Whatever they did, somehow it didn't work right on me.

I look at Kelly. "Is there any evidence," I say, speaking slowly, "any sign at all, that the cultists might have something . . ." I pause, praying that she'll take me seriously, ". . . implanted in their heads?"

Kelly peers closer, eyes narrow and focused. "Why do you ask that?"

"I've been telling people for months now that I think there's something implanted in my head, ever since the schizophrenia came on, but now I think it might actually be true." I look at her closely; her eyes are wider. "This isn't the first time you've heard this, is it? Do you know something?"

She leans back. "It's just that . . ." She stops, sighs, and runs her fingers through her hair. "It's just that it's weird you would say that, because just today—literally, just a few hours ago—this other writer and I were talking about the case, and about the Red Line Killer, and how the evidence made it look like he was . . ." She looks up. "See, he doesn't just bash them in, he doesn't just break them. Our source in the coroner's office said that he . . ." She grimaces. "He pokes the face. He prods it, like he's studying it. He cracks into the nasal cavity, and into the sinuses, and it's totally like he's just . . . looking for something."

My heart beats faster. This is the information I've been looking for. "Don't you see what this means? There's a real link now between the Killer and the Children and the Faceless Men. And me."

"How does this link anything to you?"

"The Children of the Earth kidnapped pregnant women," I say, "including my mom, but they didn't want the women, they wanted us—they wanted the babies. No one has ever figured out why they wanted us, but maybe this is it. Did you know that every one of those kidnapped kids has gone back to join the cult?"

She frowns. "All of them?"

"Everyone but me," I say. "An agent from the FBI came to visit me at Powell, he said they'd been watching me for years to see if I did the same thing."

"How can you be sure the FBI guy was real?"

"He talked to Dr. Little," I say. "You talked to Dr. Little, right?" She nods again. "Then either the agent is real or all three of you are fake."

"And you think that this . . . implant, whatever it is, brought them all back to the cult when they grew up."

I nod eagerly, standing and pacing. "It controls their minds somehow; it takes them over so they're not even themselves anymore. The implant explains everything. It creates some kind of electric field—the same thing that blurs out their faces when I try to look at them, and the same thing that lets me recognize them and see them for who they are when no one else can. I know who they are without even seeing them, and that's how I must be doing it—I'm . . . using my field to *feel* their field. And that's why other electrical fields hurt me, because they're conflicting with the field that's already in my head." I swallow. "And that's why I have schizophrenia, because my implant is broken, and it's throwing my whole brain into chaos."

She watches me. Her eyes are wet with tears. She purses her lips. "I'm so sorry for you," she whispers. "I don't know how to help you."

"You can tell me where I was," I say.

"What do you mean?"

"Before the police found me, before you and I met in the hospital, I was somewhere else—I don't know where, or why, because I lost my memory. But if I can go back there, back to where I was, then maybe I can remember. Whatever they have— whatever they're doing—the answer is there."

She shakes her head. "That's crazy."

"So am I." I crouch down, meeting her eyes. "You wanted to know their plan? *I* am their plan; me, and the other kids, and that reporter who won't come out, and God only knows how many other people. They put something in us—they change who we are. I don't know why, and I don't know how, and I don't know how far they're going to take it, but I know we have to stop them. We have to do something." I put my hand on the arm of her chair. "You have to help me find them."

She looks at me, staring intently, studying my face like she's looking for something—some visible sign of whatever the Faceless Men have stashed inside my head. She says nothing, simply watching. What is she thinking?

She takes a deep breath and nods. "It's on my computer. I'll go look it up."

I nod, backing away, and she stands up and rubs her smashed fingers. She goes into the back room and I collapse into a chair, exhausted and drained. I need to sleep. I need more food. I drag myself back to my feet and go around the counter into the kitchen, opening the fridge. A soft musical trill wafts out of the back room, a computer loading up, and soon I hear typing. I've never liked computers, and I've rarely ever used one, even before the schizophrenia. If I have something in my head that reacts to them, I guess it makes sense that it would have been there my whole life. She has a Styrofoam box in the fridge—half a smothered burrito and some refried beans. I pull it out and start eating it cold; I've never liked microwaves either.

More typing. What does she need to type? If she's searching for information that's already on her computer, couldn't she just do it with a mouse? It sounds like she's typing a whole novel—

Or an email. I drop the box and sprint down the hall, charging into the room to see an open email program lighting up the screen. She curses and grabs the mouse, and I barrel into her at full speed, knocking her from the chair. She clutches at the mouse and keyboard, yanking them off the desk as she falls. I look at the screen. The email's already been sent.

"You lied to me!"

"You need help," she says, crouching on the floor. "You are sick, and delusional, and you're going to get yourself hurt."

I shout again, an angry roar. "You lied to me! Get out of the way." I rip the keyboard from her hands, setting it back on the desk, then reach for the mouse. "Give it to me."

"What are you going to do?"

"I'm going to find where I was."

"You need help."

"Give me the mouse!"

She hands it over and I set it gently on the desk, untangling the cords. I pull the chair upright and sit down, still an arm's length away from the computer. I can use it, but I know it's going to hurt. I don't have a choice. I grit my teeth and slide the chair forward, feeling my head press into the electrical field like a pool of charged water. It buzzes like a raw current.

The speakers chirp—a short, syncopated rhythm.

I scoot back instantly, breathing heavily. "What was that?"

"It was the speakers."

I remember that sound from Powell, from Dr. Little's experiments with the speakers and the cell phone. "Do you have another cell phone?"

"You broke my phone, that's why I had to send an email."

"That sound—audio speakers make that sound when a cell phone signal passes through them. What do you have here that's sending a signal?"

"Nothing."

"Then you've been bugged," I say, "or tapped or something, because it has to be coming from somewhere. That sound only happens when one field disrupts another—" I stop. The thing in my head—if my theory is right, it creates a field of its own. I lean forward, bracing myself for the static prickling. My head enters the field around the speakers; it dances through me, sick and painful.

The speakers chirp again.

"Listen," I whisper.

"I can hear it."

"No," I say, "inside it. Can you hear it?" I stare, gritting my teeth at the pain, listening as hard as I can to a soft something in the white noise. "Buried in the signal there's a . . . something. I swear I've heard it somewhere before."

We listen, the electric fields crossing and blending, the speaker chirping and buzzing, and for one brief moment the white noise coalesces into a single word.

"Michael."

We stagger back in unison, gasping for breath.

"Did you hear that?"

She nods. "What the hell is going on?"

"It was talking to me."

"The thing in your head?"

I nod, swallowing. I almost don't dare to say it. "It's intelligent."

She steps away, watching me closely, her face a mask of terror. "Get out of here."

"Do you believe me now?"

"I don't want to be a part of this, just get out of here now."

"Give me the address and I'll go."

"I don't know how much time you have," she says, pressing back against the wall. "I emailed a friend of mine, told her to call the police—I don't know if she's even read it yet."

The speakers beep again, startling us, but it's only

a small chime. An email alert. She crouches in front of the desk and points at the corner of the screen. "She just responded. Police are on their way."

"Give me the address."

"You don't have time—"

"I have to know where I'm going. Give me the address where I was found, and the address for ChemCom."

"ChemCom?"

"They're a part of this too."

She shakes her head. "They had a victim there, but I don't think the company's involved—they were being robbed."

"Robbed?"

"On a pretty regular basis; I've got it in my notes." She clicks on a file and scans down the document. "Formamide and potassium hydroxide. The company's beside the point—you need to find whoever was stealing those chemicals."

"Why are those chemicals important?"

"Because you can combine them to make cyanide."

"No." I shake my head, pacing the small office. "This is too much. It's the Children of the Earth, it's got to be. We've got to stop them."

She clicks open another document, scrolling through page after page of notes. "Here it is." She fumbles on the desk for a pen, writing on the back of an envelope. "The police found you in an overpass, under I-34, but you ran and they chased you to an abandoned house at this address. Maybe you can hide out there again."

"Wait." My heart seems to stop, my senses tunneled in on a single phrase. "What do you mean, an abandoned house?"

"It's a whole abandoned development." She hands me the paper: STONEBRIDGE COURT. "The owner went bankrupt in the recession, and the houses were never finished."

I feel pale and weak. "It's empty?"

"Yeah," she says, staring at me in worry, "just . . . rows and rows of empty houses. Why, does that mean something?"

Sirens wail in the distance, and our heads snap up to listen.

"I need to get there *now*."

"They're almost here," she says. "I don't know if you can get away."

"Does this window open?"

She rushes to the blinds, turning off the light before pulling them open. "It's a long drop; this is the second floor." She wrenches open the window. "Be careful."

"Don't tell them where I'm going."

"I won't."

I climb through the window and leap out into the darkness.

TWENTY-THREE

THE HOLLOW CITY.

There's a chain-link fence along the outside and a sign: WELCOME TO STONEBRIDGE COURT. A suburban development, half-finished and abandoned. I ease the car slowly down the fence, watching the empty houses slip past me in the dark. There's a way in— somehow I don't just assume this, I *know* it, as clearly as if I'd been here before. I have been here before. Did I live here? Did I hide here? What will I find?

I remember a deep pit. Did I fall into it? But the policemen said I fell out of a window. . . .

There's a break in the fence, a wide, empty street that leads into the vacant neighborhood beyond. I stare at it, irrationally terrified, but I summon my courage and turn in, moving without thinking. I belong here. Don't I? A roll of chain link, once stretched across the road, is now rolled back, and I ease past it carefully; My headlights catch the first house in brilliant beams of light, a hollow shell covered in graffiti, a malevolent shroud of jagged, screaming words. The lights move past it and the house disappears again in darkness.

I drive slowly, noting each empty house as I pass it. Two. Four. Ten. Twenty. Empty mailboxes stand like soldiers; empty windows stare like cadaverous eyes, black and dead until, here and there, my headlights catch one in the distance and shine back a bright flash of reflection. Most of the homes are finished, at least on the outside, but the lawns are bare dirt and the driveways are dotted with extra lumber or bags of cement. Branded labels mark each window like a pupil, giving each house a sly, sidelong gaze. They're spying on each other.

A furtive shadow appears and disappears around a corner. I'm not alone.

I come to a cross street and pause, studying the house on the far corner—identical to the others, but different. This is where I turn right. It's not a message but a memory, and when I turn I feel a sense of familiarity: this is the way. The next street sparks another memory—turn left—but each new moment of insight increases my unease. I shift in my seat, namelessly anxious. My path is accurate, but it isn't *right*. I follow it anyway. The next intersection is a T, and I know with perfect clarity that I must go forward, off the street and between the houses.

When I followed this path before, I was on foot. I pause, headlights shining on the hollow houses, then shake my head and turn. I'm safe in the car—I don't know what's out there, or what I'm going to find. I follow the streets around and behind, twisting and turning until I catch the path again, seizing on it like a psychic scent. This way. I follow it down another row of empty shells until my mind says stop, and the house beside me feels powerfully familiar. I've been here before. I used to live here.

There's a wide picture window in the front wall, about twelve feet off the ground. It is completely shattered.

I stop the car, staring at the broken window. The bare dirt lawn is covered with footprints; most of the glass is gone, either cleaned up or stolen. I open the car and step out, locking it carefully behind me. The front door is framed by tattered yellow strips, a DO NOT CROSS police line long ago ripped away and now hanging limply by the sides. I touch the doorknob gingerly, half expecting an electric shock or a painful cell phone buzz, but nothing happens. The knob doesn't turn but the door opens anyway, and I can see that the latch is broken. The space beyond is a small landing, with stairs leading up to the window or down into darkness.

I step inside, moving around the door and the railings and the stairs by pure muscle memory, completely at home in a place I've never been. I climb the stairs and I know that Kelly was right—I did live here. I stare out of the broken window, looking across the vast field of dark and empty houses. This is where they caught up with me—I retreated here to hide, but they found me and I jumped out of this window, knocking myself unconscious. I step back from the soft square of moonlight on the floor. What else is in this house? Did I leave anything here?

I walk through the kitchen, touching each hollow space as I pass: a hole in the counter for a stove, and near it a hole for a dishwasher. The cupboards have no doors. The fridge hookups hang limp and un-used.

Each room is empty, but familiar, and as I explore I struggle to piece together not just my memories of the house but my memories of the two weeks I spent here. This is what Dr. Vanek worked so hard to help me remember—or at least this was part of it. I walk through unfinished doorways, desperate to remem-ber more.

There is a dark hole in a bedroom wall, with a jagged, exploded edge, but when I get closer I see it's not a hole but a smear, old and brown, perhaps two feet wide and three feet tall. Blood, maybe? Whose? I don't remember if it was here before or not. Did I hurt a cop? Did I hurt someone else?

If I keep looking long enough, will I find more Red Line victims buried in the floor?

I head downstairs to search the basement, finding most of the rooms unfinished—bare Sheetrock in some places, exposed cement in others, lined and fractured by a latticed wooden frame. I comb each room for clues, terrified but finding nothing. The light is too dark, nearly primordial; I'm searching by touch more than anything else. There's nothing out of place, and the fact that I know that is the most terrifying thing of all. In the final bedroom—my room, I know—I find a damp, ratty blanket and a small cardboard box. Perched on top is an old corded phone, its thin cord trailing into the closet.

I know the phone works; this is not a guess but a fact. I pick it up, hear a dial tone, and set it back down. Why does an empty house have a phone line? It doesn't have electricity, it doesn't have water—it doesn't even have sinks—but the phone line works perfectly, the power safely shielded in wires instead of broadcast through the air. It's almost too good to be true—the perfect hideout for a homeless man with a crippling physical reaction to electromagnetic fields. Where else in the city could I find a place so sheltered, so familiar, yet so distant from any type of signal? There's no civilization for thousands of feet in every direction: no cell phones, no radios, no microwaves, no wireless Internet. No people, faced or faceless. Living here I would have been free from everything that terrified me, yet retaining access to basic amenities like shelter and communication. Who set that up? Who installed the phone line?

Who maintained it?

Electricity could be stolen, leached from an overhead power line, but a phone would be impossible without service; the phone needs a specific ID, known and maintained by the phone company, or it would be impossible to connect any calls. Even the dial tone would be impossible. I move the phone and open the box beneath, hoping for some kind of clue, but it's empty. I stare at the phone in the dark. It's my link to the truth—whoever set it up is a part of this, and they set it up for me. Were They using it to watch me? Was I using it to call Them, or someone else? Who would I even call? Not the police, not my job, certainly not my father. I probably called Lucy, but I didn't need a working phone for that. Maybe I never used the phone at all.

Ring!

I stare at the phone, dull and rounded in the dark room. Who will I hear? What will it mean?

Ring!

It doesn't matter who it is; this is why I'm here. This is everything I've been trying to do. This phone.

Ring!

I pick it up.

"Hello?"

"Michael, thank goodness you're there. We've been looking everywhere for you."

I stare at the phone in shock, my jaw hanging open, then slowly put it back to my ear. "Dr. Vanek?"

TWENTY-FOUR

DR. VANEK'S VOICE IS urgent and agitated. "I didn't know if you'd find the house or not; I didn't think your memory had come back yet. Stay hidden, I'll be right there."

"Wait, wait," I say quickly, my mind still trying to catch up. "What house is this? How did you know I'd be here?"

"I told you to go there."

"No, I mean you: how did *you* know I'd be in this house? How do you even know the phone number?"

"Michael," he says, then stops. "Are you saying . . ." He stops again. "Are you saying you still don't remember?"

"Remember what?"

"Remember everything!" he shouts. "The house,

the signals, the Faceless Men. How did you find the house if you don't remember?"

"I got it from the reporter."

"I thought she wouldn't talk to you. I need you to figure this out on your own, Michael, that's why I wouldn't help you."

"I convinced her," I say, trying to think—trying to force myself to figure this out. "What are you talking about? What's going on?"

"You really don't remember anything, do you?" He grunts. "No wonder you attacked Nikolai."

"Nikolai?" I frown, then nod as recognition dawns. "You mean Nick the night janitor?"

"He was trying to help you!"

"He was one of Them, Vanek! He didn't have a face!"

"And in your idiot paranoia you assumed that meant he was evil. He was trying to help you!"

"He attacked me."

"Did he?" asks Vanek. "Did he pull out a gun, or a knife, or a vicious, killer cell phone? Did he punch you or kick you?"

"He ran straight at me."

"At you or toward you? There's a big difference."

"I . . ." My mouth moves mechanically, searching for words. "I . . ." I clench my teeth, determined not to let him cloud the facts. "He was trying to kill me."

"He was trying to rescue you," says Vanek, "though he was apparently too much of an idiot to pull it off."

"Nobody rescued me," I say. "I escaped—I saw him with no face and I ran."

"And I suppose you think you did it all on your own."

"Nobody else was there!"

"Exactly," he says. "That didn't seem odd to you? How long were you there, moving his body and stealing his clothes, and nobody walked in on you? Where was the guard? Where were the security cameras? Even the night nurse was unconscious!"

"That was . . ." I don't know what it was.

"Nikolai and the others prepared the way to help you escape the hospital," says Vanek, "but you escaped from everyone and now you're loose. And apparently very dangerous."

"He didn't help me," I say firmly. "I don't know where the guard was, but there were still people there—the nurse was still there."

"Which is probably why Nick ran toward you—to keep you from shouting and attracting her attention. How were we supposed to know you'd kill him first? We thought you'd remembered!"

"But . . . why would the Faceless Men be trying to help me?"

"Think, Michael! Why can you see the Faceless Men and no one else can? Why did the FBI try to interrogate you?"

"He wasn't interrogating me, he was . . . asking me questions. It's different."

"Why did the doctor give you so many pills?"

"I don't know."

"Why did they try to give you an MRI every time you got too close to the truth?"

"I don't know!"

"Come on, Michael, put it all together! The Faceless Men are helping you because you're one of them."

I stagger back, stumbling over the base of the phone. "That's not true."

"Dammit, Michael, you have to remember this!"

It can't be true—it can't be true. I look around, as if the walls hold some kind of answer or escape, but there's nothing; just walls, closing me in, trapping me. I feel like I can't breathe, like my lungs are being squeezed to nothing inside my chest. I back up again, pulling the phone farther, and it drags the cord out of the dark hole of the closet.

It's not connected to anything.

"Michael," says Vanek calmly, "stay where you are—I'm coming right over. I'm sorry you had to hear it this way, but we thought you already knew—we thought you'd remembered. How did you find the house if you couldn't remember?"

I pull on the cord, pulling and pulling until I hold the plug in my hand. It's right there, just hanging in the air.

"If you see anyone else without a face, Michael, please show some restraint. Don't kill anyone!"

"You're not real."

"Of course I'm real."

"This phone's not plugged in," I say, walking to the open closet and feeling in the dark for a phone jack. There's nothing there—it's not connected to anything, and it never was. "This phone doesn't work, which means this entire thing is all in my head." I stand up. "You're a hallucination."

"Just because I'm in your head doesn't mean I'm not real—"

I drop the phone and run outside; the night is clear and cold, the stars shining faintly through a choking haze of city light. I race to my car, unlocking it in a rush, running in a blind panic. I shove the key into the ignition; the engine roars to life, crackling my feet with its magnetics. My father's cell phone rings and I shout, startled. I hold up my hands to ward off the pain but there's none; the signal doesn't hurt. The phone has no batteries.

Vanek's calling me back.

The phone rings again, loud and strident, and I throw it out the window. I don't care if Vanek still wants to talk: I'm not listening.

I get lost on the way out of the empty neighborhood, just for a minute, but soon I find the exit and pull out onto the street, following the signs for Highway 34. I need to get out of here—I need to go and never come back. I take another Klonopin, just in case. I need something stronger—something to get rid of the hallucinations forever. The freeway ramp curves up and away from the street and I follow it, the city spreading out below me like a sky full of shadows, the stars below brighter than the ones above.

"I don't have to use the phone, you know," says Vanek. He's sitting in the passenger seat, right next to me, and I almost lose control of the car. I swerve back into the slow lane, my hands gripping the wheel in terror.

"Go away! You're not real!"

"As I was trying to tell you, Michael, just because I'm in your head doesn't mean I'm not real."

"Lucy said the same thing."

His voice is hard. "Lucy can fend for herself: she's a pure delusion, and a flimsy, sophomoric one at that. I'm real."

"You're not real."

"Stop saying that!" he roars. "I've been in your imbecile head for years, for your entire life, and as useless as that life is I'm not going to let you throw it away. I'm going to make something out of you if it kills us both."

"Make something? Make what?"

"Make what?" He throws up his hands. "What do you think? I'm going to make me, of course. You're a pathetic waste, Michael: a perfect, healthy body wrapped around a mind too broken to make any worthwhile use of it. I, on the other hand, am a brilliant mind with no body at all. Think what I could do with yours."

"That's . . ." I can feel myself trembling, my chest and my arms vibrating so strongly it's like the tardive dyskinesia all over again. Displaced by my own mind. "That's not possible."

"The greatest obstacle to any invading force is the outer wall," says Vanek slowly. "You either batter it down or you wait it out in an endless siege, but I'm already inside; I'm already past the wall and running through the streets, burning and slaughtering as I go. The only thing standing between me and you is your mind, Michael, and quite frankly it's not up to the task. It's weak and it's helpless—it can't even tell the difference between the truth and its own lies. There will be no reinforcements, Michael. There will be no cavalry to save the day. It's just you and me."

"Don't listen to him, Michael." It's Lucy's voice, from the backseat, and once again I'm so startled I almost swerve into the side wall of the freeway.

"Oh, please," says Vanek, grumbling low in his throat.

I wrestle the car back under control and glance over my shoulder; Lucy is sitting in the backseat, smiling kindly.

"I'll always be here for you, Michael. We can fight him together."

"I don't have time for this," says Vanek. "You're a vapid Hollywood fantasy of the worst kind—you're the most implausible delusion he has, and he thinks his water heater's trying to kill him!"

"Don't listen to him, Michael—I love you!"

"You're an adolescent pipe dream," Vanek snarls, then he points at me: "And you're a narcissistic idiot, proclaiming love to yourself through your own hallucination. It's embarrassing."

"And what about you?" I say, trying to think of something—anything—to counter him. "What does your existence say about me? That I hate myself? That I'm a fat, tactless jerk like you?"

He smiles; his teeth gleam wickedly, flashing in and out of view as we speed past giant freeway streetlights. "What do I signify? I'm here because you have potential, Michael. You created Lucy because you wanted to escape your life, but I'm here because you want to change it. I'm a psychiatrist determined to cure you; I'm the unflagging voice of improvement, always urging you to aim higher than you are. I exist because you know you can be more than yourself."

"Don't listen to him, Michael," says Lucy softly. "He doesn't want to improve you, he wants to usurp you. A change in his story is just a change in his strategy—a new tactic to make you drop your guard."

Vanek laughs. "Oh, she's good, Michael—she's very good. Why is it that your hallucinations are so much smarter than you are?"

"You're all a part of me," I say. "You're only smart because my mind makes you that way."

"Then we're using your mind more effectively than you are," says Vanek, "and you should just give it over to us and be done with it."

"I thought you were going to take it by force?"

"Wouldn't you rather do it the easy way?"

"No," says Lucy, leaning forward, "you're right, Michael. He can't take you by force because he's trapped, just like I am. He can't do or know or be anything without you doing it or knowing it first."

I glance at Vanek, who shakes his head and smiles wickedly. "In the past few months alone," he says, "how many times did I shoo away another patient? How many times did I call for a nurse, or ask your doctors a question? Either I have my own body, or I can control yours. Which is more likely, do you think, for a man who can talk on dead phones and appear ex nihilo in the front seat of a moving car?"

"You can't control me."

"Then how can I do this?" He reaches over and shifts the car into low gear; the engine lurches and roars, slowing abruptly. I swat his hand away and shift back, hitting the gas to get back up to speed. We're nearing the outskirts of the city.

Vanek folds his arms. "Was that my hand on the lever, or yours? Do you see now how your perceptions are fooling you?"

"Dr. Little knew about you," I say. "He hated you."

"He knew you talked to an imaginary man named Dr. Ambrose Vanek," says Vanek, nodding. "I was exactly what he was trying to cure you of—why wouldn't he hate me?"

"You prescribed Klonopin for years," I say, shaking my head. "You have an office on Cicero Avenue. I've talked to your secretary—is she fake too?"

"Surgically enhanced, maybe, but real in every other sense." Dr. Vanek sits back in his seat, smugly comfortable. "What you continue to forget, Michael, is that you perceive the world through a schizophrenic filter: every sight, every sound, every smell you experience is a mixture of real stimuli and your own mental constructions. If someone is talking to you, and your brain tells you it's me, you'll see me. It's as simple as that."

"That—" I stare at him, then reach into the backseat for my backpack, holding the wheel with one hand. I pull out the bag, open it, and grab a bottle of pills. I squint at the label, holding it close to my eyes, but it's too dark to read. I glare at Vanek again; he raises his eyebrow. I turn on the ceiling light and read the label: DR. LITTLE.

I look at Vanek, then back at the label. I feel enraged. "Is this bottle fake too?" I throw it at the windshield, and it bounces down to the floor by Vanek's feet. "How am I supposed to know anything?"

"You think you're the only one with problems?" he asks. "Lucy was right—we're as trapped by your skewed reality as you are. You think your own delusions are bad, try living in somebody else's and tell me how much you like it."

I stare at him a moment, then look back at the road. I shake my head again. "I don't have to see you. I don't have to hear you. You're not real."

Vanek takes off his glasses and rubs his eyes. "Not this, Michael; we don't have time."

"One, two, three, four, five, six—"

"You think Dr. Jones's ridiculous methods are going to work?"

"—seven, eight, nine, ten, eleven—"

"Is this supposed to be some kind of psychobabble exorcism? You speak the sainted words and banish me into nothingness?"

"—twelve, thirteen, fourteen, fifteen, sixteen—"

There's a fourth silhouette in the rearview mirror, a flat black outline of a man in a short-brimmed hat. There's only one thing it could be. I close my eyes, for just a fraction of a second; I glance in the mirror and it's still there. I stare straight ahead, watching the road. We're leaving the city behind, now, the highway dropping back to ground level.

"There's a man in the backseat," says Lucy softly.

"I know."

"He doesn't have a face."

I breathe in, long and slow, then puff it back out. "I know."

TWENTY-FIVE

"THE FACELESS MEN are real," says Vanek.

I ignore him, watching the road.

"Not this one, of course, and not the brief glimpse of the drug dealer you shot. They're just as imaginary as Lucy is."

"As imaginary as you," says Lucy fiercely.

Vanek chuckles. "If that makes you feel better."

I ignore him, trying to name the states in alphabetical order. Alabama, Alaska, Arizona, Arkansas . . . California . . . Connecticut . . .

"You forgot Colorado," says Vanek. "But as I was saying, this one is fake, but the Faceless Men do exist."

I try to clear my mind, to make it as empty as I can.

"They're following you, Michael," says Vanek. "They're trying to help you." He looks at me firmly. "You are, as I said, one of them."

"That's not true."

"Ah, so you're acknowledging me now?"

I say nothing. I think of nothing. It's harder than I expected. I should have taken meditation classes or something.

"I didn't really figure it out until you killed Nick," says Vanek. "It was the first time we saw one up close—the blur effect is what did it. You see, no one else saw anything wrong with Nick's face—he was just another janitor—but you were different. You saw what no one else could."

"It's called schizophrenia," I hiss. "You're the one who diagnosed it."

"Oh, that certainly accounts for the rest of your visual distortions, but not this one. You were on drugs, and one by one every hallucination dropped away. And yet you still saw a formless blur over Nick's face."

"I saw you the same morning," I say. "Obviously the drugs weren't working."

"I already told you that I'm real."

"I've had enough of this," says Lucy, leaning forward. "Michael, can't you just . . . think him away?"

"I'm trying!"

"Have you ever tried to not think about something?" asks Vanek. "It's harder than he expected." He looks at me. "You should have taken some meditation classes or something."

"Just shut up, all of you!" I look in the mirror at the dark silhouette. "What about you—don't you have anything to say?"

The figure says nothing, holding up a single finger.

"One thing? What?"

It shakes its head, turns its hand, and points toward the back of the car. I look closer and I see it: blue and red lights, far back in the distance.

"Police." I speed up. "Are they coming for us?"

The silhouette nods.

"They're getting closer," says Lucy, calling over her shoulder as she looks out the back window. "They must really be moving fast."

"Then we need to move faster," I say, pressing down on the pedal. I can hear the sirens now. "Can they track us?"

The silhouette shakes its head.

"They found us somehow," says Vanek, gripping the armrest as I swerve around a truck. "Are you sure this car isn't bugged?"

"Why would anyone bug my father's car?" I shake my head, growling in frustration and smacking the steering wheel with my hand. "My father tipped them off. He must have—he only gave me his car because he knew he'd get it right back again. He probably reported it stolen and told the police where to find me."

We've reached the farmland now, hurtling past fields and fences and long rows of wind-breaking trees. "My father's been trying to get rid of me for years. Why didn't I think of that when I took the car?"

"You're not paranoid enough," says Vanek.

"I'm on anxiety medication!" I shout. "I'm *supposed* to be less paranoid!"

"Let me out," says Lucy, eyes wide. "I'll distract them."

"They can't see you!"

"It worked last time."

Vanek shakes his head. "It worked last time because the drivers saw Michael looking at something and mirrored his reaction. It's a social instinct: if one human looks at something, every other human in the area will assume there's something there to see."

"That doesn't help us now," I say, "so just shut up and let me think."

"Us talking *is* you thinking," says Vanek.

"They're almost on us," says Lucy. I look in the window and see three police cars, maybe two hundred yards behind us, lights flashing and sirens blazing. I cock my head, thinking, and start to slow.

"Do something," says Vanek, looking at me sternly.

"There's always the chance," I say, "that they're not real either. The last cops I saw weren't. I could be having this entire chase inside my own head—for all I know I'm still at Powell, lost in a dreaming coma."

"You want to take that chance?" asks Vanek. He grips the armrest tighter.

"No I don't," I say. "That's why I brought us here."

The headlights shine on a small white sign with the single word: CERNY. I see the turnoff just in time—a break in the fence and a narrow dirt road. I shut off the lights and slam on the brakes, slowing down just in time to swerve into the gap. The car skids on the gravel, sliding to the side and spraying rocks back onto the highway, but I straighten out and gun the engine.

"What are you doing?" Lucy cries.

"I'm going to the Children of the Earth," I say, slamming down the gas pedal. "Agent Leonard said they're still on Cerny's farm, and Kelly said they're untouchable. If I can get inside the compound the police can't follow us in, and I can finally find the truth behind this whole insane mess."

"You're driving too fast."

The road is lined with a fence on each side, making it relatively easy to steer down the center, but I can't see to avoid any pot holes and the car bounces painfully over the dirt road. Red lights flash in the mirror.

"Shutting off the lights didn't work," says Vanek. "They're still following us."

I push the engine harder, listening to the transmission scream as I press the pedal to the floor. The car bounces wildly, shaking itself apart. The police are practically on top of us.

"I can stop them," says Vanek.

"I won't let you."

"I don't need your permission," he says coldly,

"but this needs to happen right now, right here, and it's going to hurt a lot more if you fight me."

"I'm not giving you control!"

"Fine," he says, and closes his eyes. The car is rattling and sliding on the dirt road, corn and fence posts whipping past in a blur on either side. Vanek frowns, furrowing his brow; he grimaces. I feel an intense pain in my head, growing in seconds to a crushing migraine.

"What are you doing?"

And then there's a brilliant flash of light and a speeding ripple of movement, like a heat distortion in the air spreading out in all directions. The engine stops instantly, grinding and catching and wrenching the wheel from my hands; the car spins to the left and slams us through the thin wooden fence on the side of the road. The planks shatter and fly and the momentum flips the car over. I hear a deafening bang and something slams into my face.

I stare at the darkness, ears ringing. I think I'm right-side up. The car is surrounded by dim shapes, thin bars crowding close around me. Corn stalks. I shake my head, trying to clear it.

I see other cars around and behind us, strewn through the corn in a chaos of destruction. The lights are gone, the engines are dead. My ears begin to ring, slowly regaining sensation after the shock of the crash, but there's nothing to hear. The sirens and squealing tires are gone.

"What did you do?"

Firm hands grab my arm, unlatch my seatbelt,

and pull me from the car; a cop, I assume, but when I look around there's nobody there. No one is near me, and no one has gotten out of the other cars. It must have been Lucy who pulled me out, or Vanek, but now both are gone.

For a few brief seconds, I'm alone.

The nearest cop car is right side up, but the windshield is cracked and bloody. I stumble toward it, peering through the window; the cop behind the wheel is dead, his head smashed and bloody. In the passenger seat is the FBI guy from before, Agent Leonard, his face studded with broken glass and his neck tilted at a horrifying angle. Why didn't the airbags work? Whatever killed the engines must have killed them as well. It was the flash of light.

I turn again, looking wildly for Vanek. "What did you do?"

I hear movement—a click and a cough. One of the overturned cars is trying to open its door. I run into the corn.

The moonlight is dim, and the corn makes it even darker. I run down the row, away from the cops, then cut across several rows and start running again. A flashlight shines behind me, first one and then another, then another, but I'm too far away to be caught in the beams. I can't see where I am or where I'm going, but the path is clear and I run as fast as I can, racing to the end of the row. I can see it now, a gap in the corn just slightly lighter than the tunnel I'm running through. I speed up, hearing shouts and cries from behind. I reach the edge and stumble down the steep side of a hill, losing my balance and falling, rolling to the bottom. My leg hits something solid and I cry out in pain. I wince, facedown in the cold mud, and struggle to right myself.

"Don't move."

I freeze. How did the police get here that fast? It doesn't make sense—they were too far behind me. I try to stay calm. "Who are you?"

"I'm the one with the rifle, son. Who are you?"

A farmer, then. I must be on his property; I look to the side and see a fence—that's what I hit with my leg. The fence around his crops, or around his home? "I'm not a burglar," I say. "I'm not here to take anything or hurt anyone. I'm just passing through on my way to another farm."

"Passing through with a swarm of police right behind you," he says. "I swear, meatbag, if you're here to kill us I will put you down right here—"

"Kill you?" I shake my head, staring down into the mud. "Why would I kill anyone?"

"We are law-abiding citizens," he says. "We will not be bullied, and we *will* turn you over to the police. Now stand up."

"'We?'" I can hear the police getting closer; I rise to my feet, and I can see faint flashes of light from the corn at the top of the hill. They're almost here. "It's you, isn't it? The Children of the Earth?"

I stop, half-turned, frozen in shock. I can see the farmer now: jeans, a dark coat, and a hat. His face is a blank void.

He lowers his rifle in surprise. "Is . . . is it really you?"

"You recognize me?"

"It is you! After all this time, you've finally come back!"

I've made it. He reaches out, gripping my shoulder, and his touch brings a crackle of electricity, painless and oddly familiar. "You're finally home again." He turns his head, and I can see the air around it ripple and distort. "Peter! Call the council together!" He looks back at me. "Tell them Dr. Vanek has returned!"

I take a step back, my hopes shattered in confusion. "Who?"

He looks at me sharply. "Ambrose Vanek. It is you, isn't it?"

This can't be possible. I touch my face—it's still there. The features feel like mine. What will the farmer do if I say I'm someone else? He still has his rifle. I take another step back, but the police are getting closer; their voices are louder now, and their lights are brighter, nearly at the edge of the field. I look back at the faceless farmer. "How do you know me?"

He leans in closer. "You're still not . . . all there? Do you have full control yet?"

In control? That's exactly what Vanek said in the car—that he wanted to take over and control my body.

It's possible—it's likely, even—that this is all in my head. That my mind has constructed this entire scenario out of thin air, taking Vanek's impossible ravings and weaving them together into a senseless yet consistent whole. I can't tell if it's real or not because I have no anchor—no outside perspective to give me context. What would I give if this were just a bad dream? If I could just wake up in my room at Powell and eat some more oatmeal and play with Linda's pretend cash register and go back to the life I had. It was awful, and I hated it, but it was mine, and I understood it, and with enough therapy and drugs it would have been mine forever. A single, consistent reality with no monsters, no murders, and no conspiracy. What I wouldn't give.

I won't run away anymore. I came here to find answers. Let's go find them.

I nod at the farmer. "I remember most of it. I've come back because I need your help. Can you protect me?"

"Of course," he says, pulling me toward the fence. "Hurry—they can't come through without a warrant. This is so exciting, Doctor! You must see the compound—we've accomplished so much!"

So much. It's a statement of change; they think I've been here before. Is this what Vanek was talking about—the two lost weeks he was desperate for me to remember? What if Vanek did take over, just like he'd threatened to, and he came here and introduced me as him? That could explain why they're calling me by his name. Then when the police found me we jumped out the window, and they gave me an

MRI and accidentally wiped Vanek back out. The MRI put me in charge again. Could that be it? Is that even possible?

I smile at the farmer as we climb the fence; the other side is lined tightly with tall, leafy trees. "You've accomplished so much in just a few months?"

He stops in surprise, cocking his head to the side. "A few months?"

Now I'm even more surprised. "Wasn't I just here a few months ago?"

"I suppose it may have seemed like two months, trapped as you were, but it's far more."

I know how long it's been. As soon as he says it I know, but I ask him anyway. "How long?" I dread the answer.

"Twenty years."

Twenty years. He's not talking about a recent visit, he's talking about me, about Michael Shipman. This is the farm where Milos Cerny lived—this is where my mother was kidnapped and murdered. This is where I was born.

He thinks I've been Vanek since before I was even me.

"Show me," I say. "Show me everything." I was right. They put something into me—they put Vanek into me—and for twenty years they've been waiting for him to take control. It happened to the others, and now it's happening to more, and I was saved by . . . by schizophrenia. A chemical imbalance in my brain. It's almost funny.

How big is their Plan? How many more people will they take over—and what, exactly, is taking us over? What is Dr. Vanek? Whatever it is, whatever they're doing, I need to find it and stop it.

"Quick," he says, "they're almost here." I climb down the fence and another man meets me—his face another blank mask. "Take him to Ellie," says the farmer. "I'll hold the police here."

"Come with me, Doctor," says the man, putting a hand on my arm. I feel that strange familiar buzz at his touch. "My name is Peter. Ellie will be so pleased to see you." He leads me carefully through a small copse of trees, holding branches aside for me to pass. Behind me I hear a terse shout.

"You! Who just crossed this fence?"

"This is private property," says the farmer calmly, "owned and lawfully operated by the Children of the Earth. You cannot enter."

"We're looking for someone," says the policeman. "We think he came this way."

"There's nobody here except our brothers and sisters of the faith."

"Then one of your brothers is a wanted fugitive!"

"I'm afraid I don't know what you're talking about."

"We'll get a warrant," says another voice. "We'll be back."

The voices fade, and Peter and I break through the trees into the commune beyond: row after row of houses—not barracks or cabins but real houses—all plain and dark and identical. The windows are dark, the yards are vacant; there are no lights or sounds. It looks like a vast, empty suburb transplanted to the middle of a country field.

Another hollow city.

TWENTY-SIX

WE WALK BETWEEN the houses, kicking up clouds of dust with our feet. There is no pavement or grass. It feels like an old Western ghost town filled with modern tract housing, and as we walk I begin to see them—faceless people in mismatched clothes, locked in a rote imitation of suburban life. A man pushes a lawn mower across a barren patch of dirt. Two women stand facing each other, holding empty brown bags from a grocery store. A child bounces a ball, up and down, up and down, and beyond him another child does the same. There is no talking; there are no lights. It is the trappings of life in a pale, lifeless body.

"What is this place?"

Peter nods. "Your predictions were right, Doctor:

we have found it impossible to integrate ourselves back into society without social therapy. Many of them have never lived on the outside—your plan has proven highly effective. Without all of this," he gestures at the houses and yards and people, "we could never hope to lead normal lives."

"You're doing social therapy?"

"Thanks to you," he says. "In another generation, perhaps, your plan will have succeeded and we will have no more need for these—ah, here's Ellie now."

"Wait, what?"

"Ellie!" shouts Peter. "Come quickly! Look who's returned to us!"

An old woman turns and I almost cry out: Lucy! But it's not Lucy; she has no face, and her long, brown hair shimmers silver and white in the moonlight. She looks at me for a moment, then shouts with joy and shuffles toward us. How do I know her? "Ambrose!" It's Lucy's voice. She takes me by the shoulders and pulls me into an embrace; her body hums like a generator, and though I can't see her face I can *feel* something—not happiness, but something like it. Pleasure, maybe, or satisfaction, but joyless. It is the pleasure of a successful calculation, cold and inert. She pulls away and the feeling disappears.

"Ambrose," she says, then pauses. "You're confused."

Don't let her know. "It's been a long time."

"It has. Thank the Earth that you've returned to us."

I nod. "Thank . . . the Earth."

"It's been *too* long, in fact, and we had nearly given up hope that you would ever come back. Then when Nikolai died and you disappeared, naturally we feared the worst." She puts a hand on my arm and turns to Peter. "Thank you, brother; call the council together. They'll all want to see him."

"Of course."

Peter jogs away, and Ellie leads me farther down the road. "We had such high hopes for Powell," she says. "Their work with you was more complete than we'd ever been able to do on our own, and the reports were immaculate. We couldn't have done better with our own doctors."

I speak carefully. "None of the doctors were . . . ours?" I need more information, but I'm terrified of giving anything away. Who knows what they'll do if they find out I'm not Vanek?

Or am I?

"We had a security guard," says Ellie, "and a janitor. The janitor tried to extract you, but he's . . ." She hangs her head. "Lost. The hospital is blaming it on you, naturally, but our man in the guard room turned off the cameras and I'm afraid nobody knows exactly how he died. We assume *he* got him."

I look at her quizzically. " 'He'?"

"The Red Line Killer. I don't know how much you've heard of him, locked away like that, but he's hunting us. He's already killed fifteen, all lost." She stops walking, worried. "We don't know how much he knows."

The Red Line murders again. But her story doesn't agree with the FBI's. "You said fifteen victims." She nods. "The agent from the FBI told me there were ten."

"There were five they never found," she says. "We were able to reach them before anyone else, and hide the bodies here. Obviously we want as little investigation as possible."

"Obviously." She doesn't seem to think I'm the killer, but I need to draw her out. "The FBI thinks you're behind the killings."

"Me?" she asks.

"All of you," I say, glancing around. "Their current theory—if the man I talked to can be believed—is that you're killing the victims yourselves. Culling dissenters from the ranks of the faithful."

She laughs. "Did you laugh in his face?"

Of course it's a ridiculous idea—there are no dissenters from the cult because their minds are literally being replaced. No dissenters but me. "Give me some credit," I say. "I'm more subtle than that."

"I assure you, Doctor, we have not diverged so far from your plans as to start murdering our own. The flesh is weak, as they say, but we are still its masters."

I nod, struggling to grasp the underlying meaning of her words. *The flesh is weak, but we are still its masters.* Is it generic religious dogma, or something more? If they're not flesh, what are they? I change tactics. "Has the killer ever come here?"

"He's tried," says Ellie. "At least we think it was

him. In thirty-odd years we've had our share of angry parents and teenage pranksters and even some garden-variety burglars try to break into the compound. There's a couple of drunk interlopers every year or two. Three journalists have been foolish enough to try to join us, thinking they could send out reports." She points to a woman by the front door of a house, pretending to sweep with a long, broomless stick. "There's the latest. I wish they were all that easy."

I watch the woman as we walk past her, sweeping and sweeping, back and forth. She's barely more than a silhouette in the dark, but Ellie steers me around the next corner and I catch a quick glimpse of the woman's profile.

"She's pregnant."

Ellie nods. "Most of us are. Phase three of your plan has proven far more successful than the others." We come around the corner and she points at a large central building. "That's the nursery, but there's no time for a tour just yet. Please, come in here." She gestures to a large house, a small crowd of faceless supplicants trickling in through the door. I take one look back at the large building—the nursery, she called it. An entire building of children, born here just like me. How many?

How long has this been going on?

She says she'll take me on a tour later; there's no need to make a scene about it now. I can't do anything to make them suspicious, or they might not show me anything. I turn back to the stairs, and my eyes slide across another house—smaller than the others, and older. A small, squat farmhouse in the middle of this already-incongruous city. I stop in mid-step.

"I know that house."

"What?" asks Ellie. She follows my gaze. "Ah, yes. The Home."

"I've seen that house in a hundred newspapers and textbooks," I say, almost to myself. "The same photo, over and over. That's Milos Cerny's house."

"Cerny," she says, dragging out the sounds as if mulling them over. She steps closer to me. "Not just Cerny," she says slowly, "all of us. You were there too."

"Of course," I say. I glance at her and see that she's watching me—even without eyes, somehow I can tell that her entire attention is focused on me. "It's just that Cerny . . ." I don't know how to finish. Will I start crying? Will I give myself away?

"How much do you really remember?" asks Ellie. "How much of you is Vanek, and how much is Michael?"

I look at her in surprise; this is the first time anyone in the compound has mentioned Michael. I shake my head, taking my best guess at what she wants to hear.

"Michael's gone," I say, "but I've been in his head for years. Some things have certain . . . associations . . . that I don't always filter very quickly from one mind to the other."

Ellie says nothing, watching me. I look back,

imagining where her eyes would be—Lucy's eyes, I think, but older and sterner. She starts to speak, but another woman plants herself between us.

"Dr. Vanek! How wonderful you've returned!"

I smile. "It's good to be back."

The woman stands expectantly, waiting for something. "Don't you recognize me?"

"I . . ." I do recognize her, the same way I recognized Ellie and Nikolai, but I can't remember how or where. Do I say yes and try to fake it? Do I use the same excuse about not quite getting all the memories back? Ellie seemed very suspicious when I said that before. "I . . . it's been a long time."

"It's Arlene," she says warmly, putting a hand on my arm. "Arlene Miller. I was in the first group, with you."

The name is familiar: in my mind I can see it in a crime report; in a newspaper article; on a list of names from the FBI. "You were one of the other children," I say. "You were born here, like—" I almost say "me"—"like Michael, twenty years ago."

She has no smile, but I can tell she's pleased—the same lifeless pleasure I felt from Ellie. No, not lifeless; not completely. Arlene feels things more warmly than Ellie does.

"Come inside," says Ellie, pushing us gently toward the door. "It's time for the meeting to start."

I climb the stairs and go inside, shooting one last glance at Cerny's old house. How do these people know me so well, and yet not know me at all? I haven't seen Arlene since we were three months old—

there's no way she could remember me, as Michael or as Ambrose Vanek. And yet she does. Whatever replaced her remembers whatever replaced me.

Then why does she still have her own name?

The room is full of people, their blank faces blurring almost imperceptibly as they whisper and turn their heads. Ellie pushes me into a back corner and picks up a lamp—not an electric light but a real, oil-based lamp. A match flares to life, the brightest thing I've seen since I got here, and she lights the wick carefully and caps it with a glass tube. The blank faces follow her as she walks to the front of the room.

"I don't like her," whispers Lucy.

"I think you are her," I whisper back, being careful that no one overhears us. "I can't see the face, obviously, but the hair and the body are pretty exact, not to mention the voice, and the . . . feeling."

"I'm not that old," Lucy protests.

"Not now, but you will be in about twenty years. I'm guessing she was here with Cerny, helping with his abductions and his murders and everything else. When I created you, I must have based you on an old memory from this place."

"Why would you do that?"

"I have no idea."

Ellie reaches the front of the room, sets the lamp on a table, and addresses the crowd. "Thank you all for coming. I'm sure you've heard the rumors, so there's no point trying to build up to a dramatic reveal: after twenty years, Dr. Vanek has returned to us."

Given how excited everyone seems to be I expect them to cheer or applaud—something to express emotion—but they simply turn and look at me, silent and watching. I smile nervously, nodding. After a moment they turn back, still silent, to look at Ellie.

"Who do you suppose she is?" I whisper.

"She might be your mother."

I shake my head, suddenly hot and angry. "My mother's dead."

"That's what they told you," says Lucy, "but how do you know for sure? You were three months old."

Ellie speaks again. "As I'm sure you're all aware, the doctor's return heralds a new age for us. There will be many blessings, but there will be work as well. We have much to do."

"The police said there were two mothers left alive when they raided Cerny's house," I say softly. "Both women were shot during the raid."

"So where was Ellie?" asks Lucy.

"I have no idea."

Ellie points at a man in the first row. "Charles, section reports."

The man stands up. "The crops are strong, the animals are healthy, and food stand sales are strong. We expect the orchard to produce a bumper crop this year, and we'd like to expand the operation to start making apple juice as well."

"And our money?"

"The Children are completely self-sustaining. With the third well finished, we don't need the city's water anymore."

"Then stop using it immediately," says Ellie. "I want every one of us drinking well water exclusively, starting as soon as possible to get us in the habit. Assign some of the Phase Threes to fetch and carry."

I ignore the words and focus on his face, musing quietly to Lucy. "Somehow the blur is replacing our faces," I say, "just like the mind behind it is replacing our minds. All my life I've seen things that others couldn't see—and it was real all along."

"That's why you solved it when nobody else could," says Lucy. "You can see what the rest of us can't."

"Can you see their faces?"

"I only see what you do."

I fight the urge to look at her, still keeping my voice down. "What do you see when you see me?"

Lucy doesn't have to hide her movement like I do; she steps in front of me, staring into my eyes. "A memory, I think. Your own image of yourself."

"Then I'm sorry." I look down. "I must look horrible."

"It's not the way you look now," she says, "it's the way you want to look. You created me to see the best in you."

I laugh—a short, voiceless huff. "Even the best can't be all that great."

Lucy puts a hand on my face, and I close my eyes at the aching softness of her fingers on my skin. "You're better than you think you are," she whispers.

"Phase Three is progressing well," says the man at the front of the circle. "Most of our women are pregnant, and there have been no miscarriages since Adrianne's in May. We think she's ready to be safely impregnated again."

"Good," says Ellie. "I trust you'll assign one of the Halseys?"

"Normally yes," the man says, "but we've grown concerned lately about the limited genetic variance we might be creating. I recommend we go with someone new."

"Very well," says Ellie. "And the Process?"

"The Process continues at full capacity," says the man. "One more generation, maybe two, and we will all be protected."

"Excellent," says Ellie. "Then it is time to begin Phase Four." She looks at me. "We've waited so long for this—nearly fifty years, though it feels like even more. At last the time has come. Dr. Vanek, would you like to do the honors?"

I grow pale, and Lucy clutches my arm in terror. "The honors?"

"Yes," she says. "It is your plan, after all, and now that you've returned it should be you who presents it. With only a few exceptions this is the full council—we would be . . . thrilled . . . if you would come to the front and explain Phase Four in detail."

TWENTY-SEVEN

ONCE AGAIN THE faces turn to me, blank and impassionate. I stare back, trying to think of what to do. I let go of Lucy's hand, afraid that they'd see the way my hand is shaped and put all the pieces together: *he's schizophrenic, he sees people who aren't there, we can't trust him.* Without Lucy's hand I don't know what to do with my arms; I hold them at my sides, too stiff to be natural. I fold them; I unfold them.

"Doctor?" asks Ellie. She's doing this on purpose—she's testing me. *How much does he really know? How much of him is Vanek, and how much is still Michael?* I look at Lucy, eyes desperate; I can't talk now that everyone's looking at me. If she's in my mind, do I even have to?

Help me.

She spreads her hands and shrugs. "I can't. I don't know anything about this."

Neither do I.

"No, you don't," says Lucy, "but he does." She points, and I see Vanek standing at the front of the room.

Vanek. I look at him, directing my thoughts and knowing he can hear them. *What did you do in the car?*

"We'll talk about that later," he says. "They're waiting for you."

I lean away from the wall, walking slowly toward the front to give myself time to think.

I won't do this.

"You have to do this," says Vanek. "Do you know what Phase Four is?"

I don't. I walk slowly. Phase Three has something to do with babies. Was I part of Phase Three? But no; it's too recent. Peter talked about it as if I'd never seen it in action. I was a part of Phase Two, maybe, or even One.

"You were Phase Two," says Vanek. I reach the front and turn to face the crowd, flanked on each side by Ellie and Vanek. "They're waiting," he says. "Instruct them."

You know I can't.

"Then let me do it." His smile is smug and self-satisfied.

That's exactly what you want—to control my mind.

"If you say no," he says, "you're exposed as a fraud and they kill you now. Or worse."

"Doctor?" asks Ellie.

"Just a moment," I say. "I'm . . . figuring out the best way to say this."

"Remember the policeman," says Lucy. "He can talk without controlling you."

How do I know you won't expose us?

"Because if you die, I die," he says. "Believe me, Michael—if I could escape you by killing you, you'd have been dead long ago."

I stare at Lucy, not daring to look to either side.

"Is something wrong?" asks Ellie.

"Phase One nearly killed us," says Vanek, addressing the council. They turn to face me, listening raptly. "Phase One taught us that imprinting ourselves on adults took too long, incapacitated us too thoroughly. We're lucky we left one of the humans empty, to take care of the bodies, or we would have starved to death. Eliska and I merged in this phase, along with Cerny and a few others."

"One of the humans," he said. What are they, if not human? I think of the maggot, shiver, and push it out of my mind. It has to be something else—the maggots aren't real. They can't be.

"They know all of this," says Ellie.

"Allow me my moment," says Vanek. "I created this plan, I'm more than a little proud of it. Plus the more I talk the more I cement my control over this schizophrenic meatbag." He rolls his head to the side, glancing at me sidelong. "They didn't hear that last part; that was just for you."

You can't control me. I can barely control myself.

"Phase Two were the babies," says Vanek. "The more we learned about human physiology the more we realized—well, the more *I* realized—that children's brains were more malleable, more open to the patterns we need to create in order to control them. The Process would take longer, but the results would be better, more complete. Most of the subjects in Phase Two were new, but I joined in again. I thought a newer, better link would be worth the time. You can't imagine how many times I've regretted that decision."

"But you're okay now?" asks Ellie.

I nod, wrestling control back from Vanek. "It's just . . ." What can I say? Lucy smiles encouragement from the back of the room. "It's so much to take in," I say. "I haven't been here since Phase Two, and to see how far you've come without me is . . . it's amazing."

"That's right," says Vanek, "feed her ego."

Now tell the rest.

"You can guess the rest," he says, speaking only to me, "can't you? Phase Two worked, in theory, but we were caught. You people get so defensive when your young are threatened, and Cerny and some of the others ended up dead, though not, apparently, Eliska. She was away from the farm, working on one of the external projects, and when the dust settled it was up to her to take the next logical step."

I look at the council, at the audience full of pregnant women. *Phase Three was impregnation*, I think, looking at Vanek, *but after Cerny you couldn't steal babies anymore, so you had to make your own.*

"All part of the plan," says Vanek. "My plan, I should say, though more than ably carried out by Ellie."

And that means Phase Four is . . .

"You still don't know," says Vanek. "All those hints, and you still can't figure it out."

Help me.

"Do you see now how you rely on me? How you can't even function without me?"

"Don't listen to him, Michael," says Lucy. "You're stronger than he is."

Tell them about Phase Four.

"No."

I pause, still resolutely avoiding Vanek's eyes. *Why won't you tell them?*

"I might eventually, but first I want to watch you squirm a little. Twist in the wind."

I look over the crowd. They'll find me out—one wrong word out of my mouth and they'll know I'm an impostor, and then I'll be sweeping the floor with a stick like that journalist—back and forth, a mind as hollow as the houses. I should have turned and run. I should have gone with the police.

The police. That's how I can do this.

"I've waited too long for this," I say, trying to keep my voice calm. "Twenty years. But tonight we have far more urgent concerns to deal with." I glance

at Ellie. "I did not come here peacefully—men on
the outside, the police, were trying to catch me and
detain me. When I crossed the fence and entered the
compound they said they'd return with a warrant.
They've wanted to come in here since we bought the
place, they've wanted to look around and see what
we're doing and put a stop to everything, but they've
never had an excuse before. I'm afraid I've given
them that excuse."

I expect them to stir and fidget, to whisper anxiously with each other, but they merely nod, accepting my words. I glance at Ellie again, looking for
her reaction; she seems bothered. I was hoping my
warning would pass her test, but does she know I
merely sidestepped it? Why would she be so dis-
turbed?

Vanek glowers at me, but stays silent.

"He's right," says Arlene. "If the police return
with a warrant to search the compound, they'll find
the nursery. They'll find the Home. We can't allow it
to happen."

Ellie's mood darkens—I can feel it like an aura
around her, sparking invisibly. She's not suspicious
of me, she's angry: I know enough of authority to
recognize its hackles when I challenge it. Vanek said
to feed her ego, and he was right; I was a leader
here, or he was, but we've been gone too long and
Ellie has taken over. Even deferring to me as she did,
asking for me to explain Phase Four, was a way of
exerting control over the group—to show them that

even Ellie can command the great Dr. Vanek. By changing the subject I've usurped her position. I need to give it back to her.

I step back and gesture to Ellie. "When I left, our group was smaller, and twenty years later I don't presume to know how best to lead it. Ellie is the expert here."

She hesitates a moment—just a fraction of a second, watching me—then steps back to the foreground. "Dr. Vanek is right—the police will return in the morning, or even sooner. We must prepare." She looks at Charles. "The nursery is our prime concern—there will be no way to conceal our plans if they find the children."

"We have procedures in place," says Charles. "Are we hiding or evacuating?"

"Hiding," says Ellie, "but ready to evacuate entirely if we need to."

"I need an hour."

"Do it," says Ellie. She clenches her jaw in a scowl. "This is not the right time for this! We can't let them discover us."

"What about the Home?" asks Arlene. "They'll use their search for Vanek as an excuse to seize everything they can. If they find our files—"

"Leave the files to me," says Ellie, "you need to deal with the nursery and the lab."

"The lab?" I ask.

"Of course," she says simply. "The last thing we need is for the police to find us with a half ton of homemade cyanide." She turns to the others. "Go with Charles—we'll need every member of the council to help corral the others. Go!"

"Cyanide?" I ask the question too quickly, too loudly; I know I've given myself away, but . . . cyanide. Kelly was right about the stolen chemicals. Ellie looks at me, sensing my shock, and I feel my charade falling apart. What are they doing with half a ton of cyanide?

"You seem surprised," says Ellie, watching me closely. "You seem almost . . . concerned."

She's onto me. I need to throw her back off. "Not concerned," I say quickly, "just surprised that . . . you were able to make that much. I was worried that Brandon's death at ChemCom had cut off your supply."

"It did," says Ellie, "but I think we have enough." She turns away, seemingly mollified, and leads me into the next room. Three people sit on a couch staring vacantly at a cardboard box; a crude human face has been drawn on it, like a child's pretend television. She speaks to them brightly, eerily reminiscent of Linda's therapy voice. "Time to go! Everybody stand up—that's right, stand up. Now come with me." She helps them to their feet, taking each person by the hand and pulling them up. The three walk stiffly, staring listlessly at the walls; one of them twitches arrhythmically. "These are new," Ellie whispers, leading me back outside. "There are dozens more like them, all still struggling with the Process. They need guidance even to eat."

The streets of the fake suburb are filled with people, half of them guiding the others in a chaotic, mindless horde. Ellie mutters in frustration.

"I don't blame you for the police, Ambrose. But I wish you'd come at a better time."

I have to find the answers. I summon my courage and ask the question. "Tell me about the Process." Ellie looks at me sharply, and I continue quickly to soothe her suspicions. "What have you done to refine it?" If she tells me how it's changed, I might be able to figure out how it works in the first place, and that will tell me how to stop it.

Ellie passes off the three human puppets to a nearby council member, and gestures for me to follow. We walk toward the nursery.

"We weren't ready for the breeding program when the disaster with Cerny forced it onto us," she says, "but it worked so well that we're more or less on schedule anyway. See for yourself."

Ellie opens the nursery door and we walk inside. As with the rest of the compound, there's no electricity, but even in the dim light from the doorway I can see them: rows and rows of beds, from cribs to full-size bunks, stretching back and disappearing in the shadows. Each bed holds a child, small and still; sleeping or sedated or comatose, I can't tell for sure. They have IVs in their arms and cloth bandages wrapped around their faces. I look at Ellie in shock, and she nods.

"Beautiful, isn't it?"

I step up to the nearest bed, a tiny cradle; the

child inside is no more than a few months old. A small card on the side says MARY. I reach toward her, trembling, touching her lightly on the arm; her skin is warm. An IV tube runs into her arm, her skin tight and crinkled under the clear tape that holds it in place. The IV stand lurks over her in ominous vigil, one of a hundred stands lined up like silent soldiers.

A light flares behind me as Ellie lights another lamp. "The IVs were one of our more successful additions," she says. "We can keep them drugged for years if we need to, though usually it's only a week at a time. Their minds can adapt more swiftly in the absence of outside stimuli—emotions have proven particularly problematic, and this process helps to negate their impact. Still, without regular exercise their bodies will begin to degenerate." She shakes her head. "It's an unfortunate flaw, but it's a flaw we accepted when we chose this path."

I nod, trying to keep my breath even and my face impassive while inside I'm screaming in rage and fear and frustration. How can they do this? I point softly at the bandage on Mary's head.

"And their faces?"

"A small amount of facial pressure seems to ease the transition; most of us sleep with masks on these days. You can remove the bandage if you want, but there's nothing to see yet—just an ugly human face."

I nod again, trying to stay calm. I think about myself as a baby, lying in a cradle just like this—maybe this very one—screaming and bawling while outside the police trade gunshots with a killer, and inside a mother murders children one by one. A slash of the knife, a splash of blood, and on to the next cradle. It's a nightmare I've lived a hundred times since I learned the truth about my birth.

This is the first time I've sympathized with the murderer.

I walk away from the cradle, too torn to stay near it any longer. They are destroying these children, implanting them with something that pushes out their minds and takes over their bodies. To kill them would be a mercy—but even the thought of it, of doing it myself in cold blood, makes me stop and clutch the wall for support. I feel light-headed and nauseous. I want to scream and cry and run away. I want to throw down Ellie and shatter her lamp and light the nursery on fire. I want to hide in a hole and never come out.

"Are you alright?"

Murderer! I scream in my head. *You did this to me!* But she didn't—it was Dr. Vanek. He started this, and then he did it to me, crawling inside of me like a hand in a puppet. And now he's trying to get back out.

"Ambrose?"

I turn to Ellie, my eyes wet with tears. I wipe them away; I have to explain them. "It's just . . ." I swallow my nausea. "I never expected that we could get this far, and in so short a time." My excuse sounds stupid and hollow, even to me. I remember her authoritarian jealousy and add: "You've done an incredible job—far more than I could have done." I curl my lips into a smile, holding back a wave of revulsion. How can I talk to her like this? How can I stand here next to a hundred tortured children? What else can I do?

She nods. "Thank you, Doctor. But I can't take all the credit. Without your research there would have been no foundation to build on."

I look across the room, trying not to think about the mass of children held silent and helpless. Of my apparent role in their horror. "What's next?"

"Phase Four."

I nod. "Of course." I need to learn more; I need to find a way to stop it. I turn to her and smile. "I hope you've improved on my plans for that as well—"

I stop abruptly, listening. There is a sound in the far darkness of the nursery, a slow, wet, scuffle. I know that sound. I try to think of something else, to imagine a faceless nanny or a lost, mindless puppet, but I can't. The image leaps unbidden to my mind.

A giant maggot.

I watch the sound, bracing myself for the sight. This is what this has all led to—this is what I've been searching for and avoiding at the same time. The answer. I put a hand on my head; I imagine I can feel the interior wriggle of a slick, larval worm.

The maggot slurps into view, a dim, writhing shape on the edge of the lamplight. "How are we going to hide them?"

Ellie follows my gaze, then looks back at me. "We'll carry them into the corn. The initiates can help, with our guidance; they can hide in the fields while the police search the compound."

"Carry them?" I ask. The thought of that maggot in my arms fills me with revulsion, and I suppress a shudder. "Is that really the best way?"

She shrugs. "There's no time to wake them up, and the lingering sedation will help keep them quiet."

"No, I mean the . . ." I stop. Something's not right. "The what?"

"The . . ." What do I say? I can't talk about them without revealing my ignorance—Vanek would know so much more than I do; what they are, what they're called, what they're capable of. "The others." The maggot crawls farther out of the darkness, a shadow coalescing into mucus and muscle. I point at it. "Them."

Ellie watches the aisle as the maggot slumps slowly toward us. "Tell me something, Michael."

"Yes?"

She looks at me. "What exactly do you think you see?"

Too late, I realize what I've done: she called me Michael, and I answered to it. She knows.

I take a step away. "What do you mean?" Can I play this off? Can I salvage this?

Ellie advances one step. "The schizophrenia is still in place, isn't it? Dr. Vanek hasn't escaped at all, you're simply playing us for idiots."

The maggot's a hallucination—there's nothing there. That's how she knew it was me. I watch the monster come closer, ringed mouth gaping open.

"I'm—I'm Vanek, Ellie, I'm Ambrose Vanek. You know me."

"You know me *now*," she says. "Just like you know everything else. And now that you do, we can't let you leave again."

I try to sound innocent. "What are you talking about?"

"Dr. Vanek, can you hear me?"

"I'm here," says Vanek. He's standing near me, maybe ten feet away; I glance at him and Ellie follows my eyes.

"Can you speak?" she asks.

"Not through him," says Vanek. He scowls at me. "Not right now."

"Of course I can speak," I say. "I've been talking to you all night." The worm shuffles closer.

"If you can hear me," says Ellie, walking slowly toward the spot I glanced at before, "I want you to know that I'm doing this to help you, not to hurt you. I have no desire to usurp your position."

I step toward her. "What are you talking about?"

"Hit her," says Vanek, his face growing pale. "She's going to attack you."

"What?"

"You're a threat, Michael, to her power and to the entire plan. She's going to kill you, now hit her!"

"We've suspected for years that you might be trapped for good," says Ellie. She stops right in front of Vanek, looking near him without looking at him. "I apologize that it has to be this way."

"Now, dammit!"

I dive to the side, hiding behind a wooden table as a flash of blue light fills the room. I feel a pain in my shoulder, like a bright electric shock, and my mind spins wildly at the contact. I turn to Ellie; she's braced with her feet wide apart, breathing heavily.

"Traitor!" Vanek shouts, his face a red mask of rage. "How dare you use the power against your own kind!"

A blue bolt of lightning arcs out from Ellie's face, and for a split second the blur snaps into focus and I see Lucy's face, old and lined but perfectly recognizable, and then the electrical surge slams into me and I choke back a scream, losing control of my muscles and collapsing to the floor. The world warps and curdles around me; my body grows and shrinks and my senses explode in a hail of sparkling shards. I gasp for breath, struggling to remember that I even have lungs, that I need them to keep me alive. The world swims back into focus and I feel pressure on my back—Ellie is kneeling on me, pulling my arms behind me to tie them.

"Get up," says Vanek, growling through clenched teeth. He swallows the pain and snarls again. "Get up and *hit her.*"

Ellie leans forward, reaching for a rope, and I throw my arm backward, twisting my torso as much as I can to slam my elbow into her face. Her arms flail out and she tumbles to the side. She hits the ground and the rope flies out of her hand, skittering across the wooden floor to stop in front of the maggot. It sniffs it, glistening maw sucking at the air. I roll over and leap on Ellie, trying to pin her to the ground.

"Children!" she shouts, trying to wrestle me away. I punch her in the face, feeling my hand hum with a surge of energy. The contact brings pain— both mine and hers, impossibly transferred with a swirl of fear and desperation and hot, rabid rage. "Get off of me!" She raises her head and I slam it again with my elbow, hammering her head against the floor; she slows, coughing for air, and I grab her head in both hands. Emotion runs up my arms like bolts of electricity, emotion and thought and memory and rage. I see darkness and earth; I feel confusion and pain; I wail with a desperation so ancient my mind crumbles to ruin at its touch. The sensation locks me in place, holds me in a vise of unknowable sadness, and I struggle to escape. I can't let go. Our minds are merged and frozen. I force my arms forward, feeling them budge a fraction of an inch. I can do it. I'm trapped in an eternity of emotionless, alien thought, and then in a burst of motion I slam Ellie's head against the wooden floor. She falls limp.

I pant for breath, letting go of her head. I scramble away, watching her body, but she doesn't move. The maggot is gone. The rope lies abandoned on the floor.

Did I kill her? I creep forward, expecting her to leap up at any moment—expecting a maggot to come bursting out of her chest in a bloody assault. But no, it's in her face, not her chest. Is it a maggot?

A microchip? I could cut her open and find out; I could discover once and for all what's hiding inside them.

Is this how the other cultists died—beaten to death by a crazy man and his living delusions?

Am I really the Red Line Killer after all?

The door handle turns. Someone is coming.

TWENTY-EIGHT

"LOCK IT!" SHOUTS Vanek. He snarls and points at the door. "Quickly! They'll see!"

The door starts to open, and I scramble toward it in an awkward flurry. A face peeks through:

"Ellie?"

I slam into the door, knocking it closed. The angle of the opening was such that whoever it was probably hadn't seen Ellie's body. Probably.

The voice is more urgent now, more confused. "Ellie?"

"Tell them you're me," says Vanek. "They'll trust you—they were raised to trust you."

"It's me," I say quickly, "Dr. Vanek. Do you need something?"

"We heard shouting, Doctor, is everything all right?"

I say the first thing that comes to my mind. "Ellie wants to call off the evacuation."

"No!" shouts Vanek, rushing toward me.

"Go and tell the others," I continue. "We need everyone to stay in the compound."

"You can't do that!" cries Vanek, reaching for the door, but I block the lock and handle with my body. "We need to evacuate," he insists. "Ellie's treachery doesn't change that!"

"Her death does," I say, staring him down. "I'm in charge now, and I want this entire thing shut down— the compound, the children, the 'Process,' whatever the hell that is. The cops are coming back, and they're going to find this, and they're going to end it."

"And what do you think they'll do to the man in charge?" asks Vanek. "Pat you on the head and send you away?"

"They don't know anything about you," I say, "and they saw me arrive an hour ago. The FBI's been watching me for years—they have so much proof I'm not involved in this that they actually sent a guy to ask me why I wasn't."

"So the council goes to jail," says Vanek. "Hooray for you. What are you going to do about everyone else?" He gestures at the shadowed nursery. "A hundred children—two, maybe three hundred others. You can't 'save' them; you can't reverse the Process. Your legal system will spread them out, drop them into hospitals and foster homes all over the world; your government will spread the Children wider than the Children could ever hope to spread themselves. Do you think we don't have people on the police force? In the courts? You've already lost, Michael."

"Are you trying to make me kill them, then? That's the only answer left!"

"I'm trying to make you see them as they are."

"What are they?"

"Inevitable."

I watch him in the lamplight, listening to the cries outside. The compound is in chaos. I look at Ellie's body, then at the rows of children. "What are they really?"

"The same thing you are."

"Then what are you?" I demand. "That thing you did in the car—that thing Ellie did to me just now. Those aren't normal things, they're barely even real things. Maybe they're not, I can't even tell anymore." I stare at him, wide-eyed. "Are you aliens?"

"We are more native to this Earth than you are. We are its Children."

"But what does that mean?"

He shrugs. "You know where the answer is."

The old farmhouse, the one Ellie called the Home— Cerny's home, certainly, but something else as well. Whatever these people are, whatever the Process is, the root of it is in there. "We don't have much time," I say. "I can't let the police find me."

"Running away again? Is that all you ever do?"

"I'm going to the Home," I say, "but I have to get out before the police come." I point at the body. "This is what, the third person I've killed now?"

"She's not dead."

I listen at the door, making sure there's no one waiting on the other side, then open it cautiously, peeking out at the compound; people wander through the dirt streets in confused, ragged groups. I glance back at the sleeping children. I can't save them, but maybe I can make sure it never happens to anyone else.

I look back at the lock on the door, fiddling with it; it's crude, but I can probably leave it locked behind me. I don't want anyone to find Ellie and raise an alarm.

I step outside and lock the door behind me.

A man walks past me, holding a leash; the collar drags along the ground behind him. I wait for him to pass and step out into the street, weaving my way between the slow rush of a dozen disorganized mobs. A woman stands in the middle of the road, holding a grocery sack upside down in her arms. She stares at the empty bag in silence, pondering it; behind her a confused swarm of people rush madly from place to place, trampling underfoot a row of toy plastic vegetables. I step around her and keep going.

"Dr. Vanek!" It's the one called Arlene—she's weaving toward me through the crowd. "Dr. Vanek, what's going on?"

I don't know what to say. I can't let them hide those children from the police, but Vanek was right about letting them be found—they'll be spread all over the city, maybe all over the country. Can the cult be spread like that? Whatever they are, trapped in our heads, can they get out? Can they make more? I have to get to the Home.

I point to the main gate. "You need to watch that, okay? You need to watch that gate and shout an alarm if anyone gets close."

"But we already have guards."

"I don't trust them in this chaos," I say. "What if someone pulled them aside to help with the evacuation? What if they got a different message entirely? We have to post a watch, and it has to be someone I can trust. Can I trust you?"

"Of course, Doctor."

"Then go."

She turns, stops, then turns back and puts a hand on my arm. "Doctor?"

"Yes?"

She hesitates, shifting her weight from foot to foot. "Is it over?"

"I—I don't know."

"There were people I used to live with."

"Your family?"

"Not mine." She frowns, looking down at her body. She shrugs. "Hers." I stare at her. She shifts her weight again. "Will I see them again?"

I don't know what to say. "Do you want to?"

She purses her lips, searching for words. She starts to speak, then stops, then starts and stops again. I put a hand on her shoulder, feeling an electric hum of confusion.

"Watch the gate."

She nods and goes. I watch her back, trying to decipher her meaning, but there's no time—they're bound to find Ellie soon, locked door or not, and then they'll come looking for me. I weave through the chaos to the Home and try the door; it's locked. Even within the cult, it seems, there are secrets. I go behind, to a back door hidden in shadow, and shatter the window with my elbow. Glass shards fall and shatter further on the floor. I reach in carefully and turn the knob.

I hear a shout in the distance: "He's here! The Red Line!" They found Ellie. I grit my teeth and open the door; maybe I can find a weapon inside to defend myself. I walk in and close the door behind me.

I'm standing in the kitchen of a small country house—at least, it was built as a kitchen, but the Children of the Earth have turned it to other purposes. Maps line the walls. A gap in the counter, probably intended for a stove, has been filled with filing cabinets. The large table in the corner is covered with papers. I walk to it and try to read some, but the room is too dark; there are lamps on the counter, but I'm trying to stay hidden and don't dare risk a light. I pick up the nearest stack of papers and carry them to the window, pulling back the curtains and holding them up to the moonlight: financial records. Birth records. Employment records for cultists in government, law enforcement, medicine, the military. Vanek is watching me from the shadows in the corner. I hold up the papers.

"What is this?"

"Gainful employment."

"But the farm's already self-sufficient," I say, leafing through the stack. "They're getting the jobs for other reasons, like Brandon stealing ingredients for cyanide, or Nick keeping an eye on me at Powell." I pull out a page. "You have a city councilman—he could help keep the farm autonomous." I pull out another. "You have a police officer to keep it protected." I pull out another, holding it to the light and tapping it with my other hand. "You have a man in Public Utilities, but . . . I don't see what he does for you. Do you get free water?"

"Water is the only thing we pay for."

"But you have wells."

"Well water is so much cleaner, don't you think?" He smiles coldly. "There's no telling what's floating around in the city water system."

So that's it. "The cyanide. You pay for water to make sure they keep it flowing through the farm, and while it's here you lace it with cyanide."

"Not yet," he says, shaking his head. "Not until the infrastructure's in place. Not until the Public Utilities director sorts out what is downstream from what."

"And then you kill everyone in the city."

"Only one city? Please, Michael, show a little ambition."

I swallow. "Phase Four."

Vanek says nothing.

"You can't possibly have that many people," I say, "you haven't been doing this long enough."

"Phase One began in the early 1950s," says Vanek. "We took an entire family: Milos and Nikolai Cerny; their sister Eliska and her husband Ambrose Vanek; a dozen more who lived and worked here on the farm. Once we adapted to the first group's physiology we split into teams—I was in charge of the merging Process, but the others set out almost immediately to infiltrate every aspect of your lives."

"By murdering the world."

"By cleansing it."

I glare at him. "You're monsters." He says nothing. "You really are—you're not human at all, you just . . . move us, like puppets." I set down the papers. "You said the answers were here, so here I am. What are you?"

He nods toward the door to the next room. "We're right in there."

I hesitate, watching him, suspicious of so much free information, but I know he won't kill me. He needs my body alive. I walk to the door, pausing with my hand on the doorknob. What will I find? I see again in my mind the row of cradles, the sprays of blood, the wild-eyed woman with the knife. I push the thought away and open the door.

It's dark in the new room—far darker than the kitchen, for the front door is tightly shut and the windows are completely boarded over. I find a lamp in the dark, and a box of matches next to it, and I fumble with them until I manage to spark a flame; the room glows orange, a tiny globe of light pressing out against the shadows, and then I light the lamp and the globe expands to a bright, wide yellow. Vanek follows me in and closes the kitchen door behind us, hiding the light from the rest of the compound. I can hear shouts and chaos echoing dimly through the walls—the Children of the Earth running in panic at the specter of their killer. Is it really me? Have I come to destroy them? I ignore the noise; I've come for answers. I push all other thoughts away.

There is no one here, but I'm not alone. I can feel it in my legs, vibrating like the hum of an engine—there is something, or someone, nearby. The true Children of the Earth are close enough to touch. But where?

The room is nearly bare, containing nothing but a few chairs, a bed, and an elaborate rig of chains and pulleys. I walk around them, touching each item; the chairs are solid wood, reassuringly sturdy. The thick, metal chains are cool to the touch, neither smooth nor rough, running up from the bed to a system of gears and wheels on the ceiling. The bed has a thin mattress and a rough woolen blanket, and the sides are fixed with strong leather restraints, just like the ones I had at Powell. I pick up one of the manacles, turning it over in my hand. I drop it. I walk around to the front of the bed—

—and then I feel it. This is where the hum is coming from, directly below my feet. It's the same pulsing jolt I feel with cell phones, the same hum I feel from touching the cultists, but a hundred times stronger—a thousand times stronger—and instead of being painful it feels sickly euphoric, like the cranial buzz of a narcotic or a general anesthetic. It calls to me; it pulls me down; it feels more familiar, and more alien, than anything I've ever felt. I realize I'm lying on the floor and I struggle to stand up. Vanek takes my hand and pulls me to the side.

"There are still so many of us down there," he says, leaning me against the wall. He's panting. "The sensation is . . . stronger than I remember."

I can see an outline in the floor—a trapdoor hinged to fold open and closed. The chains make more sense now—with the trapdoor open, the bed could slide forward and drop right down inside. I clutch the wall and pull myself to my feet.

"What are you?"

"We are the Children of the Earth."

"But what does that mean?"

Vanek stands motionless. "It means we were here before you. In ancient eons before the rise of Man we lived in the depths of the Earth; we plumbed its secrets; we thought and we watched and we learned."

"You're the maggots?"

"The maggots are a construct of your imagination," says Vanek. "They represent us in your mind;

you were aware of something you couldn't fully process, and created a hallucination to give it form. In reality we have no form at all."

"That's impossible."

"Don't be an idiot," he says. "What is intelligence but an organized matrix of electrical impulses? In you it evolved through flesh, but it is typical human arrogance to assume that it could not evolve in other ways for other forms of life."

"You don't just react to electrical fields," I say, the pieces finally clicking into place, "you are electrical fields."

"We are energy," he says, "unconstrained and, as we discovered, unprotected."

I stare at the trapdoor, still feeling its pull through the soles of my feet. They feel so powerful—what could possibly harm them? "Unprotected from what?"

"From you," he says. "Your radios, your cell phones, your entire civilization. The more technology you build, the more you attack us with it, beaming waves and fields and signals all over the planet."

I nod. "That's why those signals hurt me so much—because they hurt you."

"They distort us as painfully as a physical attack hurts your physical body, except you've filled the world with them. For nearly a hundred years your kind has been bombarding us with an endless barrage of contrary fields and foreign radiation—you've all but destroyed our ability to live."

I stare at the trapdoor, mouth hanging open. "We didn't know."

"Does that matter?" he demands. "Has ignorance ever excused murder, even in your own imbecilic society? We exist in a very specific band of geology—certain rock formations, certain mineral structures conducive to our fields. You drove us away from them, farther and farther until we couldn't survive. Our only choice was to come out."

"To steal our bodies?" I demand. "You accuse us of invasion, and then you turn around and wear us like clothes—like some kind of hazmat suits?"

He walks to the bed, grabs a lever, and pushes it down; the floor drops away and the bed lurches forward to the edge. I step closer, feeling the tingle in my legs grow stronger. I peer into the hole.

It's a deep pit, dark and hollow like an empty well. The sides are rough and uneven, full of gaps and hollows and sharp flares of rock—this wasn't built, it formed naturally, hollowed out by water or torn open by an earthquake. I gasp, my breath catching in my throat. This is the pit that's haunted me; this is the pit that's lurked in the back of my mind and worked its way into so many other memories. I know this place.

"I've been here," I say. "I've been . . . down there."

Vanek nods. "This is how we merged. The first time was an accident; one of the farmers broke through the surface and fell into the sinkhole—your friend Milos, in fact. When he finally gained enough control to realize what had happened—that he was safe, that the pain was gone—he started throwing the others in so we could join him. Imagine the pain we must have been in to agree to such a mad endeavor—to give up our lives and seal ourselves inside of a lesser creature. It would be like you choosing to live as a vegetable."

I stare at the pit, imagining the darkness, the pain, the terror on both sides. Innocent beings attacked by their own world. "I can only imagine."

"That was 1952. Now imagine how much worse it's gotten since then. Your technology has outstripped every other electrical force on the planet." He bows his head, looking reverently into the empty pit. "You stand on holy ground, Michael. You stand over the last haven of our people."

I turn on him, angry and frightened. "And now what? How does it end? With traitors in the right positions and a massive stash of cyanide? Why not just nuke the world and kill us all?"

"If our host body dies, we die, because our electrical patterns become dependent on yours during the merging. We can leave a body voluntarily, but we must immediately enter another."

"So you're protected," I say, "but you're trapped."

He nods. "A necessary evil."

"Then what happens next?"

"We will undo you. We will destroy your capacity to hurt us. We will return you to the pastoral life you used to lead, before you poisoned the sky."

"You can't."

"We already are. The poison is already in place, the water system already mapped and routed exactly the way we need it—in this city and in dozens of others, scattered to every corner of the country. In a matter of days your glorious city will be a ruin, quiet and empty, home only to shadows and echoes and a vast, open grave."

TWENTY-NINE

I STARE INTO the pit, searching for some sign of life—a flicker of movement, a glimmer of color—but there's nothing to see. Instead I feel it, vibrating through my body like a wave of energy. *We are here. We are your brothers. We are your death.*

A hundred faceless spirits, intangible and invisible, hell-bent on the destruction of all mankind.

What can I do to stop them?

Vanek smiles in grim satisfaction. "You see now that there's *nothing* you can do to stop us. We're smarter than you; we're more prepared than you. And the only human being who knows of our plans is a dangerous schizophrenic, well-known for his ridiculous delusions and, now, wanted for murder." He smiles. "We've already won."

"The police will come," I say. "They'll come to look for me, and they'll find your nursery and they'll put you all in jail forever."

"Forever is a very long time," he says, "and we can afford to wait much longer than you. Do you know how old we are, Michael? Do you have any idea the things we've seen—the glories my mind contains? I was here when the Earth cracked open and the continents split apart; when the dinosaurs rose and fell; when the first man raised his spindly arms to deify the sky. I watched him do it, or one like him, squirming like an insect in a jar, railing idiotically against a world he couldn't possibly understand." Vanek walks toward me, seeming to grow larger as he approaches. "Do you have any idea how insignificant you are compared to us? How little it would bother us to snuff you out like candles? We've seen your infantile political systems: you'd kill yourselves if we gave you an excuse." He looms over me, malevolent eyes mere inches from my face. "You're alone and you're helpless. There is nothing you can do to stop us."

I feel a hand on my arm; Lucy is here. "You're not alone, Michael. Don't listen to him."

Vanek laughs. "An imaginary friend: how terrifying."

"You're just as imaginary as I am," Lucy snaps.

"I am more real than any human could possibly be."

"Then why am I still in control?" I look up, meeting his eyes, forcing myself not to shy back from the force of his gaze. "If you're so powerful, why are you still trapped in my mind?"

He hits me, a shocking blow across the face that sends me reeling against the far wall. "Do not mock me!"

Lucy tackles him from behind, but he throws her off with ease; she nearly falls into the open pit, but catches the edge of the bed and pulls herself away. I steady myself against the wall.

"You're a prisoner in my head, Vanek. You said so yourself." I let go of the wall, legs still shaky, and step toward him. "That means you're weaker than you say you are. It means I can beat you."

"It's not my weakness," he says, rushing toward me, "it's yours!" He hits me again, knocking me into the chairs; they clatter to the ground around me, bruising my arms and slamming solidly against my chest. "Your mind is broken!" Vanek growls. "I can't control your body because no one can control it— it's a hopeless wreck of faulty connections and crossed wires." I try to stand and he hits me again, slamming my head against the wall. "You're a useless bag of meat!"

I crawl away from him, scattering the chairs and trying to keep them between us. Lucy meets me, crawling from the other direction, and wraps her arms around me protectively. She has a cut on her cheek from when Vanek threw her.

Dr. Vanek shakes his head, looking down at us with disdain. "If I'd known twenty years ago that your mind was this twisted and useless, I'd have killed you on the spot and merged with someone else."

I'm shaking, trying to regain my breath and bearing. Lucy strokes my cheek, whispering, "It's all right—you're still in charge. He can rail and yell all he wants, but you're still in charge."

"You're trapped in here with me," Vanek snarls at her. "Don't make me angry."

"No," I say, shaking my head, "she's right."

"Shut up!"

"You're trapped," I say. I brace myself on a fallen chair and stagger to my feet. My left eye feels swollen, and my ribs throb with pain. "I thought my schizophrenia was part of what you did to me, but it's not—it's an accident you weren't prepared for. You can't even choose a new host, the way the others can, because you can't find your way out of my mind." I stand up straight. "For all your talk you're still just a prisoner, and I'm not useless because I'm your prison."

"I can control you."

"Sometimes," I say, "but not often enough, and not consistently. The other . . . Children of the Earth, whatever you are . . . they could take over their hosts' bodies in just a few years because they figured out how the nervous system worked: which electrical pulses connected to the senses and the muscles and the memories. But I'm schizophrenic—none of the systems you've tried to master make any sense, and half of them are complete fabrications. You hear things that aren't there, you see people that don't exist. You trace mental signals that start no-where and end in another nowhere completely dif-ferent from the first. It's a web you can never hope to untangle." I set my jaw and stare him down. "I can see you and hear you, I can feel your attacks, but no one else even knows you exist. You can't talk or act or communicate with anyone. As far as the real world is concerned, you're just another halluci-nation."

He roars and charges me again, but this time I stand my ground and deflect his swing with my arm, throwing him back.

"You live in my mind, Vanek! You can't hurt me!"

"But I can," says Ellie. I look to the kitchen and see her standing in the open doorway, one arm limp at her side, the other hand holding a gun. Her blank face is smeared with a blur of blood, like I'm look-ing through a cloud or a TV pixilation.

"I thought you were dead."

Vanek barks a humorless laugh. "I told you she wasn't."

Ellie steps forward. "I'm sorry, Dr. Vanek, but this is the only way to stop him. It pains me that you will die with him, but I will not sacrifice our people to save you." She swallows. "I'll use a gun to avoid any more . . . unpleasantness."

Lucy steps in front of me, blocking the path be-tween me and Vanek. "I can't protect you from her," she says, nodding at Ellie, "but if Vanek attacks you he'll have to get through me first."

"I don't need to attack anyone but Eliska," says

Vanek. "I have not come this close just to let her kill me!"

"Don't attack her!" I shout. "She'll shoot me and kill us both."

"I'm sure he's enraged," says Ellie, leaning tiredly against the door frame. "He was never as selfless as the rest of us—that's why he insisted on claiming one of the newer, younger bodies." She smiles cruelly. "I guess we see what greed will get us, don't we?"

"Just think about this," I say, fixing her with my eyes. "You're talking about the destruction of an entire civilization. Can't we find some kind of compromise?"

"Do humans compromise with cattle?" asks Ellie. "Do they make deals with insects? Humans are nothing but a nuisance to us—an infestation to be culled and farmed, as casually as you would watch a goldfish in a bowl."

"We can communicate with each other!" I say. "Do you have any idea how incredible that is? To find intelligence right here, right under our noses! We have ideas to discuss with each other—cultures to share and explore."

"We have explored your culture since the day your invasive technology forced us to pay attention to it, and we have found nothing of any value." She glances at the ceiling, as if looking at the sky beyond. "We heard the stars singing, Michael; before you drenched the world in electrical blather we felt the Earth stir within us, we felt the movements of the sun and the moon as they danced across the sky.

What could you possibly have to compare with that?"

"We have . . ." I stop. What do we have? I've lived a life of fear and hatred and neglect; I was teased at school, tossed helplessly from job to job, beaten by my own father. I have lived for twenty full years without ever experiencing peace or happiness. Now, I search for an impassioned defense of humanity, and I can find nothing.

"We have love," says Lucy.

I look at her standing in front of me, her clothes ripped and bloody, her small frame dwarfed by Vanek's terrifying bulk. She's a nothing—a frail figment of a diseased imagination—and yet she's prepared to sacrifice everything to save me. Me. The child no one cared about; the man everyone wanted to forget. She loves me.

Her voice is firm and fierce. "Do you people even know what love is? Do you have any idea what love can do to you—how it can crack you open, how it can beat you down and scour your soul and leave you more joyful than you've ever been before?" She talks proudly, and I realize that I am talking with her, mirroring her words. "You were married, Ellie: Ambrose and Eliska Vanek. Did that mean anything to you at all? Even if your kind have no emotions of your own, did you gain nothing from your hosts—no feelings, no memories, no hopes or dreams?"

Ellie snarls. "Nothing."

"But he felt something for you," I say, stepping forward. "Vanek's thoughts were in my head, his memories mingled with mine, and one of them must have been his love for you." I look at Lucy and she turns to me, brown eyes brimming with tears. "Why else would my ideal girlfriend—the most perfect woman my mind could imagine—have your face?"

Ellie's arm falters. Vanek looks at her. "There was something," she says, "long ago. It was not love but loss, a sadness I couldn't understand."

"Loss?"

"When Ambrose left—when he merged with the child and his old host died—I felt . . . grief." She shakes her head and snarls. "I felt my host's *weakness*." Her arm straightens, the pistol again trained squarely on my chest. "It was not a sensation I have any desire to repeat. I've raised every child since then to ignore it."

"But you can't," I say, remembering Arlene. She missed her human family. "It's a part of you now. You didn't feel emotions as spirits, or fields, or whatever you were, but you feel them now—your entire race, everyone who's bonded with a human host. They were raised with us, they feel a kinship with us." I step forward. "When the time comes, and you give the orders to destroy us, will they even follow you?"

Ellie hesitates, her arm wavering. I watch her closely, fists clenched in anticipation. Put down the gun! She shakes her head.

"I don't have time for this," she says. "The Red Line Killer is here—I must go and deal with him, and I can't risk you getting away. Whatever this means for our plan, whatever changes I'll have to make . . . either way I still can't let you live."

"Wait," I say, confused. "The Red Line Killer? When I heard the shouts I thought they were talking about me."

"You?" asks Ellie. "You're not the Red Line Killer, it's your—"

Her chest explodes with a deafening boom, spraying blood against the wall. Her body slumps to the ground, blank face staring vacantly at the ceiling, and as I watch it the smooth blur over her features starts to distort. Light and color swirl and fuse, and all too soon they dissipate and die. Lucy's face stares blankly from the floor, old and wrinkled.

"No!" Vanek wails.

A figure steps into the room: first a shotgun, then a pair of black-clad legs stepping over the corpse, then a face: my father. He trains the shotgun on me.

"Are you one of them?"

My father. I look at Ellie's corpse, then back at his face. "Is it really you?"

"Answer me, Michael." He raises the shotgun to his cheek and sights down the barrel. "Are you one of them?"

"They tried," I said, glancing at Vanek, "but I'm still me."

He doesn't move. His finger hovers over the trigger.

"Father?"

"Prove it," he says.

"You can't even stand up to your father," says Vanek. "Give me control and be a man for a change."

My father barks: "Answer me!"

I shake my head, steeling my courage. "No, Dad, it's your turn to talk. You gave me your car, then you called the police and told them where to find me." I pause, frowning. "And you wanted them to find me here, or near here. You told me to take this road. Is this is a setup?"

"You watch your mouth, boy."

"You planted your cell phone in the car with me—if you're the Red Line Killer, that's evidence."

"I told you to answer me!"

I stare at his gun, terrified and liberated at the same time. I've never stood up to him; I've never had the courage. But now I've seen something even scarier, and he's only a man with a gun. "What else did you plant in the car, Dad? I didn't check the trunk—is there more evidence in there? The gun you used to kill them, or the knife you used to cut off their faces?"

His expression is flat and emotionless; his mouth a thin, tight line. "The police wanted you anyway, so I figured you could take the blame for me, too; take some of the heat and let me keep working."

"But what were you doing?"

"I was trying to find what they were," he says. "You saw her die just now—there's something in their heads, something behind their faces. I could never find what it was."

I swallow. "Do you want to know?"

He tightens his grip on the shotgun. "I want to know how to kill them."

"But we don't have to kill them. You just shot one ringleader, and the other is trapped in . . . ," I stop myself, eyeing the shotgun. "He's trapped. They're the ones behind all the bad stuff. The rest are innocent. They're practically children, just like their name."

His voice is firm and heartless. "Tell me how to kill them."

"We're already killing them! Everything we do, everything we have, we're strangling them right out of existence." I look at Vanek. "The man on the council said what, two more generations? That's not very many people—eight hundred maybe, in their entire species. In their entire form of life. We should be trying to save them."

"I won't hear that talk from you!" he shouts. "I won't hear that talk from her son!"

I straighten, standing as tall as I can. "You saw the people out there—they're scared, and they're lost, and all they want to do is live. They're not the people who killed Mom."

He takes a step forward. "Your mother was the best thing that ever happened to me, and now I am making them pay. I thought maybe I'd done the wrong thing, letting her only son go down for my crimes." He pauses, swallowing his tears, and when he speaks again his voice is cracked and husky. "But if her son has joined her killers, I swear to God I will end you." He steps forward. "Prove it now, or die where you stand."

"You can't win," says Vanek, watching me. "You join us and he kills you, or you join him and commit genocide."

I shake my head. "There's another way." I point at the pit, and look desperately at my father. "I think I can end this without killing anyone."

He glances down, steps back, then looks back at me, keeping the gun level. "What's down there?"

"The thing that destroyed our lives." I walk toward the bed. "I was born in this room—they put me in that pit, and through it they put something into my mind. And now I'm going back in."

Lucy puts a hand on my arm. "You think Vanek can get out?"

"I'm not going to get him out, I'm going to trap the rest of them in here with him."

"No!" cries Vanek, and Lucy grabs my arm.

"They'll destroy you," she says. "With that many minds in one head you won't even be able to move!"

"Then neither will they. They'll be sucked in—I'll pull them in if I can—and they'll be trapped."

"You wouldn't dare!" shouts Vanek.

"I've lived with a false reality my whole life," I say, pointing at him, "but you and the others will be trapped and helpless."

"You're insane!" my father growls.

I whirl to face him. "I'm insane but I'm right. And that makes me the perfect prison."

Vanek lunges at me, shoving Lucy aside and punching me square in the face. I reel backward. My father cries out and Lucy tackles Vanek, trying to pull him off, but he's too strong; he comes at me again, pounding my head against the floor.

"Michael," my father shouts, "what are you doing to yourself!"

"Grab me!"

Vanek kicks me in the chest, knocking the wind out of me. I struggle for air, gasping desperately as soon as I can breathe again. "It's not me, just—hold me down!"

My father reaches for me, fending off a flurry of kicks and punches from Vanek, and then he has me by the leg; he's dragging me across the floor; he's pulling me toward the pit. He catches both my feet, holds them tightly, and suddenly Vanek can't hurt him anymore—he simply stands to the side, seething with rage.

"You can't do this!" Vanek shouts. "Even if you trap them all in your mind, there's hundreds more outside! You can never stop us!"

"I don't need to stop them," I say. "Without you or Ellie the others will change their minds—some of them already have. They won't destroy a species they've become a part of."

Vanek lunges, but my father clutches my feet tighter, holding me in place, and Vanek can't hurt him.

I look at Lucy. "I don't know what this is going to do to me, but . . ." I pause. "I love you."

Her eyes are wet with tears. "I'm not even real."

"You're real to me." I stare at her a moment longer, not daring to pull my eyes away.

My father holds my twitching feet in an iron embrace. "I can't strap you down with you fighting like this."

I look at the edge of the pit. I look up, seeing the room and the farm and the great city beyond—teeming with life and light, only to be snuffed out and left empty. A monument to a lost world. It's the only way to stop it. "You'll have to throw me." I'll be broken, but I'll be alive.

"It's okay," says Lucy, kneeling next to me. "We'll do this together."

I keep my eyes on hers; she holds me tightly, and I clutch her hands in mine. "I'm ready," I say calmly. "Throw me in."

My father heaves, Vanek roars, and I fall into the deep black pit.

EPILOGUE

THE HOUSE IS enormous—a mansion, really. Lucy calls it a palace, but it doesn't really have the appearance. I think she just likes to think of herself as a princess. She sits across from me at a long, narrow table and raises her glass.

"Dinner looks delicious."

"It does."

I smile. There are footsteps in the room above us, slow and ponderous, but I ignore them. I ignore everyone in the house these days, keeping most of the doors closed so that Lucy and I can enjoy our solitude. Most of the others are too lost to find us anyway. It is, as I said, a very big house.

Even Vanek can't find his way out.

I pick up my spoon—polished silver, intricately

carved—and scoop up a bite from the delicate china bowl. Oatmeal. It seems like oatmeal is all we get anymore, though sometimes there are other things: applesauce. Jell-O. Cream soups if it's a special occasion. I'm never sure what the special occasions are, but I don't mind. I have a luxurious mansion, the food is delicious and free, and my best friend is the woman of my dreams. We've spent our lives this way for ... I lose track. A very long time. I'm happier than I've ever been.

A shape walks past the door, dark and half-formed. I watch the empty doorway, waiting, and a moment later the shape returns. Its voice is dull and distant.

"Who are you?"

I glance at Lucy, then back at the shape in the door. "I am the master of this house."

It stands silently, doing nothing; it is a shadow made real, its outline fading at the edges. It raises a black, translucent limb. "Who am I?"

"You are my guest," I say softly. "You may go anywhere you wish, but you may not leave this house."

"Then you are a jailer."

"In a sense."

"And what is my crime?"

I set down my spoon. "When you have discovered that," I say, "return to me, and we will discuss it."

The shape turns, wisps of unreality trailing as it moves. It leaves without farewell, and I turn back to my food.

"They're learning," says Lucy.

"They are."

"And they're getting braver. More forward."

I say nothing. I stare at the table, playing with my fork.

"Dessert is here." She holds up a silver tray and gracefully removes the lid. "Peaches."

I smile. "I love peaches." I pierce one with a silver fork, watching the juices run. I place it in my mouth.

It is delicious.

TOR

Award-winning authors
Compelling stories

Please join us at the website
below for more information
about this author and other great
Tor selections, and to sign up for
our monthly newsletter!